ALSO BY DARRYL BOLLINGER

SATAN SHOAL

A Novel

DARRYL BOLLINGER

JNB
PRESS

Copyright © 2016 by Darryl Bollinger

JNB Press
Tallahassee, FL

www.jnbpress.com

Printed in the United States of America

First Trade Edition: February 2016

ISBN 978-0-9848432-8-2

In memory of Regina.

Prologue

The sun was less than an hour away from sinking into the blue-green waters of the Gulf of Mexico. With daylight fading, it was time to think about stopping for the night. Kenny and Valerie were in their sailboat just northwest of Satan Shoal about twenty miles from Key West. The waters in the Florida Keys could be treacherous and with the *Black Swan* drawing four and a half feet, Kenny wanted to be anchored before dark.

"Let's go ahead and get the sails down," he said. Kenny was at the helm while a naked Valerie sat close by. "We'll motor from here."

"Too bad Jack and Molly had to turn around," Valerie said as she stood, stretching. Kenny couldn't help but admire the view. The two couples had left Key West that morning on their way to the Dry Tortugas, a seventy-mile journey. Less than two hours out, the refrigerator on Jack and Molly's boat had quit, so they had returned to port.

Kenny turned his attention back to the task at hand, starting the small diesel engine before turning the boat into the light breeze. Clouds were gathering and he saw lightning in the distance. They got the sails down and stowed, then turned toward the Marquesas Keys, where they planned on spending the night on the western side of the horseshoe-shaped group of small islands.

When he arrived at his destination, he cut the throttle back and turned east. He was surprised there were no other boats around since this was usually a popular anchoring spot. When the depth sounder showed ten feet, he put the engine in neutral and told Valerie to take the helm while he went up to the bow.

He got the anchor ready and when the boat's forward momentum slowed almost to a stop, he released it. As the boat drifted backward with the current, he played out the anchor line until the mark on the line showed seventy-five feet. Satisfied the anchor was set, he tied it off and told Val to shut down the engine.

The quiet was conspicuous as he made his way back to the cockpit. Very little breeze was stirring, which was unusual for the Keys. The only sound was made by birds finding a place to roost on the small island in front of them.

"Going to be a beautiful sunset," Val said, handing him the customary end-of-day beer and sitting next to him. Dusk was beginning to settle on the water.

"Looks that way," said Kenny, taking a drink of his beer and looking out at the empty ocean. Val put her hand on his thigh, tracing circles with her fingers. Smiling, Kenny turned his attention to her. Suddenly, she stopped.

"Is that a boat?" she asked.

He cocked his head and heard an outboard motor in the distance. He turned to see a boat approaching, heading directly toward them.

As it got closer, he could see that it was a center console, somewhere around twenty-five feet long. Two people were at the helm, and he could see fishing rods upright around the T-top above the console.

"Fishermen," he said, relaxing. "Maybe we can score some fresh fish for dinner?" Val handed him his bathing suit, then wrapped a cover-up around herself and tied it.

The powerboat slowed as it got closer, turned, and idled parallel to the *Black Swan,* eight or ten feet away. The captain, a heavyset dark-skinned man, jockeyed the transmission and throttle, keeping them even with the anchored sailboat.

The other man, who was taller, waved. "How's it going?" He was a pale, thinner guy whose face had gotten too much sun in spite of his blue ball cap. From the way he was standing and holding on, he didn't appear to have a lot of boating experience.

"Not bad," answered Kenny. "You guys have any luck today?"

Blue cap held his hand out, palm down, and waggled it. "So-so. We fished Satan Shoal and landed a couple of dolphin. Where is the other boat?"

"Other boat?" Val asked.

"Yeah, there was another sailboat with y'all earlier."

"Oh, they had some refrigerator problems and—"

"Did you know them?" Kenny asked.

Blue cap shook his head. "Not sure. From a distance, it looked like a friend of mine."

"What kind of boat does he have?"

The man hesitated, his eyes shifting from Kenny to Val and back. He held up his hands. "Sorry, just wanted to say 'hello' to him. Did he go back to Key West?"

Kenny noticed their boat was drifting closer to them. That and the fact that the man didn't answer the question about what kind of boat made him uneasy. Val looked up at him and he could tell by her expression she had the same thought. *This is starting to feel wrong.*

He reached down and grabbed the microphone for the radio. "Maybe I could—" Kenny froze when he looked up, the microphone halfway to his mouth. Blue cap was pointing a gun at him.

"Don't key that mic. Very slowly, put it back."

Kenny gulped. He stared at the guy, his mind racing. His and Val's only hope was the microphone in his hand. He slid his thumb toward the TRANSMIT button.

Blue cap glared at him. "Put the fucking microphone down. Now."

Kenny dove to his right, away from Val, pressing the button and yelling, "Mayday."

The shot slammed into the left side of Kenny's midsection, knocking him back against the fiberglass seat, the microphone falling from his hand. Val screamed, and he felt a burning sensation, the shot echoing in his ears.

It was like watching a movie in slow motion, everything seemed to move at half speed. He wanted to say something, but his mouth wouldn't form the words. He looked down to see blood coming from a wound just above his waist. His hand moved over it, blood pouring through his fingers.

He looked over at the other boat and the captain's eyes were as big as saucers.

"Goddammit," blue cap shouted.

"You shot him," Valerie screamed, as she put her hand over Kenny's, pressing it onto the wound. "We've got to get help." She reached for the microphone.

No, Kenny tried to shout, as the movie sped up, out of control. He strained to grab her hand.

Another shot rang out. Kenny saw Val fall over his feet in the floor of the cockpit, part of her head missing. He looked up to see the man with the gun shaking his head.

"Goddammit. Now see what you've done."

"You bastard," said Kenny, raspy words finally escaping his lips.

"I din't sign up to shoot nobody," said the captain in an unsteady voice, shaking his head, and speaking for the first time. "We got to get help."

Blue cap turned to face him, lowering the gun halfway. "It's too late for that."

Still shaking his head, the captain said, "We got to call somebody."

"Listen to me. You call anybody, you go to jail—forever. Understand?"

"I din't shoot—"

Blue cap edged closer to him, the pistol still in his hand.

"We are both in this—together. You realize what I'm saying?"

The captain glared at him. He glanced at Kenny, and then looked at the gun before returning his eyes to the man holding it. At last, he gave a slight nod, giving in to the reality of the situation.

Kenny was feeling light-headed and knew he would soon lose conscience. He willed his bloody finger to scrawl a message on the boat beneath the seat. On the last letter, his finger slipped, sliding down in a crooked trail and then he, too, was gone.

1

Jack Davis stirred and cracked one eye open. Daylight streamed through the tinted hatch above him. He smelled fresh coffee and heard Jimmy Buffett singing "Come Monday." *How appropriate,* he thought, even though it was Saturday. Of course, when you were retired, every day was Saturday.

His head throbbed. He stumbled out of the berth and stepped into the head. As he stood there, he heard Molly in the main cabin, moving things around. When he finished his business, he went back into the forward stateroom and picked up a pair of shorts. Still standing, he struggled to get them on, but the challenge of standing on one leg while he lifted the other foot proved impossible. Finally, he sat on the berth so he could get dressed.

Adjusting his shorts as he stood, he walked into the main cabin, wondering what Molly was doing. He stopped short when he saw her. She was on her knees, bent over and looking in the locker underneath the settee. He recognized various items from the locker setting on the cabin floor. She had not yet removed the ratty blue sail bag he knew was at the bottom of the locker.

"What are you doing in there?" he asked, a little more sharply than he intended.

She turned to face him. "Good morning to you too. I'm looking for those bamboo trays we had. I thought they might be under here."

He reached to pick up one of the sail bags on the floor and handed it to her to put back in the locker. "They're in the aft stateroom, not in here."

She frowned, then took the bag from him. "Don't worry, I'll put everything back. Why don't you get a cup of coffee and go topside to de-grouch."

He watched her for a minute, making sure she was replacing the items in the locker. He poured a cup of coffee and climbed up the stairs to the cockpit. The bright sunlight made him wince and he wished he'd brought his sunglasses, but didn't want to go back down below to retrieve them. Still unsteady, he made his way over to the cockpit table and sat.

Molly rummaging around had caught him off guard. He'd never seen her in that locker before, which is why he chose it. The ratty blue sail bag contained almost $400,000 in cash, untouched since he'd put it there.

In Clearwater, he had stolen close to a million dollars from Peabo Watson, the drug dealer responsible for kidnaping Molly and a young teenage girl named Wren. That had been Jack's leverage to get them back. It had worked, and in a bizarre turn of events, the drug dealer had been killed and Jack ended up with the money, minus a hundred thousand dollars the cops recovered.

He'd found the women, drugged and unconscious, in a cheap motel room on Clearwater Beach. Exactly what had transpired in that room was still not clear. They had been given Ketamine, so the events were buried forever.

He took half the money, set up a trust fund for Wren, and bought her a nice boat to live on. That he felt good about. She'd been in an abusive relationship with Peabo and she deserved it. His faith was being borne out, as she was going to nursing school.

The rest, he'd kept, rationalizing at the time that it was restitution for the ordeal Molly had been through. It was a hasty decision and one he regretted. He hadn't spent any of it and was reluctant to do so. Molly was doing better, and he felt that the money should go to a good cause. However, legally getting rid of almost a half a million dollars in cash was more difficult than he realized. Compounding the problem was the fact that no one, including Molly, knew he had it.

"What's so important about that locker?" Molly said, coming up the steps a few minutes later to join him.

"Nothing. You just had crap strewn all over the place," he said, studying his wife. Her long red hair framed her thin face, with a few freckles showing. Her green eyes were beginning to regain their sparkle. He took a sip of coffee and said, "Sorry I snapped at you. I'm just bummed we're not on our way to Fort Jefferson."

He looked around Key West Bight, where they were docked at A&B Marina. It was another gorgeous day in the southernmost Florida key, with the temperatures already creeping into the eighties. A light breeze stirred and a brown pelican sat on the piling across the dock, pretending to be asleep.

They had enough money saved up for a couple of years and had decided to spend a year in Key West recuperating.

His only complaint was that Key West was expensive. The income they got from renting their boat slip in Fort Myers didn't come close to covering their space here at A&B. For *Left Behind*, the 38 foot Island Packet that was home, the slip was $1,900 per month plus utilities, substantially more than the $500 a month they got for subleasing their slip in Fort Myers.

This morning, they should have been halfway to Fort Jefferson on Garden Key in the Dry Tortugas. They had set sail yesterday morning with another couple, Kenny and Valerie, who were on their boat, *Black Swan*. The two couples had planned on spending the night in the Marquesas Keys, about a third of the way.

Two hours out of Key West, just north of Satan Shoal, *Left Behind's* refrigerator had conked out, which meant no place to keep ice and cold items. Kenny and Valerie didn't have enough room on their boat and with no marinas in the Tortugas, Jack had reluctantly decided to return home to Key West.

"You sleep okay?" he asked.

She nodded.

"I had some really weird dreams," he said, shaking his head.

"Not surprising, given the shots of El Tesoro you and Nick had last night."

He nodded. The tequila could explain the headache. Nick, a muscular, tanned Texan with short brown hair, had lived in Florida for the last ten years, but still retained his west Texas accent. He'd left Tampa for Vero Beach, over on the east coast of Florida. Stopping in Key West on his way around the bottom of the peninsula, he decided to stay. That was three years ago.

He lived on his forty-six-foot sportfisherman next door at the Galleon Marina. Surprised when Jack and Molly had returned yesterday afternoon, he came over to find out what happened. Discovering they'd lost their refrigerator, he told them to bring all of their cold items over to his boat until they could get theirs fixed. He'd insisted they stay for dinner, lamenting the fact that they were in Key West instead of on their way to the Tortugas. After dinner, Nick had brought out the tequila and, as they say, the rest was history.

"Any ideas on the refrigerator?" Molly asked.

Jack shook his head. "Not a clue. Great time for it to crap out, though. When I finish my coffee, I'll go ask Terry for the name of a good mechanic." Terry was the dockmaster at A&B Marina.

"Could have been worse. It could've died after we got there," she said.

He nodded. Molly was right. Fort Jefferson was remote, with no services at all, not even fresh water. The Tortugas are at the western end of the Florida Keys, closer to Cuba than the mainland. Many a boat captain, when stranded there, had taken the fast cat back to Key West for supplies.

"Maybe if we can get it fixed, we could catch up to them?" Molly said.

"We'll see, but I wouldn't count on getting a mechanic out here on a weekend." He hated having to turn around yesterday. Molly enjoyed sailing, and being back out on the water had been therapeutic for her.

"I've still got some time off. Maybe we can get it fixed and go back out, even if it's just for one night."

Molly, a nurse, worked part-time at Lower Keys Medical Center, the only hospital in Key West. Since they'd planned on being gone for a few days, she wasn't scheduled to work again until Wednesday night.

"That may be a possibility. Let me eat a little something, and we'll see."

Two cups of coffee and a bagel later, Jack started to feel human again.

"I'm going up to see Terry. Want to go for a walk when I get back?" he asked.

She shrugged, not enthusiastic about the idea.

Jack had always been a runner, but this morning he was in no shape to run. Since moving to Key West eight months ago, he'd tried to get her to walk with him, wanting to get her out and about and back to some sense of normalcy. She'd gone with him only a few times since they'd been here, but recently she'd become more receptive.

He reached out and put his hand on her arm. "Come on, Molly. It'll do you good."

She looked up at him giving him a hollow smile, an expression he'd seen too often since they'd left Clearwater.

He tugged lightly on her arm. "It'll be fun, okay?"

She hesitated, then nodded. "Alright. Go see Terry and I'll change."

He watched as she got up, taking her iPad and going below. He tried to convince himself that she was improving, but deep down, he was beginning to fear he was in denial. Her therapist had told them it was going to take time—lots of time—for the scars to heal.

Jack stepped off the boat onto the dock and glanced across the water toward the Galleon Marina. Nick's boat was berthed directly across from them, probably no more than fifty feet away. There were no signs of life stirring, so he turned and headed down the dock toward the office.

A&B was a small marina, essentially just one large T-shaped dock, with stern-to slips on each side of the main dock. Their slip was the furthest one from shore, just inside the top of the T, across from the fuel dock. It was quieter there and more secure, away from the bars and foot traffic on the boardwalk alongside the waterfront.

At the boardwalk in front of Alonzo's Oyster Bar, Jack turned left and then right. Terry was standing out front of the dockmaster's office talking to a man in a blue ball cap.

"Morning, Jack. You look surprisingly well, considering," Terry said.

Jack shook his head. There were no secrets in the bight. "Morning." He stuck his hand out to the stranger. "Jack Davis."

The man shook Jack's hand and introduced himself. "Randy Jenkins. I was just talking to Terry about maybe leasing a slip here."

Jack nodded. "Good place. His rates are outrageous, but good neighbors." Terry chuckled. No marina in Key West was cheap, but A&B was one of the most reasonable around and everyone knew it. Jack turned to Terry. "In my defense, I was overserved by Nick."

Terry snorted. "I've heard that one before. Shame you had to cancel your trip, though."

"Yeah, that sucks." Jack turned to Randy to explain. "We were on our way over to the Tortugas with our friends. Our refrigerator went out, so we turned around and came back. That's why I'm here. Either of you know a good marine mechanic?"

"A couple," Terry said. "Penny's Boatyard is good."

Randy nodded. "Keys Marine is good, too. Guy there named Evens, he's top notch."

Terry agreed. "That was the other place I was going to recommend. I've used Evens several times, and I know he's done work for others around here. I'll give him a call if you'd like, though it'll probably be Monday before he can get here."

"That's fine. Nick's got all of our cold stuff, and we've got an ice chest to get by on, but the sooner the better." Jack turned to Randy. "Nice meeting you. Stop by if you end up getting a slip here. I'm the Island Packet out on the end."

He turned back to Terry before leaving. "Molly and I are going to walk downtown for some lunch. Give me a call when you talk to this Evens guy."

2

Knowing Jack and Molly were going out for lunch, Randy had hung around A&B, out of sight until he saw them leave. After waiting a few minutes, he walked out on the dock to snoop around, spotting Davis's boat at the end.

He pretended he was looking the place over, like a prospective tenant. *Left Behind* was in the last slip inside the transient dock, which formed the top of the T and abutted the main entrance into the bight. Opposite the main dock or the base of the T was the fuel dock.

Randy shook his head. This was an exposed location and would be hard to break into unnoticed. He dared a closer look at *Left Behind*. The lock on the main cabin was a hefty, industrial-strength combination lock, unlike the small, dinky locks usually found on boats. Even on *Left Behind,* the cockpit lockers had only small padlocks. There was also an alarm system sticker on the bulkhead. That seemed like a lot of security for a live-aboard in a highly visible marina.

He was certain the money was still on Davis's boat, but getting it wasn't going to be easy. Looking beyond the boat to the waterfront, he saw a convenient bar with a clear line of sight, a perfect spot for lunch.

Halfway around the boardwalk, he stopped where a homeless man sat in the small patch of shade provide by the building. The thin, scruffy man held a cardboard sign that read, "Homeless vet. Please help."

Randy chuckled, then reached into his pocket. He pulled out a wad of cash, fished out a five, and handed the man the money. The guy looked at it, then up at Randy. "Thank you, sir. I appreciate it."

Randy smiled and said, "Good luck," before walking on. Randy had lived on the streets before. When he started digging his way out, he swore two things. One, he'd never go back to that existence. He was probably one of the very few dealers that had a nest egg stashed away. Unlike most in his profession, he lived a modest lifestyle, preferring to sock money away for leaner times.

The second thing he vowed was that he would never ignore a homeless person again. While he was amused at the various tricks they employed to ask for money, he never forgot the way people would look past you on the street, pretending you didn't exist. A homeless person was a non-person. That was the worst feeling he'd ever felt, and he would never subject anyone to that again.

At the waterfront bar, he found a table overlooking the small harbor. As he predicted, it had an unobstructed view of Davis's boat. He sat there eating lunch, studying the sailboat and watching the hordes of tourists walk past.

His phone chirped and he looked at the screen. Evens. Randy answered the call.

"You doing okay?" he asked.

"Dis ain't good."

"Just be cool. Everything's going to be fine. I was just down at A&B, and you're going to get a request to do some work on a refrigerator. Get to it as soon as you can. I'll fill you in later."

"Okay."

Randy hung up and signaled the waitress for his check. The big man was still shaky. Yesterday evening had been a disaster. He'd talked Evens into taking him out to intercept Davis's boat at dusk. Come to find out, Davis had returned to Key West. Then, the fools on the other sailboat had to go and reach for the radio.

They had dumped the bodies in the ocean and washed the sailboat down as good as possible. He knew the chances were almost certain the bodies would never be recovered. He had considered towing the boat out into the Florida Straits where the currents would take it somewhere far away, but he was afraid of running across a Coast Guard patrol or a fishing boat.

Randy wasn't worried about Evens saying anything to anyone. Prisons meant something entirely different to someone from Haiti, so the threat of going to prison was enough to keep his lips sealed forever.

Evens was proving to be quite an asset. Randy had befriended the big, quiet man several weeks ago when he'd first tracked Davis here. He'd hired Evens to take him out and teach him how to navigate the waters around the Keys. When Randy had started to get queasy on the boat, Evens had offered him a cup of tea that his sister brewed. It had settled his stomach immediately. When Randy inquired about it, he discovered it came from a plant that she had brought from Haiti.

Based on Evens's description of the plant, Randy figured it was angel's trumpet or *Brugmansia*. Randy had worked for a tropical plant nursery in Naples, so he was familiar with the plant. He reasoned that if Evens's sister knew how to properly make the tea, it could be a gold-mine in Key West. With the cruise ships stopping weekly, he could sell it to the tourists, who were gone in a few days.

He'd pressed Evens to introduce him to his sister, a palm reader named Mysterie. Randy was hoping to enlist her as a supplier. It was an understatement to say it didn't go well. She was, however, devoted to her baby brother, so Randy had persuaded Evens to get the tea.

When the waitress walked over and asked if he needed anything, he handed her a twenty and told her to keep the change. She rewarded him with a big smile and thanked him twice for the six dollar tip.

He wiped his mouth, then rose to leave. Outside, he smiled as he looked at the horde of tourists. A cruise ship had docked earlier, and he knew his two guys were already working the new arrivals down at the pier. They were hawking the special blend of "herbal" tea.

There was nothing illegal about the tea itself, containing dried parts of the flowers from Mysterie's plants. However, the plants contained substantial amounts of scopolamine, a very potent though largely uncontrolled drug. A powerful, dissociative medicine, scopolamine had a reputation as the "zombie" drug. The right dosage had the capability to make a person compliant, willing to do almost anything and not remembering afterward—the ideal date-rape drug, which made it popular with the cruise ship crowd.

Randy understood the illegal drug business, but he preferred plants. He had concentrated on what he called "botanicals," drugs that could easily be made from plants. It was a small, but profitable trade and he was constantly on the lookout for new products to sell to an eager clientele.

He had come to the west coast of Florida to work with his half-brother, Peabo Watson. Peabo worked for Dr. Devo Drager, a successful pain management physician in the Tampa Bay area who also ran a thriving illegal prescription drug trade. Prescription drugs were hot in Florida, but, unfortunately, attracted a lot of attention from law enforcement. Too many people involved and too many trails ultimately led to Drager's downfall. The only thing that saved Randy is that he had never met the doctor. With Peabo dead, there was no connection to Randy.

What happened at Big Cat Rescue, Randy didn't know. Before his ill-fated trip to Big Cat Rescue, Peabo had told Randy someone stole a million dollars from him and he was going to make that person pay dearly. That person was Jack Davis, who had a sailboat named *Left Behind* at the Clearwater Marina.

Randy did know two things: the police only recovered a hundred thousand dollars from the deal and Jack Davis was responsible for Peabo's death.

Family was everything.

3

After locking up the boat, Jack and Molly decided to brave Duval Street. Most days, they avoided the busy tourist thoroughfare. Since they had no plans for the afternoon, they walked over to the crowded street, checking out the tourists and always-interesting locals.

"Terry figures it'll be Monday before the mechanic can come," he said. "He said he'd call as soon as he talks to him."

As they passed a side street, Molly said, "I've always wanted to do that."

"What?" He looked around, trying to figure out what she was talking about.

She nodded to her left and he saw a neon sign a few doors down.

"Get my palm read," she said. "Remember when I tried to get you to do it in New Orleans at Marie Laveau's?"

He chuckled. "I don't remember much of that night."

Three months ago, Jack had suggested they fly to New Orleans for a long weekend, thinking a change of scenery might do Molly good. They'd eaten some great food and gone down to Decatur Street to listen to music. He vaguely remembered eating beignets at three a.m.

He'd forgotten about her wanting to go to the famous voodoo queen's storefront on Bourbon Street. Unfortunately, he recalled that the trip hadn't made much of a change in Molly's disposition.

"Why would you want to do that? It's just a scam."

Molly frowned. "I'm sure some of them are, but maybe some are legitimate. It's possible, you know?"

He started to argue, then shook his head. "I think it's a waste of money. How about a lobster roll for lunch?" he asked, changing the subject.

A block later, they stopped at DJ's Clam Shack, a popular local spot for lunch. Most of the places on Duval were tourist traps, but DJ's had the best lobster rolls in town. They ordered and found a seat in the back on the small deck, where they waited for their food.

"They're probably at Fort Jefferson by now," Molly said, referring to Kenny and Val.

"I'm sure they are, anchored and snorkeling. Too bad there's no cell service out there—I'd give them a call and harass them."

"Can you reach them on the radio?" Both boats had a VHF radio, standard equipment on any boat in the Keys.

Jack shook his head. "Too far."

"I was so looking forward to a couple of days out on the boat."

"Me, too. I'll make it up to you. We'll go out as soon as the refrigerator is fixed."

Wanting to lighten things up, he said, "I can read palms, you know?"

Molly looked at him without answering and cocked her head.

"No, really," he said. "I never told you about the gypsy who lived in our neighborhood in Jacksonville? She taught me."

Molly rolled her eyes, but couldn't withhold a thin smile. "I suppose she was related to the one-legged pirate you told me lived on the next block?"

Emboldened, he held out his left hand, palm up. "Give me your hand."

She looked at him, then put her right hand in his, opening it up to face him. He took his index finger and started tracing lines on her palm.

She jerked. "It tickles."

"Be still. I have to concentrate."

Her green eyes stared at him, trying to discern whether to believe him or not. "Okay. I'll try."

"This is your heart line," he said, tracing the line closest to her fingers. "You have fallen madly in love with someone. Hopefully me."

She giggled, and he gave her a reproachful look.

He traced the next line down. "This is your head line. You are spontaneous and adventurous."

She was listening now and paying attention, the frivolity fading.

Moving down to the next one, still tracing with his finger, he said, "This is your life line. You are energetic and healthy."

He glanced at her. She was studying her palm, focusing on the movement of his finger. He picked out another line.

"This is your action line." He traced it back and forth several times. He paused and wrinkled his brow before speaking. "You want to rip your clothes off and make mad, passionate love to your husband."

She snatched her hand off of his and slapped it.

"You had me going for a minute," she said.

He laughed. "Hey, I just tell what I read." He reached out and put his hand on her arm and arched his eyebrows. "So, whadda ya think?" he asked, leering at her.

She grinned. "Maybe. We'll see how nice you are the rest of the afternoon."

It was nice to see her smile, and he beamed at the possibility of more to come. Her decreased libido since Clearwater had been noticeable, but she was getting back to her old self. He missed the intimacy. Lately, things had seemed to slip back into the familiar, and he could only hope they were getting back to normal.

After lunch, when they got back to the boat, Jack unlocked the companionway and they went below. He opened the cooler to see if they needed more ice while Molly checked her phone for messages. As he closed the lid, she held up her phone to Jack. "You've got a message. Tony wants you to call him," she said.

"Tony?"

She nodded, and he realized it must be Tony Budzinski, their detective friend from Fort Myers. "Tony from Fort Myers?" he asked, to confirm they were talking about the same person.

She nodded again.

"Wonder what he wants?" He fumbled around and found his phone on a shelf over the small table. He picked up the phone and pressed the HOME button. Nothing. He pressed it again and realized the battery was dead. He shook his head and looked around for the charger.

"Your phone dead? Again?" Molly said, a slight edge to her voice.

He started to respond but decided better of it. He knew she was getting concerned about their financial situation. Truth was, they were in pretty good shape.

He found the charger, plugged it in and connected it to his phone. "I'll call him later."

She shrugged. "He said it wasn't urgent, but you can use my phone if you'd like." Her eyes were questioning and daring him at once.

He was about to reach for it when she continued. "Maybe he's got some work for you."

He and Molly didn't have enough saved to retire permanently. Sooner or later, he was going to have to find a way of generating at least some modest income. With Molly now working part-time, he felt the pressure to contribute.

"It can wait," he said. He set his phone down and went back topside.

A few minutes later, Molly emerged from the cabin. "I'm going over to Fausto's to pick up a few groceries. You need anything?"

He shook his head.

"I'll stop by the seafood market to pick up something for dinner," she said.

As she stepped off the boat, he felt bad about being such an ass. "Be careful. Love you."

She hesitated, then over her shoulder said, "Love you, too. Later."

He smiled. She didn't sound angry, which was good. He knew he was being ornery and chalked it up to a serious lack of conjugal relations. They had always had an active sex life, but since Clearwater, it had dropped to an unhealthy low.

After giving his phone another thirty minutes to charge, he went down below, grabbed a bottle of water, and unplugged the phone from the charger. Turning it on as he made his way back up on deck, he scrolled through his contacts, found Tony's number and called.

"It's about time. I thought you were blowing me off," Tony said when he answered.

"My phone died and I had to charge it. How are you?"

"Good, thanks. Molly?"

He hesitated, not sure how to answer. "Better, I think. She's doing some part-time work at the hospital down here and that's good for her."

"She still seeing someone?" Tony asked, referring to her therapist.

"Yes, and the therapist keeps saying it's going to take time, but she's pleased with the progress Molly's making."

"She's been through a lot, but she's strong and a survivor. She'll make it. How about you? What are you doing?"

"Running. Reading. Eating and drinking, though not necessarily in that order."

Tony laughed. "Sounds like the good life to me."

"Doesn't pay well, but yes, Key West is not a bad place to hang out."

Tony's voice took on a serious note. "Be careful, Jack. It's easy to slip into bad habits." He paused. "I know."

Jack nodded, even though he was on the phone. When Tony had retired a year ago, he'd slid into a depression and started drinking too much. It had affected Tony and Connie's marriage. Connie had called Jack, begging him to intervene.

He'd spent a couple of days in Fort Myers, most of it in Tony's face. He'd persuaded his friend to get help and ease up on the booze.

"I will, Tony." Uncomfortable with the direction of the conversation, he changed the subject. "Everything okay in Fort Myers?"

There was an awkward silence on the line. "I need your help, Jack."

Jack's first thought was that the depression was back, but then he realized Tony wouldn't have just made the comment he had if that was the problem. But he was still worried. For Tony to call and ask for help, it had to be something serious. He and Tony were alike in that respect and asked for help only as a last resort.

"What's the matter? Connie alright?"

Tony cleared his throat and exhaled. "We're fine—I mean, health-wise, we're okay. It's not that. And, no, I'm still on the wagon." He paused, then said, "It's a long story."

"Time is something I've got plenty of these days, Tony. Talk to me."

Over the next forty-five minutes, Tony told him a classic tale of financial imprudence. Several years ago, Connie had inherited a small sum when her mother passed, and they had invested it in a friend's medical equipment business, along with the bulk of their lifetime savings. Now, that investment was in jeopardy, and Tony didn't know where to turn.

"This happened before we met you, Jack. At the time, I didn't have anyone to ask for financial advice."

Jack shook his head. He'd heard this before. He just hoped it wasn't too late.

"I was wondering if you would come up and go through everything with me. Give me some advice on what to do," Tony said.

Fort Myers was a five-hour drive, on a good day. From Key West to the mainland, there was only one highway,

US 1, which was mostly two lanes. Flying was a reasonable alternative, providing the weather cooperated. It was a fifty-minute trip and there were two direct flights each day. Last, there was the ferry, with one trip a day. While it was half the cost of a plane ticket, it was a three and a half hour trip and some weeks didn't operate on certain days.

"When?" He couldn't refuse Tony.

"As soon as you can. I hate to impose, but this kind of caught me by surprise."

"Monday okay? I'll check and see if I can get a flight up. Easier than driving."

"Monday would be great."

"I'll call you back after I know my arrangements. Give my regards to Connie."

"I will, and love to Molly. Thanks, Jack."

He set the phone down and went below to get his laptop, figuring he might as well try to learn a bit about the durable medical equipment business.

On paper, DME was a simple business. Someone would buy medical equipment like wheelchairs, beds, or scooters, and rent it out. The margins were incredible. A wheelchair could be purchased for several hundred dollars and rented out for that much in one month's rental fees, usually billed to Medicare or Medicaid. With a three-year life expectancy, that meant an investment of $300 would return $72,000—an obscene gross profit of thousands of percent. Higher ticket items, such as electric scooters, meant even bigger returns.

Companies that weren't reputable were known to bill for phantom patients or recruit homeless people to "rent" equipment, pushing the returns to even higher levels.

He was so absorbed in his research that he didn't hear Molly come back. He felt the boat move as she stepped aboard, and looked up to see her carrying two bags.

"I've got it," she said, halfway joking.

He stood and took the bags from her. "Sorry I was such an ass earlier." He pointed to the computer. "I was doing a little research and didn't hear you."

She kissed him on the lips, leaving her hand on his chest. "Maybe we can have an early dinner, with a nice glass of wine," she said when she pulled back.

He smiled and nodded, believing he saw a bit of sparkle in her eyes. "That can easily be arranged. What'd you get at Eaton's?" he said, holding up the reusable shopping bag.

"I picked up a nice piece of grouper. Maybe you could grill it?" She looked at the computer. "What kind of research are you doing?"

"I talked to Tony. Long story short, he wants me to come up and go over his financial situation. He and Connie invested in a medical equipment business and it seems to be going south. I was just getting some background info."

"Interesting," she said.

He shrugged. "Too bad this gig doesn't pay," he added, trying to make amends.

She smiled, leaned over, and kissed him. "They're good friends, and that's more important."

Halfway through the wine and dinner, as Jack had hoped, they did indeed remove each other's clothes and make love. Reminiscent of earlier days and more passionate than it had been in months. Maybe things were getting better. Afterward, they cleaned up the galley and went back topside.

"Hey guys," said a familiar female voice from the dock. They turned to see Doug and Lisa, a couple who lived around the corner at Key West Bight Marina on a Catalina 355. Along with Kenny and Val, the three couples were close friends and kindred spirits. Lisa and Val worked at Lower Keys Medical Center with Molly. Doug was a computer guru and worked as an IT consultant.

"What are you guys up to?" Lisa asked.

Jack looked over at Molly and they both grinned.

"Uh-oh, did we interrupt something?" Lisa said, giggling.

"We've already had dessert," Jack said, winking at Molly. "Come on up. How about a glass of wine?"

"Thought you'd never ask," Doug said, as they stepped onboard.

Jack went below and brought up two more glasses. Most boat people, as liveaboards called themselves, used plastic, but he insisted on real glass for wine. After pouring everyone a glass, they all took a sip and relaxed as Jack told them about his new "job."

"How long is this job going to last?" Lisa asked.

Jack shrugged. "Hard to tell. I'm planning on going up for a couple of days next week. Unfortunately, this is a freebie."

"That's okay, they're good friends," Molly explained, patting Jack on the leg. "Besides, right now I'm enjoying him being my galley slave."

"Whoa," Doug said. "Starting to sound a bit kinky."

"We didn't come over to bum a drink," Lisa said, as Jack refilled her glass.

"Maybe she didn't, but I did," Doug said, laughing.

Lisa rolled her eyes, shook her head, and continued. "We thought you guys might want to walk down to the Square for the sunset. I know it's not Garden Key, but it's not too shabby."

Every evening before sunset, like lemmings, people in Key West gravitated toward Mallory Square for the sunset and the street performers. Jack and Molly hadn't made that trek in weeks.

"Don't remind us," Jack said. "Kenny and Val are probably grilling steaks about now."

"We'll just have to plan another trip when they get back," Lisa said. "Maybe next time, I can get off work, too, and we can have a three-boat flotilla."

"Weather is perfect, and the best part—no cruise ships tonight," Doug said. "The one in this morning has gone."

The cruise ships had been a source of controversy for the residents of Key West. While they brought in thousands of tourists—and dollars—they were not welcome by everyone. Key West, while still a unique and quirky place, had lost lots of its charm from years past.

Jack put his hand on Molly's arm and said, "We'd love to. We haven't been in forever."

They finished their wine, then locked up the boat, and headed over to Mallory Square.

They made their way through the throngs of people, pausing for a few minutes in front of the Westin to watch Dominique, the cat man. The busker had been doing his routine in Key West for over thirty years. His shtick was training ordinary housecats to do extraordinary feats, like jump through a ring of fire. Rumor had it, he lived in a mansion overlooking the Atlantic.

As they watched Dominique start working the crowd, Lisa piped up and said, "Somebody at the hospital told me he lives in a house next to Louie's." Louie's Backyard was one of the nicest restaurants in town, situated in an oceanfront home.

"I heard that, too," Molly said. "He also put a daughter through college." They watched Dominique for a few minutes, then wound their way back to the other end of the pier.

They browsed the various vendor booths as they walked. They passed an exotic looking woman sitting at a table, advertising palm readings. She had short brown hair and large, gold hoop earrings. They paused and watched her for a few minutes as she was reading a person's palm.

"Molly's dying to do that," Jack said.

"Really?" Lisa said, looking at Molly in surprise. "I didn't figure you as someone who'd be into that."

"I don't know that I am, but I'd like to try it," Molly said.

As they walked off, Lisa said, "She works as a bartender over at the Green Parrot. Normally, she only comes down here when a cruise ship is in. She also does body painting during Fantasy Fest. She makes more that week than she makes the entire summer. If you want a real palm reader, you should go over to Mysterie's just off Duval."

Molly looked at Jack. "That was the one we passed today at lunch."

Doug and Jack looked at each other and rolled their eyes.

Lisa ignored them. "Doug thinks it's all 'hocus-pocus' and a lot of it is. I'm just saying Mysterie is the real deal. I've been there several times and she is amazing." She looked at Doug. "You should try it, you might be surprised."

"I'd rather open up a body-painting booth for Fantasy Fest. What do you think?" Doug said, looking at Jack and grinning.

Fantasy Fest was a ten-day festival of debauchery the end of October, culminating with the Saturday night parade on the last Saturday of the month. On Friday and Saturday, most of Duval Street was closed to vehicle traffic and mobbed with partygoers well-lubricated with alcohol and God-knows what else. Public nudity was supposedly banned, but many people tested the limits, wearing as little as possible. Some brave women wore nothing but body paint.

"I'm in," Jack said.

Molly slapped him on the arm. "Don't even think about it."

Lisa shook her head. "They are so full of it."

They squeezed in and found a place for Lisa and Molly to sit on the edge of the pier, legs dangling above the water while the guys stood behind them. It was going to be a gorgeous sunset. Oranges and reds streaked the sky as the sun neared the horizon. A sailboat passed in front, and some of the onlookers jeered, wanting it out of their picture. Others oohed and aahed, snapping selfies on their phones.

Jack squeezed Molly's hand and whispered in her ear. "Wish we were out there with Kenny and Val."

4

Early Monday morning, Molly watched as Jack left on his bike to go to the airport on the southeast side of Key West. Yesterday, he'd made reservations to fly up to Fort Myers for the day to see Tony.

She was bored, not scheduled to go back to work until Wednesday evening. Jack had tried to get her to go with him, but she wasn't interested in going up just for the day and they agreed to make another trip when they had more time. She'd called her manager to tell her that her plans had changed and she be available if they needed her to work.

Molly liked working at the small hospital in Key West. Even though she and Jack were far from broke, the money came in handy. Compared to her last few positions, she enjoyed the variety of working in different departments, and not having the management responsibility.

Key West had been good for them. She didn't remember anything about what happened in Clearwater. She'd asked Wren, and the young girl claimed she didn't remember anything either. It was like the experience had been erased.

Molly's intuition told her it was ugly. Some nights she would awake in a cold sweat from horrible nightmares.

Certain smells or when Jack touched her a certain way triggered a strong negative reaction which she couldn't explain. The good news is it was happening less frequently and she was beginning to feel more like her old self.

She wondered if it was worse not knowing than knowing and being able to process it. She'd been seeing a therapist in Key West since they'd moved down, and that had helped some. Yet, Molly was the type of person who wanted to know details, good or bad.

Jack had said he'd stop and grab a coffee and a bagel before he left the island, but she hadn't had breakfast yet. Last night, she'd picked at dinner, not eating much, but this morning, she was hungry. She headed over to the Cuban Coffee Queen only a few blocks away for an egg and cheese sandwich and coffee.

After eating, she decided to walk over to Duval Street. It was almost ten, so most of the shops would soon be opening. It was different in the light of day, especially in the morning. Duval was for creatures of the night, not the day. After lunch, as the hung-over tourists stumbled out of bed, the numbers would start growing. By late night, the street would be packed with amnesiacs, starting all over and repeating their mistakes of the previous evening. She enjoyed the peace of the morning as opposed to the bedlam of dark.

When she got to Duval, she turned left and walked along the famous street, to many the heart of Key West. The shops were opening, and many of the bars were already open, though only occupied by a few hard-core partiers. A few blocks further east, the mix changed from predominately bars to more retail shops and galleries.

She stopped at Petronia Street and looked over at the palm reader's sign a few doors down. It was the shop she and Jack had passed a few days earlier. The sign was lit, so she turned and walked that direction. The door was open, and she considered going in.

She knew Jack thought it was all baloney. Although he wouldn't have minded, she would rather go by herself. She wasn't sure about it but wanted to try it. Now was the perfect opportunity, with him on his way to Fort Myers.

Taking a couple of steps inside the bead covered doorway, she paused and peeked around. The walls were covered with all sorts of mysterious paraphernalia that she didn't recognize. Various objects hung from the ceiling. There was a young girl behind the counter, sitting on a stool and reading a book. She sensed Molly's presence, looked up, and said, "It's okay to come in and look around."

Molly smiled, feeling a little embarrassed. She stepped inside the shop, not knowing where to start.

"If you have any questions, I'd be happy to help you," the young girl said.

"You do palm readings?"

Shaking her head, the girl smiled, and nodded toward a curtain pulled across a doorway leading to the back.

"I don't. Mysterie does, but she's busy right now. I'll be happy to schedule a reading if you'd like?"

Molly hesitated. "No thanks. Just curious. Maybe some other time."

She turned and looked at the items on the shelves. There were charms, books, and what she assumed to be voodoo dolls. Totally foreign to her, but her environment in the hospital would probably be equally daunting to someone not familiar. As she perused the curious items in the shop, she heard a rustling and looked up to see a tall woman come through the doorway and stop, looking at her.

She was striking, her skin the color of a well-prepared cappuccino or café con leche. She wore a single, large, gold hoop earring dangling from her right ear. A green print scarf was wrapped, turban style, around her head.

"Are you here for a reading?" the woman asked. Her voice was soothing, with a lilt to it that Molly recognized as coming from the Caribbean. Molly hesitated, almost unsure if the question was directed to her. A quick glance around the little shop confirmed she was the only customer there.

"There's no need to be nervous," the woman said, seeming to sense Molly's reluctance. "Relax. Be comfortable. I'm Mysterie. And you?"

"Molly," she answered at last.

Mysterie smiled, and Molly found it calming. "You've never had a reading before, have you?"

She shook her head.

"There's nothing to fear. Come on back." She motioned to Molly to follow her, and turned, walking back through the beaded curtain.

Molly walked through the doorway and found herself in a dimly lit room. Mysterie was taking her seat on the opposite side of a small table, covered with a colorful cloth. She beckoned to Molly to sit in the vacant chair, the only other place to sit in the room.

"Would you like some tea? Maybe it would help you relax."

Molly nodded, and Mysterie turned to a small table behind her, where a small teapot sat on a hotplate. She poured Molly a cup and handed it to her.

Molly noticed the fragrance as she brought the cup to her lips, but couldn't place it. She took a small sip and swallowed. The tea tasted of flowers and chamomile. She took another sip, and then set the cup on the table.

"I didn't have an appointment and I haven't paid, yet."

Mysterie smiled. "That's okay. You can pay when you leave or pay next time."

Next time? Molly started to say something when Mysterie held out her left hand, palm up, and elbow just above the table top.

"Please, give me your hand, Molly."

Molly hesitated but felt drawn to comply. It was like a struggle was going on inside her head. One voice telling her to run, and the other arguing to stay.

She stretched out her arm, and turned her hand over, presenting her palm. As she lowered it to Mysterie's unwavering hand, she felt a slight charge the instant the back of her hand touched the woman's palm. It felt like a current had passed between them, and her hand twitched.

Molly relaxed as if a warm blanket had been gently pulled over her. In a soothing voice, Mysterie asked some simple, non-threatening questions, and it was as if the voice was coming from a third, unseen person. The palm reader then proceeded to tell Molly things, things she thought she'd forgotten, and things she'd tried to forget, but oddly, it wasn't upsetting.

An hour later, after they'd finished, Mysterie rose. "I'm sorry Molly, I have an appointment coming in a few minutes."

"How do you know . . ."

Mysterie laughed, but it was a gentle laugh, not mocking. "It's a gift. I'll tell you more when you come back, but you

and I are kindred souls. I knew it the moment your hand
touched mine."

5

Before her next appointment, Mysterie went back to her living quarters to get more tea. As she walked through the breezeway from the shop, she noticed her brother's diving gear was gone. He worked in a boatyard and also cleaned boat bottoms on the side. She thought he was off today, so maybe he'd gone out spearfishing.

At her kitchen window, Mysterie closed her eyes and took a deep breath, inhaling the pleasant fragrance of the towering shrub outside. It was so large it looked like a tree. The soft white flowers, tinged with pale pink, resembled trumpets, all obediently facing down. The plant appeared to be raining flowers.

Her yard contained several other smaller copies, all originating from this one. She'd rooted it from stock she'd brought over from Haiti—from a plant at her Aunt Hattie's house. The common name was angel's trumpet, native to tropical or semi-tropical environments. It had the most beautiful and sweet-smelling flowers. But the beauty masked its true nature.

It was no secret that the plant produced scopolamine, a powerful drug with a variety of medical uses but most well-known for its effectiveness in preventing motion sickness.

Mysterie smiled as she remembered taking a cup of Hattie's tea before getting on a boat to Florida.

Hattie was the one who'd taught her the magic of the plant. The leaves could be used as a poultice since the chemical was readily absorbed through the skin. Various parts of the plant could be boiled in water, creating a tea.

Either way, the problem was gauging the amount of scopolamine. There were substantial variations in potency from one plant to another. All parts of the plant contained the drug, with widely different levels. Even the same plant, under different conditions, could produce wide variations in the strength.

At the weakest level, the drug could prevent motion sickness and nausea. One tiny step up produced the dosage known on the street as the Zombie drug. It was odorless, colorless, and used as a "date-rape" drug. A person taking it was powerless to resist. Scopolamine was different from other such drugs in that the person literally couldn't remember what happened. It was as if the memory was never recorded. It simply didn't exist with scopolamine.

The last step up was deadly. The range between effectiveness and death was very small and to further complicate things, alcohol exaggerated the side effects of scopolamine.

This plant was unusual in that its consistency was extremely reliable. While the seeds and leaves still contained the highest concentration, it was measurably uniform. Hattie showed her how to determine the strength by varying the amounts and proportions of the plant parts.

Mysterie opened the cabinet over the sink where she stored the tea in large tins. She took one off the shelf and thinking it felt too light, she opened it. The tin was half full.

She'd noticed the tea was disappearing at an alarming rate. When she questioned Evens, her younger brother who lived with her, he said people at work were asking for it.

Darker than her, he was simple-minded but loyal and strong. He had a good job at the boatyard, where he had a natural mechanical aptitude that served him well. Still, she worried about him. He was naive and others were quick to take advantage of him. She was afraid that was happening again.

She'd been in Key West for almost two years, coming over with Evens from Haiti via New Orleans. Haiti was where she learned voodoo and palm reading. After spending five years in New Orleans working at Madame Leveau's House of Voodoo, she felt it was time to move on before her juju ran out.

Key West was perfect, full of transients and tourists. Everybody here was running from something or someone or both. As long as a person kept their nose clean and stayed under the radar, the authorities generally left you alone. They had more pressing problems to deal with, such as cruise ships full of drunk tourists.

Mysterie had a gift, one she'd inherited from her mother. Of all the fortune tellers in Key West, she was authentic. She wasn't infallible, but many things she could foretell. Her gift was so genuine, she had to be careful to sprinkle deliberate falsehoods in amongst her predictions. Being too right too often would draw unwanted attention.

It was ironic, she thought. One of the people she had the hardest time reading was Evens, her brother. He'd been acting strange the last couple of days, quieter than usual. She knew something was bothering him, but she couldn't see any farther. Smiling, she guessed he was feeling guilty about taking so much tea.

Mysterie looked at the time. She needed to get back to the shop. A cruise ship had docked this morning, and she knew the day would be busy. She made a mental note to have a talk with Evens the next chance she got.

She had just sat on the stool behind the counter when the chime on the door sounded. A young couple walked in, looking around. Tourists for sure. She could sense their hesitation, especially his. Typical. Usually, the female was the one that wanted to have a reading, dragging the male along.

The girl was young, probably late teens. She was attractive, wearing short shorts, and a skimpy, revealing top. Her long, blonde hair was tied in a ponytail.

Her boyfriend had the thick neck and stocky build of a farm boy or wrestler or both.

"How much is a palm reading?" the girl asked.

"Forty-five dollars."

"Do you take credit cards?"

Mysterie nodded.

The girl looked at her boyfriend with expectant eyes, squeezing his hand.

Without a lot of enthusiasm, he shrugged, as if to say, *whatever*. He pulled out his wallet and handed the young girl a credit card.

"I'll be next door," he said as he turned and walked out.

Mysterie knew he was referring to the bar. She indicated for the girl to follow her back behind the curtain to her reading room.

"Have a seat," she said, as she sat in her chair and extended her arm to indicate the comfortable seat opposite the small round table. "What's your name?"

"Tammy," the girl said as she sat. She handed her the credit card.

"I'm Mysterie. Relax while I run this, and then we'll get started."

The girl scrunched up her shoulders and smiled. "I've never done this before, but I've always wanted to. How does it work?"

Mysterie swiped the credit card and asked the girl to sign the form on the iPad with her finger.

"It's simple, really. Are you here on vacation?"

She nodded. "Brad and I are on a cruise—our graduation present. We left Miami yesterday. I picked this cruise because I'd always wanted to come to Key West. It's so different down here. Brad didn't want to come. I figured I'd probably never get another chance."

"Did your parents come, too?"

She giggled and lowered her voice. "No, thank goodness. My mom thinks I'm with my girlfriend, Kay. Kay's with her boyfriend, Todd. We're covering for each other."

Mysterie held out her left hand, palm up.

"Relax, and place your right hand in mine."

Tammy did as instructed.

She felt a slight tingle when Tammy's hand touched hers. It always did when she touched another person.

When she was a child, it scared her, until her mother explained it was part of the gift. Her mother told her she knew she had the gift when she was in her belly before she was born. That was why she named her Mysterie.

Her mother had the gift, but not as powerful as hers. Over the years, she taught Mysterie how to manage it. That all changed one night when she was thirteen.

Her mother was sick with the fever and sent her to her uncle's shack to stay so she wouldn't catch it. In the middle of the night, Mysterie awoke and found her uncle touching her while she was lying on a mat in the kitchen. He whispered in her ear to be quiet or her mother would die.

She was afraid. She tried not to make a sound as she felt her uncle's hands touching her all over her body, in places where no one had ever touched her before. She whimpered as she felt his fingers entering her.

When he climbed on top of her, she covered her mouth as she felt him press his thing inside her. It was too big and it hurt. When she cried out in pain, he covered her mouth with his. She remembered the bitter taste of tobacco and rum in his mouth.

After he finished, he lay there on top of her, breathing hard against her chest. Before he rose, he whispered in her ear again. *Don't tell anyone. If you do, she will die.*

Two days later, her mother came to get her. She was better, and Mysterie was convinced her silence had worked. She tried to avoid being alone with her uncle, for every time she was, he would take her again.

Two months later, she didn't bleed at her normal time. When she missed the second month, she noticed her breasts were more tender than usual.

When she told her mother, she never forgot the look on her mother's face. Her mother wanted to know who she'd been lying with, accusing the neighborhood boy who'd grown up with Mysterie.

"You're with child," her mother said.

The next day, her mother took her to the neighboring village, telling her she was taking her to see a nurse who would help her.

Mysterie remembered going into the nurse's shack. She was an older woman with wrinkled skin, long hair, and rotten teeth. The nurse asked her mother to wait outside.

She asked Mysterie a few questions and then told her to take off her dress. She did, embarrassed as she felt the bare, cold fingers of the woman touching her belly and her breasts. The woman instructed her to lie on the dirty mat in the corner and gave her a thick piece of leather to put between her teeth.

She remembered the woman telling her she needed to examine her down there, and it might be painful. Mysterie lay there, the filthy piece of leather in her mouth, looking up at the holes in the tin covering the roof. She didn't look at the woman or what she was doing.

She felt fingers entering her, and then the cold intrusion of metal, pushing and probing. She bit down on the leather. Finally, she heard the woman tell her to get up, that she would be fine.

It was only later that she realized the nurse had aborted her baby.

She turned her attention back to Tammy. She went through the ritual of tracing the lines on her palm, even though it wasn't necessary.

Tammy was madly in love with Brad. They'd been having sex for some time, and she wanted to get pregnant and marry him. She wanted to be a teacher.

Mysterie couldn't know what Brad was thinking without touching his hand. But, based on her experience and observation, Brad was using the girl to fulfill his physical needs and had no intention of marrying Tammy.

It made her sad, and she was tempted to cast a spell on him. That was the downfall of having the gift, wanting to right every wrong. But, she'd learned that she couldn't fix everything and sometimes she had to let fate take its course, good or bad. This was one of those times.

What Tammy didn't know, but would soon find out, is that she was with child.

6

Molly got back to the marina, still in a daze. As she turned to go out the dock, she saw Terry coming toward her.

"Hey, Molly. I was just coming down to tell you the mechanic will be over in an hour or so to fix your refrigerator."

"Great, I hope he can get it fixed this afternoon. It's been a pain without it the past few days."

Terry laughed. "Evens is good. He's with Keys Marine. Big fellow, from Haiti. Kinda quiet, but he knows what he's doing. He'll have you back up in no time. Let me know if you need anything."

Later, Molly was sitting out under the bimini, reading, when she heard someone approaching. She looked up to see a large, dark-skinned man standing on the dock next to *Left Behind.*

"Ms. Davis?" he asked in a soft-spoken voice that seemed out of synch with someone his size. He was wearing shorts and a logo shirt with KEYS MARINE over the pocket, carrying a large toolbox that matched his stature.

"Yes. You must be Evens, the mechanic Terry was telling me about. You're here to fix our refrigerator, I hope?"

He smiled, displaying a single gold tooth on the upper right side of his mouth. "Yes, ma'am."

Molly welcomed him aboard and showed him where the refrigerator was. He asked where the propane tank was, and she led him back topside to the stern locker.

"I'll need to shut off the gas," he said.

"No problem. Let me know if you need anything," she said and settled back down to read.

An hour later, Evens emerged from the cabin, sweat glistening on his brow. "It's working. Just a bad relay. I figured that's what it would be, so I brought one with me."

"You just made my day. I didn't realize how spoiled we are."

"Yes, ma'am." He presented her with the bill and said he needed to turn the gas back on. She gave him her credit card and he copied the information down on the form, asked her to sign, and gave her a copy.

After he left, she texted Jack that the refrigerator was working and walked over to Nick's boat to retrieve her food.

That evening, she had dinner over at Doug and Lisa's. She couldn't stop talking about her session with Mysterie.

"It was amazing. It was like she was inside my head," Molly said.

When Doug couldn't hide his disbelief any longer, Lisa turned to him and said, "Hey, don't knock it till you try it. I know exactly what she's talking about and it's true."

"Whatever," he said. "Sorry, but my computer beckons. I've got some work to finish for a client. If you two will excuse me."

As he walked away, Lisa said in a not-so-soft voice, "Yeah, World of Warcraft beckons."

After Doug was gone, Molly lowered her voice and said, "She told me things about Ambrose. She knew I wanted to kill him."

Ambrose Clark, her first husband, was a sociopathic doctor. She'd left him in the middle of the night after he'd threatened to kill her. She was afraid of him but more afraid of what she knew she was capable of doing to him. She drove non-stop from Boston to Savannah, Georgia, and the next morning to Florida.

Lisa nodded, not surprised. "I told you she was the real deal."

After dinner, Molly went back to *Left Behind* and sat in the cockpit, waiting for Jack to get home. She was anxious to see him but hadn't decided if she was going to mention seeing Mysterie.

"Hey, good looking. Mind if I join you?" Jack said. Engrossed in her book, she hadn't heard him walk up.

Smiling, she put her book down and stood to greet him.

"How was your trip?" she asked.

"Interesting. I'll fill you in. Glad to have your refrigerator back?"

"Oh yes. It didn't take the mechanic long this afternoon. He said it was a relay or something, but he had one with him. I went and got our food from Nick, then had dinner with Doug and Lisa. How're Tony and Connie?"

"Good. Not sure about their investment. I'm tired. I've been looking at accounting records and financial statements all day and my eyes are crossed. Let me put my bag up and get a glass of wine. Good day?"

"Yes, it was."

A few minutes later, Jack came up with two glasses and an open bottle of wine. He poured them each a glass and sat next to Molly.

"How are Tony and Connie doing?" she asked.

Jack frowned. "Tony's not looking good. I don't know what's going on. He's gained some weight, doesn't seem to be feeling well. I asked him about it, and he shrugged it off, saying he was going to the doctor this week. Connie looks great, as always. They both said to give you their love."

"What about their investment?"

He shook his head. "I got the background from Tony and looked over financial statements and everything they had. First glance, and I need to do more research, but the company looks solid. I thought about it on the way back and what I don't understand is why they're selling. I told him I'd check it out and try to get back to him in a few days. Maybe you can go up there with me next time."

"I'd like that."

Jack stretched his arms out, took a sip of wine and asked, "What did you do today?"

She took a deep breath and said, "Went for a walk downtown this morning. Got my palm read, came back—"

"Got your palm read? So you went to that kook on Petronia?"

"She's not a kook," she said, folding her arms across her chest. "You're as bad as Doug."

"What did she say? You going to win the lottery or something?"

"Forget it."

"No, really. Tell me about it."

She glared at him, trying to determine if he was serious.

"She told me things, things she had no way of knowing."

"Like what?"

"She told me about Ambrose."

Jack cocked his head, clearly skeptical. "She told you about Ambrose? By name?"

Molly thought for a moment. "Well, she didn't mention him by name, but she said I'd been with someone before my current husband, someone who'd abused me."

Jack snorted. "Oh, well that's very profound and detailed. A lucky guess, probably based on some introductory chit-chat you'd had. That's the way those people work."

She started to say that there was more, but she knew this was headed toward a quarrel and she wasn't in the mood to fight.

"Just forget it, okay? You believe what you want."

Jack started to snap back, then shook his head. "If you want to waste your money, then go ahead. I don't care."

7

Tuesday morning, Jack walked up to the office to thank Terry for getting the mechanic out to fix the refrigerator. When he rounded the corner at Alonzo's, Jack saw Terry standing out front talking to an official-looking woman dressed in pants and blazer—unusual in Key West. Short and trim with shaggy brown hair, she was nodding. If he had to guess, he'd say she was law enforcement.

"Jack," Terry said when he saw him, motioning him over. "Got a minute?"

Jack sensed this wasn't a request, as the woman turned to study him. He approached with caution, wondering what was going on.

Terry introduced her as Detective Cally Stevens with the Monroe County Sheriff's Office. As they shook hands, Terry continued. "Sunday morning, an abandoned sailboat was found adrift near Satan Shoal." He hesitated, cleared his throat, and looked at Jack. "It was the *Black Swan.*"

Jack shook his head in disbelief. *Black Swan* was Kenny and Valerie's boat. It was the only boat he knew of with that name. "Are they okay?" he asked. The somber faces surrounding him gave him the answer he feared.

Detective Stevens spoke. "Have you got a few minutes, Mr. Davis?" Her voice was firm, with a trace of New England in the roots.

Still processing the news, he nodded. Terry excused himself as the detective escorted Jack over to an empty table at Alonzo's, facing the water. The bar was empty, and Stevens waved off the hostess as they sat.

"What happened?" Jack asked.

"Terry told us that you left Friday morning to go to the Dry Tortugas with Kenny and Valerie Wilkins and you returned that afternoon?"

Jack nodded. "Yes, we—my wife and I—had planned to go out there with them for a few days. About two hours out, our refrigerator died, so we decided to turn around and come back. They decided to go ahead. That's why I was coming up to see Terry, to thank him for getting the mechanic out yesterday."

"Two hours from Key West? About where were you when you turned around?" Stevens asked, her voice husky and all business.

He thought a moment. "We were just out of the channel, on the southwest side of Key West, not far. We'd decided to go over on the outside and spend the night at Marquesas Keys. Where are Kenny and Valerie?"

"No one was on the boat when it was found," she said. "What time did you last see them?"

He squeezed his chin, trying to remember. "Uh, probably around one o'clock Friday afternoon, when we turned around to come back. I don't understand. What happened to them?" Jack asked, growing frustrated.

"We're not sure, yet." She leaned across the table and fixed Jack with a penetrating stare. "Did your friends use drugs, Mr. Davis?" She watched him closely, waiting for a reaction.

Jack glanced away for a few seconds, then returned his eyes to the detective. "They occasionally smoked a little marijuana, but that was it. What has that got to do with anything? If you went after everyone that smoked dope down here, you'd have to arrest practically the entire town."

She sat back in her chair. "I'm talking more than marijuana. We found a Ziploc full of pills on their boat."

Jack shook his head. "No way. They didn't use—"

"Maybe they were dealing?" she said, leaning back over the table.

Jack stared at her. She was deliberately trying to throw him off guard with her questions.

"Kenny and Valerie didn't use pills and they didn't sell them." Holding her stare, he stuck his hand out toward the bight. "Ask anybody here who knew them. They'll tell you the same thing."

She allowed a thin smile to cross her lips. "Don't worry, I'll be speaking with the other boats, too." Her phone pinged, and she picked it up to read something.

Scowling, she rose to leave. She handed him her card and said, "I'll be in touch."

As she started to walk away, she stopped and turned around, fixing him with a parting stare.

"We found your name scrawled in the cockpit. It appears to be written in blood."

"I thought you got lost," Molly said when Jack got back to the boat.

He looked down at the business card Stevens had given him. He realized he'd completely forgotten to thank Terry for getting the mechanic out so soon.

"What's the matter?" Molly asked when Jack didn't answer.

He sat, turning to look into Molly's eyes. "They found the *Black Swan* Sunday morning, out by the Marquesas. She'd been abandoned and no sign of Kenny or Valerie."

Molly cocked her head, a look of bewilderment on her face. "Where were they? What happened?"

"They don't—"

"They? Who's they?" Molly was getting agitated. He grabbed her forearm, and she jerked as if shocked by an electric current. "Don't do that," she said. Her eyes flashed and her voice was hard, sounding like someone else.

He watched her. She was rubbing her arm where his hand had been. She had reacted this way shortly after they had arrived in Key West when he'd grabbed the same arm to keep her from touching something hot.

In a low, calm voice, he said, "I'm sorry. Are you okay?"

"I'm fine, just upset about Val," she said, her voice indicating she was still agitated.

"There was a detective up at the office."

"Detective? What's going on?"

He explained to her the detective didn't know. Both of them were missing.

Molly had a puzzled look on her face. "They could've fallen overboard. Maybe they had mechanical problems and caught a ride with someone?"

"I asked about that. According to the Coast Guard, there had been no calls from the *Black Swan* on Channel 16."

VHF Channel 16 was the universal communications channel for mariners.

He took a deep breath and told her about the detective's comments concerning drugs.

Molly snorted. "That's ridiculous. Everyone knew they would smoke a joint from time to time, you could smell it on their boat. But, they didn't do anything else. What did they find?"

"A baggy full of pills."

"What kind of pills?"

"She didn't say." He paused for a minute before continuing. "That's not all."

Molly gave him a questioning look. He told her about his name scrawled in the cockpit. When he told her the detective thought it was written in blood, a gasp emerged from deep inside her.

"My God, Jack, we were supposed to be with them."

He nodded, unable to speak.

Molly put her hand to her mouth, shaking her head. "Why your name? Why would they be writing your name?"

Jack shook his head and shrugged. "I don't have a clue. The detective wants to talk to you, said she'd come back later." He handed her Stevens business card.

"That could've been us," she said, leaning her head against his shoulder.

He put his arm around her. *Maybe it was supposed to be us,* he thought. He tried to push the notion out of his mind, but a sinking feeling in the pit of his stomach was beginning to form. Somehow, this was linked to the money.

He wanted to believe it wasn't, that it was drugs or trafficking or anything but what was gnawing at him. Trafficking had surpassed drugs on the local smuggling scene. While drug running hadn't ceased, the cartels had shifted some of their efforts over to moving people. Maybe it was drugs. Maybe they didn't know the couple as well as they thought.

"What are you thinking?" Molly asked, turning her head to look up at him.

Jack shook his head, avoiding her eyes. "I wonder if Nick knows anything."

As if on cue, he saw Nick walking down the dock toward their boat, more of an amble, Jack thought. The Texan never seemed to be in a hurry.

"Your ears must've been burning," Jack said as Nick stepped aboard, rocking the sailboat.

"Good things, I hope," Nick replied, taking his usual seat across from them. "I saw Detective Stevens talking with you at Alonzo's. She'd already talked to me."

"What do you think?" Jack asked.

Nick looked at Molly, then back to Jack. "Bullshit," he said, letting the word settle over them.

"Did she mention the drugs?" Jack asked.

Nick nodded. "More bullshit."

"I called a friend, a Coastie," Nick said. "He told me a commercial fisherman had spotted the boat. It was riding low and the fisherman didn't see any sign of anyone on board, so he reported it to the Coast Guard. They sent a crew out to investigate."

"They find anything?"

"Their sailboat. Nobody on board, no sign of anything missing. They called Monroe County Sheriff's Office. I called another buddy over there. He confirmed the five letters—j-a-c-k-y—written on the bulkhead in the cockpit.

Wouldn't tell me anything else, but he did hint we'd read about this one in the news."

Jack wondered what that meant. It had to involve drugs or bodies or both to make the news. Abandoned boats weren't news in the Keys.

The Florida Keys could be a dangerous place for boaters. The weather was unpredictable, and strong currents could be problematic. The area was also littered with wrecks and shoals. While a beautiful place to be on a boat, it wasn't for the inexperienced. He hoped it was drugs and not bodies.

"Maybe they had problems and hitched a ride with someone?" Molly asked.

Nick shook his head. "Radio was working. Engine started. All electronics worked."

"Smugglers?"

"Doesn't make sense. If Kenny had spotted something, why wouldn't he have called it in? Smugglers don't like to attract attention. They obviously didn't want the boat, and nothing on board was disturbed. They don't operate that way."

Jack looked at his friend. "You sound like you know how they operate?"

Nick shrugged. "I had a lot of interesting assignments in a previous life. Let's just say I'm pretty familiar with how they operate."

He studied Nick, wondering what he was talking about. He knew Nick had worked for a government agency, but couldn't remember Nick ever saying more than that. Now, Jack was wondering what he actually did and who he worked for.

"What do you think happened?" Molly asked.

"Somebody wanted to get rid of them. Cops just don't know *who* or *why*." He looked at Jack. "Any ideas on why either of them would write your name?"

Jack shook his head. "I don't have a clue. My response is that if something bad happened, then why wouldn't they write the name of the killer?"

Nick raised his eyebrows. "That's exactly what Detective Stevens said."

Jack sat up in his seat. "Don't even joke about that. Is she thinking—"

Nick raised his hand. "Calm down. I know you didn't do it, and that's what I told her. The cops are just covering the bases."

"Covering the bases? I was with you Friday night—both of you."

"Jack. Chill, okay? They're just doing their job. Even you said the logical conclusion would be for the person to write the name of the bad guy. You and Molly were with me, so they've got two witnesses as to your whereabouts."

Jack eased back into his chair but was still upset. "Do they know who wrote it?"

Nick shook his head. "They're doing some additional tests to see if they can determine *who*. All they know at this point is that it was written in blood. Whose blood and who wrote it aren't known."

Molly straightened up, clutched Jack's hand, and looked directly at Nick. "You think they're dead, don't you?"

Nick hesitated, looking first at Jack, then back at Molly. He nodded twice.

8

Tuesday evening, Randy and Evens sat in a dingy bar at the edge of Old Town. The small, nondescript tavern was a truly local place unknown to the tourists. It was the kind of place that if a tourist stumbled across it, they would keep going.

By now, everyone on the island had heard about *Black Swan*. Key West was still a small, tightly knit community with relatively little violent crime. Two residents missing on a boat that close to Key West was major news.

Evens was freaking out. His hand was shaking as he took a long drink from the beer he was holding.

"What did you see on the boat?" Randy asked. He was quizzing Evens about *Left Behind*.

"I tole you, I was only in the locker with the propane. I fixed the refrigerator and I put that thing you gave me on the propane tank. De woman she was up top the whole time."

Randy nodded. The tracking device was in place, he'd verified that already. He was hoping Evens would have a chance to nose around a bit, but that didn't happen.

"I got to go somewhere," Evens said.

At first, Randy thought he was talking about leaving the bar but then realized Evens was talking about leaving Key West. That wasn't going to happen.

He glanced around to make sure no one was nearby, then lowered his head and leaned across the table.

"You can't do that. Nobody has any reason to suspect us. You leave all of a sudden and that will attract attention. Understand?"

Evens was shaking his head. "They gonna find us."

"Stop it," Randy said. "There ain't no way. I talked to somebody I know with the police. They have nothing, okay, nothing at all." It wasn't a complete lie, at least the part about talking with a cop. Randy had befriended someone with the sheriff's office and occasionally had a beer with him. Of course, they hadn't talked about *Black Swan*.

"What we gonna do?"

Randy straightened up. "What we're going to do is what we usually do, nothing different. You get up and go to work every morning like usual. Don't change *anything,* you hear?"

"My sista, she gonna know."

Randy snorted and shook his head. "How's she gonna know if you don't tell her?"

"She knows tings, she does."

Randy knew the rumors about Mysterie and he knew Evens was convinced she had supernatural powers. Randy didn't believe it for a minute. She was just a good con artist and nothing more.

He finished his beer, pulled out a twenty, and laid it on the table. "I've got to go somewhere else. Remember, stay cool. Don't be talking to no strangers, okay?"

Randy walked out of the bar, headed a few blocks away to meet with Bobby and Mike, his tea distributors. He had to set a trap.

9

Wednesday afternoon, Molly had gone to work and Jack had insisted on riding out to the hospital with her. It was a nice day and a pleasant ride back to the marina. After he secured his bike to the rack at the foot of Front Street, he walked out the boardwalk next to Alonzo's, still thinking about Kenny and Val when he heard a familiar voice call out.

"Hey, Jack. Come on over and have a beer."

He turned to see the smiling face of Nick, sitting in the open-air bar, raising a glass. Glad for the distraction, he walked over and pulled out a stool.

"Molly working?" Nick asked.

Jack nodded. "I rode out to the hospital with her." The bartender brought Jack a beer.

"Your buddy came by," Nick said. "Asked a bunch of questions about Friday night."

Momentarily confused, Jack realized he was talking about Detective Stevens.

"They found some illegals on the Marquesas who'd been brought in Friday," Nick said. "They're figuring Kenny and Valerie either saw something or stumbled across the smugglers. I'm still not buying it."

"Why not?"

"Doesn't work." Nick explained how a sailboat wouldn't just stumble upon a transfer. The smugglers would've seen a sailboat headed their way in plenty of time to finish what they were doing or move. Plus, as he pointed out, if Kenny and Valerie had seen something, why wouldn't they have radioed it in?

"Makes sense."

"They're still trying to figure out why your name was written in blood on their boat. Kenny's blood, apparently."

"Kenny's blood? How do you know that?"

Nick ignored his question and nodded. "They found traces of Valerie's blood and . . . her brain tissue in the cockpit. The doers had washed the boat down with salt water, trying to erase the evidence. The blood stains were still visible with the right tools and it's almost impossible to make sure you get everything out of all the nooks and crannies. Since forensics matched the brain tissue with her DNA, they're assuming she wasn't the one doing the writing."

A chill ran down Jack's spine. "Jesus. What do you think?"

"I think they're both dead. The doers probably dumped the bodies in the ocean, so doubtful they'll ever be found. Back to *who* did it and *why*."

"Nobody's thinking I did it, are they?"

Nick shook his head. "No, your alibi is solid. Plus, it'd be hard to say what your motive was."

"Why would Kenny write my name? I still wonder if he was trying to write something else."

"What else could 'Jacky' mean? That's the question."

A bell went off in Jack's head. "Jacky?"

Nick nodded. "Yeah, that's what was written. Five letters. J-a-c-k-y. Remember, I told you that last night."

"My name doesn't have a *y*."

Nick looked puzzled. "What are you saying?"

"The last person who called me 'Jacky' to my face got punched. Of course, that was in high school. My point is Kenny wouldn't have written 'Jacky.'"

Jack finished his beer, pulled out his phone and called Detective Stevens. When he got her voice mail, he hung up.

"The detective's voice mail," he explained to Nick. "I need to see how it was written. Something doesn't make sense."

Saying he needed to do some work, Jack left and walked out to *Left Behind*. He picked up Tony's file, grabbed a beer, and went back outside.

Not much of a breeze was stirring as he sat, drinking his beer. Music drifted over the water from several different directions, a product of the many bars surrounding the bight. He'd opened the folder but couldn't stop thinking about what was written on *Black Swan*.

The odds of the killer having the name "Jacky" were almost impossible, yet no one had called Jack that in decades. *Kenny had tried to tell him something, but what?*

After taking another swallow of beer, he peered over the stern down into the water, where he could see several large tarpon swimming underneath the end of the dock. He remembered the first time he'd seen a tarpon. He didn't know what it was.

That's why Kenny didn't write the killer's name—he didn't know who it was. It still didn't explain why his friend had written Jack's name. There had to be a reason.

The next morning, he got up for his run before Molly got home. Before he left, he called Detective Stevens again.

"Mr. Davis," she answered.

"Do you have a picture of the name scrawled on the boat?" he asked, not bothering with a greeting.

Stevens hesitated, then said, "Yes, why?"

"I need to see what he wrote."

"Capital J, followed by a-c-k-y, Jacky."

"Doesn't make sense, that's why I want to see exactly what you saw." He repeated what he'd told Nick.

"Come by around 9. I'll show you what we've got."

He hung up and stretched before he left. As he made his three-mile loop around the island, he thought about Kenny writing his name. He was hoping an answer would come to him, but all he could think is w*hat was Kenny trying to tell him?*

Back at the marina, he showered, and when he got to the boat, Molly was home from work.

"You're up and about early," she said, welcoming him with a hug and kiss.

"I'm going out to meet with Detective Stevens. Something's been bothering me about how my name was written."

Molly yawned. "I'm going to try to get some sleep. Long night. Maybe we can get a late lunch."

"Get some rest," he said, giving her another kiss before leaving. "I'll be back for lunch."

He rode his bike out to Stock Island, where the Sheriff's office was located. At the front desk, he signed in and stated he was there to see Detective Stevens. The deputy picked up the phone and called. In a few minutes, Stevens walked around the corner, holding a folder and a large, loose-leaf notebook.

She led him to a small conference room where she explained what they had found.

"The doer had washed the boat down with salt water, trying to remove any trace. However, the blood had dried enough that the forensic techs were able to bring it out by spraying it with Luminol. What we have is a picture of what was scrawled as illuminated by the chemical. We know it was blood, Kenny's blood. And based on other findings, we believe it was Kenny that wrote it."

She left out the part about the other findings being Valerie's brain tissue and Jack didn't say a word. She pulled an 8x10 photo out of the file folder and slid it over to Jack. He studied it for a minute, confirming what he was seeing.

As Stevens had told him, the letters J-a-c-k-y were scrawled at an angle in the middle of the photo. He had expected to see red letters against the white fiberglass, but on the photo instead were black letters on a bluish-gray background. It appeared to be on the vertical side of the seat in the cockpit, just above the deck.

Something was off. There was more space between the *k* and *y* than between the other letters. And, the tail on the *y* was excessively long, extending several inches below the rest.

He looked up at the detective. "He wrote this with his finger?"

"That's what forensics said."

He looked back at the photograph and tilted his head to the side, trying to imagine Kenny lying on the deck, writing with his finger. He held his finger up, tracing the letters in thin air. Then, it clicked.

Shaking his head, he looked up at her. "It's not a *y*."

She looked puzzled. "What do you mean?"

"The *y* threw me. No one calls me 'Jacky' with a *y*. Neither of them ever called me that. It's not a *y*, it's a *u*. Plus, look at the spacing between the *k* and *u*. It says, 'Jack u,' not 'Jacky.'"

"I don't understand," Stevens said. "That makes even less sense."

"Kenny was trying to warn me. Get it? Jack. You."

Jack picked up the photo and stared at it. There was no doubt it was "Jack u." Kenny used to point at him and say, "Jack. You." to get his attention, then follow it with the reason for the interruption. Just one of those idiosyncrasies between friends that turns out to be a trademark. He smiled as he recalled Kenny saying that, then frowned as he realized Kenny would never utter those words again. He explained to Stevens.

"Who would be after you?" she asked. "And why?"

He set the photograph on the table. "I don't know. But I am positive this is what Kenny was trying to say."

It had to be connected to Clearwater and the money. It was blood money and it was coming back to haunt him.

But who knew about it? Peabo, the drug dealer, and Wren's boyfriend, was dead. Peabo's sidekick, Shorty, was in a hospital psychiatric unit. As far as Jack knew, he hadn't spoken a word since that rainy night at Big Cat Rescue.

There were only two other people who knew. Tina Marshall and Devo Drager, the doctor Jack worked for and the kingpin of the entire pill mill operation. Tina was the doctor who had helped him rescue Molly and Wren. She wouldn't have told anyone. That left Drager.

"Maybe it was related to Clearwater?" He told the detective about what happened up the western coast of Florida, leaving out the part about the cash he took.

When he got to the part about Peabo getting killed by the tiger, she said, "Oh yeah, I remember hearing about that. You were the guy that worked for the doctor, what was his name?"

"Drager. Devo Drager. Maybe he's out for revenge? Or someone else involved with him?"

Stevens scribbled some notes. "We'll check with Pinellas County. See what they have. I'll get back to you."

He left the station bewildered. As he pedaled back to the marina, he pondered the problem, turning it over and over again. Someone was after the money.

He stopped at the Cuban Coffee Queen to get some breakfast. Molly would still be asleep, and he didn't want to disturb her. After getting his food, he found a seat in the shade and sat, eating his sandwich. He pulled up Tina Marshall, M.D., on his phone and called. No answer. It went straight to voice mail. He left her a message, asking her to call. "Nothing urgent," he said, not wanting her to panic.

The tourists were starting to stir as the crowd picked up. It was an interesting place to people watch. People of all shapes and sizes milled about, anyone of who could be looking for him. He hoped Tina would have some ideas.

By the time he finished his sandwich, he'd given up on figuring out *who*. It was not somebody he'd known, and therefore not someone he'd guess.

As he sipped the last of his coffee, he turned to the question of *why*. That was easier, or at least he thought so. Someone was after the money. If they'd been after him, there would have been ample opportunities over the last eight months. Although cautious, he'd never felt like anyone was watching him.

The money was in a locker on *Left Behind,* wrapped inside an old headsail and stuffed into a well-worn sail bag. He was always surprised at how little space that much cash occupied. Half a million dollars in hundred-dollar bills took up less space than ten books, and he had less money than that. Although he had a small safe onboard, he figured that would be the first place someone would look. A person would have to go through the entire boat before they'd think to look in a musty old canvas bag.

He felt his phone vibrate and pulled it out of his pocket to see who was calling. It was Tina.

"Hey," he answered, "how are you?"

"Good." They caught up on small talk for a few minutes, then he asked about Wren.

"She's doing great. Making As and Bs in nursing school. She's going to make an awesome nurse. We get together every week for dinner. She's a smart girl with a good head on her shoulders."

Tina was proud of Wren, and so was he. She'd overcome a lot of adversity, and he knew she would turn out fine.

"Anything unusual happened lately?" he asked.

She laughed. "Something unusual happens almost every day in my business. Just yesterday, I had a woman come in complaining of abdominal pains. She was two months pregnant and didn't know it."

He had to chuckle at that. "Didn't she understand what caused it?"

"You would think, but to answer your question, no, nothing out of the ordinary. At least not that I've noticed. Why? What's going on?"

"Someone's looking for the money," he said, lowering his voice.

"I thought you were giving it away."

"I am—I mean, I was. I can't just walk in and hand somebody a bag of cash."

"Jack . . ."

"I haven't touched it, Tina. I don't know what to do. I'm afraid I'll get in trouble if I report it to the authorities now."

"What are you going to do?"

"I don't know." He told her about *Black Swan* and his name being written in blood on his friends' boat.

"My God, Jack."

"The cops think it was smugglers."

"Maybe it was. Maybe you're being paranoid."

"Could be, but my gut tells me not. I just wanted to give you a heads-up. Be careful and keep an eye out."

"I will. What does Molly think?"

He paused for so long Tina started to repeat the question.

"She doesn't know."

"What?" She screamed into the phone and he had to hold it away from his ear.

"I was going to tell her. I was just waiting for her to get better."

There was a long silence, then Tina said, "You need to talk to Tony."

He'd thought about that earlier. Even though Tony was retired, Jack was concerned that he couldn't be completely honest with the former cop about an illegal activity.

"I've thought about doing that." He didn't mention that he'd seen Tony Monday.

"Jack, he's a good friend, *and* he's an ex-cop."

"I know, and that last part may be the problem. I'll keep you posted."

"You need to come clean on this." She let the words sink in, then added, "Before it's too late."

"I know. I will. Thanks," he said before hanging up.

He set the phone down on the bench next to him. Tina was right, this was spiraling out of control. He was going to have to tell Tony. And Molly. The question was *how?*

When he got back to the boat, Detective Cally Stevens was sitting out in the cockpit with Molly, having a cup of coffee.

"Hello again, Detective," Jack said as he sat down next to Molly. "I'm surprised to see you here." She seemed to delight in keeping him off guard.

"We checked with Pinellas County Sheriff's Office. I talked to the detective who worked your case. I thought you were headed back home and since I needed to speak with your wife anyway, I dropped by."

Stevens shook her head. "It appears to be a dead end. Drager's awaiting trial in federal court. He's on a very short leash, looking at the distinct possibility of major jail time. PCSO thinks it's highly unlikely he's involved in anything down here and we agree."

Molly grabbed Jack's hand and squeezed it.

"What about Shorty?" Jack asked.

"Watson's sidekick is in Chattahoochee, still bat-shit crazy. There's nobody left. Everyone up there has closed the book on that operation. We're back where we started. Smugglers, either drugs or people. Your friends saw something they shouldn't have."

Jack shook his head. "I'm telling you, Kenny was warning me—I know it."

Stevens narrowed her eyes. "Warning you about what?"

He felt Molly's eyes on him, and both of them waited for an answer.

He shrugged. "I'm just saying . . ."

Stevens held his gaze until he looked away. "Yes?"

"Nothing," he said. "Why do you think he wrote my name?"

Stevens was silent for several beats, then stood, putting her coffee cup down on the table. She stared at Jack.

"I don't know. Based on what we *know,* it doesn't make any sense."

She looked at Molly and said, "Thanks for the coffee—and the talk." After she stepped off the boat onto the dock, she turned toward Jack. "Give me a call if you think of anything else."

Jack watched her walk down the dock.

"What was that all about?" Molly asked.

"I told you I was going out to see her." He explained that he figured out Kenny was trying to warn him, and his first thought was that the people involved in the prescription drug ring were behind it.

She folded her arms across her chest. "Thanks for telling me. I felt like an idiot, not knowing what was going on."

Jack exhaled. "I'm sorry. It didn't occur to me until I saw the pictures. What did she want with you?"

"She just wanted my version of what happened Friday. Do you really think what happened out there was related to . . . to what happened back in Clearwater?"

"I don't know," he lied. "Look, it was my name Kenny scrawled on their boat. I'm just trying to understand why."

Somebody was looking for him, and he was convinced it was somehow connected. He needed to talk to Tony before telling Molly.

10

The marina community was abuzz with speculation about what happened to Kenny and Val.

"Smugglers," Doug said. "I heard the Coast Guard picked up some immigrants who'd been dumped in the Marquesas." He and Lisa were at the Half Shell, having lunch with Jack and Molly.

"That's what most people at the hospital are saying," Molly said.

Jack shook his head. The prominent theory so far was human traffickers. Even the sheriff's office had implicitly endorsed that. He wanted to believe it, but based on Nick's comments, it didn't sound likely.

"I still can't believe they're gone," Lisa said, shaking her head. "The Keys are getting as bad as the Bahamas."

For many years, the Bahamas had a reputation for being unsafe for lone boaters. The Keys hadn't shared that before now, but finding *Black Swan* had everyone on edge. Even Jack was leery about going out alone overnight on the water.

"No, but I'm not sure about either of you riding bikes out to the hospital," Doug said.

Like Molly, Lisa rode her bike to work at the hospital since neither couple owned a car.

"We don't ride after dark," Molly said. They usually worked twelve-hour shifts, from 7p to 7a. "Besides, most of the time we ride together anyway."

"Well, you still need to be careful," Jack said as he rose to leave. "I need to get back and finish up my work, so if everyone will excuse me." He was flying to Fort Myers tomorrow to meet again with Tony. Jack had spent most of the morning wrapping up his analysis of 1AAA. Frankie Crispino, Tony's friend and the CEO, had been pestering Tony for a response, so that gave Jack a good excuse to go back.

He got back to the boat and went below, where he'd left everything spread out on the table in the main cabin.

Everything looked in order. Jack had contacted a CPA friend of his who worked for a large accounting firm in Miami, asking for her opinion. Although they had not done the financial statements for 1AAA, his friend was familiar with the firm that had. "Totally on the up and up. I'd trust them," she'd told Jack.

When Jack had pressed her, she told Jack that if anything, Frankie Crispino was too honest from all reports. It was hard to make a go of the medical equipment business in south Florida if you didn't fudge.

Based on Jack's analysis of the financials, the valuation of the company seemed to be justified and the price Crispino was offering for Tony's stock was fair, even though it was less than Tony's initial investment.

What bothered Jack is why Tony was selling if he didn't really need the money.

* * *

The next morning as he boarded the small Silver Airways turboprop sitting on the tarmac, Jack thought about what he was going to discuss with Tony. He knew what he was going to say about the medical equipment company; that part didn't bother him. What troubled him was how to handle the conversation about the tainted money.

Tony was retired, but Jack still didn't know what the ex-detective might think about the money he took from Peabo. Friendship or not, Tony was one of the most principled men Jack knew, and he didn't want to put his friend in an awkward position.

He took his seat and buckled his seat belt. The last few passengers were boarding as he unfolded his copy of the *Key West Citizen*. On the front page was an article titled "No News on Missing Couple." He read the article, but it contained nothing new. Kenny and Val were presumed dead, ostensibly the victims of an unfortunate encounter with smugglers.

He refolded the paper, stuck it in the seatback pocket, and looked out the window. The short flight didn't get very high on the way to Fort Myers and he had a good view of the Florida coast. Thousands of islands dotted the waters below. Maybe he was being paranoid like Tina suggested.

When he got to Fort Myers, Tony was waiting for him on the other side of the security checkpoint at the terminal. He didn't look any better, Jack thought.

"How was your flight?" Tony said, giving him a bear hug.

"Uneventful, the best kind," Jack said, looking at his friend from head to toe. "What did the doctor say?"

Tony shrugged. "Getting older. He's tinkering with my meds. Put me on some new stuff. He doesn't have it dialed in yet."

"Have you lost some weight?" In truth, he did look thinner.

Tony patted his stomach. "Eh, maybe a little. Certainly not because I've quit eating. Besides, I could stand to lose a few pounds."

They made their way to Tony's car for the short trip to their condo. Connie greeted him with a hug when they arrived. She was petite and quiet, with beautiful silver hair. An attractive woman still, in her late sixties, she and Tony had been married for over forty years. Her size was deceptive, Tony had told him one time. She was not one to get angry easily, but when she did, watch out.

"Would you like something to drink?" she asked.

Jack shook his head. "No, thanks. I'm fine."

"Sorry to rush out on you, but I need to run to Publix to pick up a few things. I'll be back shortly."

Tony and Jack moved out to the screened lanai, a common fixture in this part of Florida.

"Sure I can't get you something?" Tony asked, taking a sip of his coffee.

"I'm good."

Tony set his cup down and asked, "I hate to be so abrupt, but before Connie gets back, tell me, how bad is it?"

Jack shook his head. "Bottom line, the valuation seems fair, based on everything I looked at."

"That's not good," Tony said, visibly disappointed. "It's less than what we invested."

"Well, it's good in one sense. There certainly doesn't appear to be any funny business going on with the books."

He paused for a moment, then asked, "How well do you know Frankie?"

Tony laughed. "He's like a brother. We grew up together in Chicago. Trust him with my life." His expression turned serious. "Why do you ask?"

Jack thought back to a grandmother he'd caught early in his career. Active in the church, she was the model of propriety. The only problem was she'd been embezzling money from the hospital for years.

Her secret was that she never got greedy, keeping the amounts low enough so she'd be below the radar. The only reason she'd got caught is she'd missed a day at work—her first in years. As an entry-level accountant, Jack tried to help out by reconciling the bank statement and discovered the fraud.

"Just curious. I checked with a friend of mine who works for a big accounting firm in Miami, asked about Frankie. She said he was as straight as they come and that was the problem: hard to make a good profit in the DME business competing with all the crooks."

Tony laughed again. "That's my boy."

"What I don't understand is why are you wanting to sell?"

Tony shrugged. "I was talking to Frankie after we got the last report. He knew I was disappointed. Told me he'd be willing to buy us out. Connie and I talked, and figured maybe we should take the bird in the hand. That's when I called you."

"Excuse me for being so direct, but do you guys need the money?"

Tony cocked his head. "We can always use a little extra, but no, we're doing okay. Why?"

"If you don't really need the money, I wouldn't sell. The company's sound, somebody may make them an offer. Hang on to it."

Tony took a sip of coffee from his White Sox mug. "We'll talk to Connie about that when she returns. I don't want to get too far out in front of her."

"Sure." Jack rested his chin on his hand. "I need to talk to you about something else before she gets back."

Tony had a puzzled look on his face. "Okay, what's going on?"

"You remember that conversation we had in the hospital cafeteria? In Clearwater, when Molly was unconscious?"

Tony nodded. "I remember. We talked about Peabo and you asked me some 'hypothetical' questions."

Jack laughed. "You've got a good memory."

"I was a detective, Jack. Let me guess, you've got some more 'hypothetical' questions."

Over the next two hours, Jack told his friend everything about what happened up there, relieved to be able to unburden himself. He didn't leave anything out. Tony listened attentively, occasionally interrupting to clarify a point.

When Jack finished, Tony leaned back in his chair. "Why didn't you put all of the money in the bag you took to give Peabo?"

"I didn't trust him. I was afraid he'd take the money and I wouldn't get Molly and Wren back. So, I put just enough money in the bag to convince them it was all there. Once I knew they were safe, then I was going to give him the rest. It was the only leverage I had."

Tony nodded. "Then, the whole deal went to shit at Big Cat Rescue."

"Exactly. Peabo was dead, Shorty couldn't speak, and I didn't know where Molly was. When I found her, all I had on my mind was getting her well. Later, once I knew she was going to be alright, I realized I still had the money. By that time, I was afraid to mention it to anyone."

"That's when you set up the trust fund for Wren."

Jack nodded. "Wren deserved that much. Peabo was abusive and took advantage of her. The rest of the money, I planned on Molly and me giving away to deserving causes."

"But you never told her."

Jack lowered his head and shook it. "I was afraid it would set her back, reliving what happened when she had been kidnapped. Her getting well was and is my priority."

He raised his head and looked Tony in the eyes. "The money's all there. I haven't spent a dime of it. Now, I feel trapped and don't know what to do."

Tony stroked his chin while he thought, then said, "The cop would tell your hypothetical 'friend' to go to the authorities and come clean."

"You're telling me that's what I need to do?" Jack asked, leaning forward.

Tony took the carafe from the middle of the table and refilled his cup before speaking. "Sit back and let me tell you a story."

He told Jack about growing up in a Polish neighborhood on the south side of Chicago.

"My mother, God rest her soul, was the most honest and ethical person I've ever known. To her, right and wrong were easy—it was black and white. There was a family who lived next door, the Kaminski's. The mother's name was

Adriana. Oswald, her husband, was a drunk and beat her regularly. Neighbors would call the cops, they'd come, and Adriana would say she fell or tripped or something, but would never blame Oswald. This went on forever.

"One day, uncle Leo, my mother's brother, came by. His day job was at a trucking terminal, but everyone knew he worked for one of the organized crime families on the South Side.

"Anyway, I heard my mother mention to Leo about Oswald beating Adriana. Just a casual reference, she didn't belabor the point."

Tony cocked his head. "Leo looked at my mother for a few seconds, then nodded. That was all I saw or heard.

"The next day, Oswald came home, drunk as usual, and started to use Adriana as a punching bag. Two men came in the front door, beat the ever-loving shit out of Oswald. Rumor was that they told him if he ever laid another hand on Adriana, he'd never see another sunrise. He kept drinking, of course, but as far as we knew, he never hit her again."

Jack had a puzzled look and started to interrupt. Tony held up his hand. "Several months later, Mother was dressing me down for doing something wrong. I made the mistake of saying that she told Uncle Leo to take care of Mr. Kaminski. She got real quiet and a look flashed over her like I'd never seen before. I knew I'd screwed up and for the only time in my life, I was scared of her. She sat me down, looked at me and said, 'Do right and God will know.' I never forgot that moment."

Tony rose from his chair. "Too much coffee. I've got to go get rid of some. I'll be back in a minute."

Jack thought about Tony's story. He was still thinking about what he needed to do when Tony walked back out on the lanai.

"Back to your friends that were killed," he said as he sat. "You have nothing to support your allegations and the locals are thinking smuggling, right?"

"All the way. I told them about everything that happened except the money. But I have no names, no evidence of anyone looking for me, and no reason for someone to be looking for me that they know."

"I can't blame them. If you came to me with what you have, that's probably what I'd think, too. What do *you* think happened on that sailboat?"

Jack had given this a lot of thought since he'd seen the picture of Kenny's message. "I think whoever did this knew Molly and I were taking *Left Behind* to the Tortugas with Kenny and Val. Based on what time we left Key West, they expected to find us at the Marquesas. There was no way we could've made it to the Tortugas before dark, and only a complete idiot would try to take a sailboat into Garden Key after dark.

"The bad guys pull up next to their boat with some excuse, wondering where we were. Remember, the only reason we weren't there with them is we had the refrigerator problems and had to turn back. Totally unplanned."

"Yeah, but why kill them?"

Jack shrugged. "I don't know. Something obviously went wrong. Kenny and Val could identify them. Maybe Kenny smelled a rat and tried to call for help or pulled a gun on them. Who knows, but I think Kenny was trying to warn me."

"Believable." Tony nodded. "But who? And how would they know you had the money with you? The money could be in the bank."

"The money part is easy—an educated guess. They know I never mentioned the money, so it's a safe bet that I never deposited it in my bank account. Maybe I could've put it in a safe deposit box, but doubtful. Access would be limited, and besides, $400,000 doesn't take that much room. That leads back to 'who.' I've racked my brain trying to figure that out. It's someone I don't know, but they know me."

Tony nodded. "Someone who knew about the money. Someone you didn't figure. Who would Peabo have told about the money? A trusted lieutenant you never met?"

"How do I find someone connected to a dead person?"

"They've found you. They're in Key West, you're just not looking in the right place."

"Food for thought," Jack said, nodding. "You never answered my question about what to do."

Tony smiled. "Remember, Jack. You don't always get answers, but you always have choices. Do right, and God will know."

11

It was a beautiful morning, typical Key West, and Molly decided to walk the length of Duval and back. At the upper end, she stopped at the window of a new shop. It had an eclectic collection of everything from furniture to art to knick-knacks. She liked to look in places like that but seldom bought anything. That was one of the advantages of living on a sailboat—room for "stuff" was extremely limited, which made it easy to avoid the temptation to buy things.

When she walked in, a pleasant young man asked if she was looking for anything in particular. She explained she was a local and just killing time.

"That's quite alright. My name's Seth," he said, extending his hand.

"I'm Molly," she said. "You're new here, aren't you? I've been watching your shop take shape over the last few weeks and was anxious to see what you were doing."

Seth smiled and nodded. "Well, Lee and I have been down here for a year, but I've just opened this shop."

She looked around. "Very nice. You have a great eye."

"Thank you," he said, bowing. He told her to make herself at home, and let him know if she needed anything.

She wandered through the shop, occasionally pausing to look at something. She stopped to admire a watercolor of a sailboat silhouetted against a sunset. It was a beautiful piece of art and made her long for a wall to hang it on.

Seth walked over. "That's a beautiful painting. It's done by a local artist, a friend of mine. She is marvelous. I try to showcase local people whenever I can."

"It is gorgeous. Unfortunately, my husband and I live on a sailboat, so I don't have a place to put something like that."

"Ah, that explains your interest."

They chatted further. Seth's partner, Lee, was a former chef in New York. "Thank goodness," Seth said. "I can barely boil water."

Molly laughed. "But, you do have impeccable taste." She stuck out her hand. "I enjoyed talking with you, Seth."

"And I enjoyed meeting you as well. Please come back. And bring your husband. I'd love to meet him."

She walked out on the sidewalk and put her sunglasses on. Since she was almost at the end of Duval, she turned left and headed back toward the marina.

When she got to Petronia, she looked to her right to see if Mysterie's was open. The sign was lit, so she crossed Duval and walked down to the shop.

She walked in and recognized the girl behind the counter, with stringy black hair and the tattoo of a snake circling her left arm. The girl looked up and smiled, apparently recognizing Molly from a few days ago.

"Mysterie's free if you're interested in a reading," she said, nodding to her right toward the open curtain framing a doorway.

Molly looked through the door but didn't see anybody. It wasn't time for lunch, and she didn't have anywhere else to be.

"I still owe you from the other day."

The girl shrugged. "Forty-five dollars a visit. We take credit cards."

Molly reached into the pocket on her shorts and pulled out her folding money. Flipping through the bills wrapped around her credit card, she counted them. A one, a ten, and three twenties.

She didn't want to charge ninety dollars, in case Jack looked at the bill, so she peeled off the three twenties and handed them to snake girl. "Is it okay if I bring the thirty dollars later? I don't really want to use my card."

"Sure." She asked her to wait while she went and told Mysterie she had a reading.

"She'll be out in a minute," the girl announced when she came back out through the doorway. She returned to her perch behind the counter and sat.

"Hello, Molly," Mysterie said as she came out. "How are you?"

Molly was again struck by the woman's presence. Something about her countenance put Molly at ease. She smiled and said, "Fine, and you?"

"I'm doing well, thank you." Mysterie turned and walked through the doorway, Molly close behind.

She didn't hesitate, this time, almost anxious to get started.

As they sat at the small table, Mysterie said, "You seem much more relaxed today. Would you like some tea?"

After Mysterie served them, she sat back and chatted, not asking for Molly's hand this time.

"You're troubled by something that happened to you. It's like a curtain. You want to be able to pull it open to see, but you're scared."

Molly could only nod at first. "I don't know what to do. Maybe I shouldn't look?"

"I understand. When I was a child, I was raped by my uncle."

The frankness of Mysterie's admission startled Molly.

"For too long, I refused to confront it. Eventually, I did. And for me, it helped."

They sat there, in silence, drinking tea as Molly considered what to do.

"Can you help me remember?" Molly asked.

Mysterie nodded. "If that's what you want."

Later, when she walked out of Mysterie's, Molly wasn't sure how long she'd been there. She felt tired, but also a strange sense of peace. Mysterie had said they should take it slowly, a little at a time, allowing Molly a chance to process things which was part of the healing. Passing a clock in a shop window, she realized she'd been in the palm reader's for over an hour.

Her head was spinning from what the woman had told her, yet she felt strangely relaxed and at peace.

Back at *Left Behind*, she got a bottle of water and sat out under the bimini, thinking about her session with Mysterie.

It was almost like Molly had been hypnotized. Mysterie gently led her back to when she'd been kidnapped by Peabo, back to the dingy motel room on the beach. She saw the room with incredible detail, from the soiled curtains to the stained bedspread. Yet, she wasn't frightened. Mysterie kept reassuring her she was safe, and Molly believed her.

Molly saw Peabo and Shorty. They'd tied Molly and Wren to the beds. Molly remembered how scared she was, but it was like she was watching a movie.

Her phone rang, and she jumped, startled by the sound. "Hello?"

"Hey, what are you doing?" It was Jack.

It took her a moment to get grounded. "Sitting on the boat, drinking water and thinking about lunch."

"Are you okay?"

"I'm fine, just surprised to hear from you in the middle of the day."

"Bad news, I'm afraid. Silver Airways has canceled my flight. Next flight is not until morning."

"That sucks. So much for a nice, romantic dinner."

"Hey, do I get a raincheck?"

She laughed. "We'll see. Call me later, okay." As she ended the call and put her phone down, she felt a tinge of guilt about not mentioning Mysterie. Maybe this weekend, she thought.

12

Molly decided to ride over to the fish market on Eaton Street to pick up lunch and something for dinner. When she walked in, Yvonne, the proprietor, smiled and greeted her. Molly was the only one in the small shop, a converted gas station, which was unusual.

"Hey, girl. Haven't seen you in a while," Yvonne said.

Molly laughed. "Because you're never working anymore when I come by. Business must be doing well. I thought you'd retired."

Yvonne snorted. "Business is good, but not that good. I've been working on the books. Sales tax returns, tax deposits, payroll taxes—it never ends. How about you?"

"I'm okay, working some out at the hospital."

"That was bad about Kenny and Val. I heard you and Jack were supposed to be with them."

Molly nodded. "The four of us were going to Garden Key for a few days. We had a problem with our refrigerator, turned around and came back."

"Geez, that's scary. Can't be too careful these days."

Molly looked around, and seeing that Yvonne and she were still alone, she lowered her voice and asked, "Do you know Mysterie, the palm reader, over off Duval?"

Yvonne cocked her head and stared at her, frowning. "What are you doing hanging around her?"

Molly shrugged. "Just getting a few readings, is all. Do you know her?"

Yvonne's brown eyes narrowed. "I know enough to know you don't need to be spending time with her." She looked around and lowered her voice. "That woman is evil. A friend of mine's cousin had her life ruined when she put a curse on her. You should stay away from there."

About then, the bell over the door rang as a couple walked in.

"Well, well," Yvonne said. "This must be the day for people I haven't seen in a while. How are you, Seth? Lee?"

The shorter one just threw up his hand and walked over to the counter, looking at the fresh seafood on display behind the glass.

Molly recognized Seth, the taller one, as the shop owner she'd met a few days ago.

"Hey, Yvonne," he said, coming over to give her a hug. He turned to Molly and stuck out his hand. "And, Molly. We met a few days ago."

"I remember, Seth. Good to see you again."

"Well, I see you two know each other," Yvonne said.

Molly nodded. "I met Seth at his shop the other day."

Seth extended his hand toward the shorter man, obsessed by the fresh seafood in the case. "That's my partner, Lee—the chef, as you can tell. His first stop is to check out what's in the case."

Before Seth could say another word, Lee turned, gave a slight bow, and said, "Pleased to meet you, Molly." His deep baritone voice took Molly by surprise. It seemed incongruous with his diminutive stature.

"Hey, I can cook, too," Seth said, laughing.

"He can cook as long as the directions are clearly stated on the package," Lee said, turning back to study the contents of the refrigerated case.

Yvonne shook her head, obviously used to such banter between the two. "Lee was the executive chef at a five-star restaurant in New York before they moved to the Keys. Seth was wasting away down here, living on frozen dinners. He's gained ten pounds since they've met."

"Molly," Seth said, feigning disgust and waggling his index finger toward her. "Don't believe a word either of these two say. They're just jealous. When we met, Lee's entire wardrobe consisted of sweatpants, t-shirts, and Crocs—hardly what anyone would call fashionable attire. And this one," he said, pointing to Yvonne, "wasn't much better. Heaven knows what they'd do without moi."

By this time, they all were laughing, including Molly. Lee had picked out a beautiful piece of mahimahi and was debating between Florida lobster tails and stone crab claws for an appetizer. Molly had settled on grouper and asked Yvonne to bag her a small filet and a crab cake sandwich to go.

Lee nodded, approving her choice, and asked how she intended to prepare it.

She shrugged. "Probably just grill it."

Lee frowned, shaking his head. "Rather plain, if you want to know, especially for a small portion." Without waiting for her response, he proceeded to give her an easy recipe for parmesan-crusted grouper. "And, no more than three minutes on each side. More people ruin fresh seafood by overcooking it."

"Sounds wonderful," she said. "Plus, I can save the rest for lunch tomorrow."

Seth glanced at her left hand and raised his eyebrows. "Hubby working late?"

Molly nodded. "Hubby, who goes by Jack, is stuck in Fort Myers, working. He'll be back tomorrow."

Seth frowned. "Well, we can't have that. You are not dining alone tonight, my dear. You're coming to our place for dinner."

Lee turned to Yvonne. "Make that a pound and a half of mahi. She won't be needing the grouper tonight." He turned back to Molly and said, "I'll show you how to prepare the grouper."

Molly started to protest, and Yvonne started laughing. She was already putting the grouper back in the case. "These two will not take 'no' for an answer. Besides, Lee is a fabulous cook. Anybody in town would kill for an invitation to eat at his table. Consider yourself lucky."

Molly laughed and nodded. "It sounds like my dinner plans have improved."

"We're only a block from here. How about six?" Seth said.

"Six would be perfect. What can I bring?"

"Nothing," Seth said. He wrote down the address and his phone number. When he handed it to her, he said, "We'll see you this evening."

Yvonne handed her a small bag containing the crab cake sandwich and gave Molly her change. "Don't forget what I told you," Yvonne said, giving her a stern look.

Molly wanted to pursue it but realized the shop was now full of customers. She nodded, turned, and walked out, telling Lee and Seth that she'd see them later.

Holding the sandwich, Molly tried to get her aqua beach cruiser out of the rack in front of the market. She'd not bothered to lock it, but the front wheel was binding. Giving it one last tug, the wheel came out and the bike slipped out of her grasp, falling on the pavement.

"Shit," she said. The bike wasn't brand new, but she hated to acquire more scrapes on it. As she leaned over to right the bicycle, a man stepped over and picked it up for her. She hadn't heard him approach and looked up to see who it was. He wore sunglasses, blue cap, and the island uniform of t-shirt, shorts, and sandals.

"Thank you," she said. "The wheel was binding and when I jerked it, down it went."

"No problem. How's the seafood here?"

"Great, best on the island and very convenient. You must be new around here?"

"Still learning my way around Key West. Somebody at work told me about this place."

"Work, huh? So you live around here?"

He nodded. "I've got a little house over on Stock Island. Nothing fancy. You live close by?"

"Over at Key West Bight. A&B Marina."

"You live on a boat?"

"Yeah, an Island Packet." Seeing his puzzled look, she continued. "It's a sailboat."

"Oh. Sorry, I've never been sailing."

Molly put the bag containing the sandwich in the small basket on the front of the bike. "Well, I better get back. Nice meeting you, and thanks again."

Back at A&B, Molly chained her bike to the rack and walked toward the dock. Lisa was coming toward her, a book in her hand.

"I brought your book back. Hey, what's for lunch?" Lisa asked, nodding toward the bag in Molly's hand.

"Crab cake sandwich from Eaton's. Come on with me and I'll share. Jack's stuck in Fort Myers. They canceled his flight."

Lisa fell in step next to her as she walked out the dock toward *Left Behind.*

"I've been invited out for dinner tonight," Molly said.

"Oh, really?" Lisa said, a conspiratorial grin appearing.

Molly shook her head. "No, not like that." She told her about Seth and Lee. "Seth just opened that new shop on Duval, up above Petronia. You should check it out, a lot of really nice things. His partner, Lee, was a chef at a five-star restaurant in New York. He's going to teach me a new way to prepare grouper."

"Shucks, I was hoping for something juicier," Lisa said, laughing.

"Sorry to burst your bubble. I did run into a stranger at Eaton's. He picked up my bike for me."

Lisa turned and looked Molly over. "What happened? You okay?"

Molly chuckled. "I'm fine, just dropped my bike trying to get it out of the rack. Some new scars for the cruiser." She looked around, then leaned closer to Lisa. "Guess where I went this morning?"

Lisa shook her head. "I give. Where?"

"Mysterie's."

"No shit?" Lisa looked surprised. "Tell me about it."

When they got to *Left Behind,* Molly went to the companionway to go below. The padlock was hanging on the clasp, unlocked.

"Shit," Molly exclaimed.

"What?" Lisa said.

Molly turned around, pointing to the lock. "I left the boat unlocked. Jack would have a conniption fit."

Lisa waved her hand and shook her head. "I do that all the time. Doug complains, but it's pretty secure here, especially where you are on the end of the dock."

Molly got a couple of glasses of lemonade. They sat out on the deck sharing the crab cake sandwich while Molly told Lisa about her session with Mysterie.

"It was incredible. There's no way she could've known about some of the stuff she told me."

"I told you she was the real deal. You going back?"

Molly nodded. "But don't say anything to Doug. Jack doesn't know."

"Don't worry. As you probably picked up, Doug's skeptical anyhow. Guys," she said, shaking her head and frowning.

13

The twin-engine Silver Airways turboprop banked to the right, then leveled the wings and extended the landing gear on final approach to EYW. Jack was sitting in a single seat on the left side of the plane, looking out at Key West. It was near sunset and lights were beginning to blink on. He was amazed at how small the island appeared from the air.

The morning flight was overbooked, so he had to wait for this one. He'd been thinking about his conversation with Tony concerning 1AAA. Something didn't smell right. Why would Frankie want to buy out his partner for a depressed price? He was convinced there was something else going on.

Tony had not given him a clear answer regarding Peabo's money, not that he was expecting one. Tony reminded him of his father and wanted you to come to your own decisions. The immediate problem was trying to find out if someone was after him, and if so, who?

When he got to the boat, he changed and checked everything out. Nothing was out of place, so he locked up and went over to see Nick. As usual, his friend was out on the deck of his boat, drinking a beer.

"Traveling Jack. Welcome back," Nick said, reaching into the small cooler for another beer for Jack.

"Everything okay here?" he said, taking the bottle from Nick. He took a long swallow before sitting.

"No problem. Molly left for work about an hour ago, but everything's been quiet around here this week."

"Good. Hey, I was wondering. Is there a shooting range around here?"

Nick frowned. "Yeah, why?"

"I haven't shot since we've been down here. I was thinking about carrying again, and yes, I have a valid permit."

"Big Coppitt Gun Club, up on Big Coppitt Key, about ten miles up from us. What did you carry?"

"SIG 229, forty cal."

Nick nodded his approval. "Nice gun. I used to tote one of those when I was working. Kinda big for shorts and t-shirts, though."

"True. It was fine when I was wearing suits, but it is a bit bulky. You recommend something else?"

"Lot of choices. SIG makes a nice compact, pricey but you can't go wrong with SIG. Glock's always solid. Ruger makes a nice affordable compact 9mm, as well as Beretta."

Guns were like cars, everyone had their favorites and many times the choice was totally subjective. Every gun owner had his preference of guns and ammo. As Jack's instructor had always told him, as long as you go with mainstream manufacturers, aim is more important than brand or ammunition.

"My advice is to try a few and go with that's comfortable and something you'll carry. Doesn't matter how good it is if you don't carry it and don't know how to use it," Nick said. "We can take a ride up there sometime if you want. I can introduce you to the owner."

Jack nodded. Nick had a car, so he intended to take him up on the offer.

Nick finished his beer. He held his empty up toward Jack with a question in his eyes. Jack nodded, and Nick fished two fresh ones out of the cooler. He twisted the tops off and handed one to Jack. "How was your friend in Fort Myers?"

Jack told him about his suspicions regarding Tony's business partner.

"What did Tony say?"

Jack shook his head. "He trusts him totally. Maybe I'm getting too cynical, but something feels wrong about it."

"Over the years, I've learned to trust my gut."

"Yeah, well speaking of that, I think I know what happened to Kenny and Val," Jack said, looking at Nick for a reaction. Nick didn't say a word, just took a long drink from his beer and waited for Jack to continue.

"I've told you about what happened up the coast with the drug dealer, Molly getting kidnapped and all." He took a swallow of his beer, then continued. "I left out a few minor details."

Jack told him about taking the money, not hiding behind the 'hypothetical' framework he'd used with Tony. He wasn't sure of Nick's employment status, but he felt the man operated in an area considerably less black and white than Tony.

Nick listened, taking it in and saying nothing until Jack finished.

"How much?"

Jack shrugged. "Close to a million."

Nick whistled and shook his head. "Minor, huh? That would explain a lot. So you don't know who's looking for it?"

"Nope. And . . . there's less than half of it left." He explained about setting up the trust fund for Wren.

"This would make a hell of a book. Somebody you don't know is looking for money you don't have. I'd say you're in deep shit, my friend."

They sat there for a few more minutes, finishing their beer in silence.

Finally, Nick said, "All this has made me hungry. Let's go over to the Half Shell and figure out what we're going to do."

Jack smiled. Hearing Nick say "we" made him feel better.

The Half Shell Raw Bar was across the bight, only a five-minute walk. Nothing fancy, the seafood was fresh, and the prices reasonable, at least for Key West.

Nick locked the boat, and Jack noticed him give his waist a cursory pat as he turned to leave.

"You carrying?" Jack asked.

"Don't leave home without it."

Jack shook his head, puzzled. "I didn't think you could legally carry in a place that served alcohol?"

The Half Shell wasn't named "Bar" for no reason. Florida law was somewhat ambiguous when it came to restaurants that served alcohol, but it was generally agreed that persons carrying should stay out of the bar area, where serving alcohol was the primary function.

"Most people can't," Nick said as he stepped off the boat.

At the restaurant, they sat at a table overlooking the bight. Karen, their server, who also drove a taxi part-time, came over to take their order.

"Gentlemen. Nick. How are you?"

Jack laughed, and Nick shook his head. "We gotta find a better restaurant," Nick said. "Surely somewhere on this island is a place where we can get some decent food and not be harassed."

"You're a masochist, Nick. That's why you keep coming back. Too bad I'm not into guys—we could have fun," she said, winking as she turned to Jack. "How's Molly? She stopped by the other day."

"Doing well, thanks. Still working some out at the hospital."

"Good to hear." She shook her head, holding her order pad. "That was awful about Kenny and Valerie. Damn smugglers are getting bolder."

They each ordered a grouper sandwich with fries. Nick ordered his usual beer while Jack ordered something from the local brewery.

When Karen walked away, he said, "I think she's got the hots for you, Nick."

Nick just scowled and gazed around the bar. He hesitated at one point, then continuing scanning the surroundings.

"Looking for someone?" Jack asked.

Nick shrugged. "Habit. Your theory makes a lot of sense. Somebody found out about the money and tracked you down. Did you know any of Peabo's associates, besides Shorty and the doctor?"

"No, not really. All of my dealings were with them."

"Don't turn around," Nick said in a low voice, barely audible above the din in the crowded bar. "There's a guy sitting at the bar watching you."

Jack resisted the urge to turn his head, instead asking Nick to describe him.

"My two o'clock. Dark blue ball cap, shorts, and a butt-ugly green t-shirt. About your height, medium build, short brown hair, no facial hair. He came in about five minutes ago, and keeps looking your way."

Jack started to make a wisecrack, then realized Nick was dead serious. He shifted in his chair, turning his head past the person as if he were looking around for his server. When he turned back to look the other way, he let his gaze linger a few extra seconds on the person Nick had identified.

"I know that guy," he said, facing Nick. "Give me a second, I'm trying to remember his name."

Karen walked up with their beers. "Your food should be out in a few minutes," she said, putting the beers down, then walking away.

"He's coming over," Nick said, his expression still intense.

"Jack?"

Jack turned to see the man from the bar standing there, his hand extended. "Sorry for interrupting. I thought that was you, but wasn't sure. Randy. Randy . . . Jenkins. I met you over at A&B Marina the other day."

Jack shook his hand, then introduced him to Nick. "Randy was talking to Terry about a getting a slip."

Randy shrugged. "Just thinking about it. How've you been?"

Jack nodded. "Doing a little consulting work in Fort Myers. Just got back."

Randy turned to Nick. "What do you do, Nick?"

"Retired." There was an awkward silence when Nick didn't say anything else.

Randy cleared his throat. "Well, I better get back. Just wanted to come over and say 'Hi.' Good seeing you, Jack." He turned to Nick. "Nice meeting you."

Nick just nodded as Randy walked away.

After a few minutes, Jack looked around to make sure Randy was back at the bar, then turned to Nick. "You didn't care for him, I take it?"

Nick shrugged. "He's alright. Just another Cayo Hueso wannabe. I give him a year." He used the Spanish name for Key West, which literally translated as "Bone Island." Many fell in love with the island, but relatively few stayed any length of time.

Jack laughed. "You think Molly and I will last?"

Nick's face softened and he nodded. "You're boat people. And, you love the ocean. Yeah, you could make it down here if you choose."

"Back to my question. How do I find out who might be watching me if I don't have any idea who it is?"

Nick took a long swallow of his beer.

"Maybe we should go sailing?"

14

When he got back from his run the next morning, Jack smiled when he saw Molly's bike in the rack. At the boat, she was sitting out under the shade of the bimini with a cup of coffee, waiting for him.

"Hey stranger," she said, rising to give him a hug and kiss.

He could feel the curves of her body under the thin sundress, and knew she was wearing nothing else. "I hope you don't greet all strangers like this," he said, his hands still on her hips as they separated. Her green eyes twinkled.

"I missed you," she said, her arms still around his neck.

"I missed you, too."

"Would you like a cup of coffee? What do you want for breakfast?"

He gave her a lecherous grin and she blushed.

Placing her hand on his chest, she said, "Maybe after you take a shower."

He raised his eyebrows. "You've got my attention. Water first. I need to cool down before I shower."

He filled his water bottle, came back topside and sat next to her.

"How was work?"

"Pretty quiet, which is a good thing. How was your flight?"

"Fine, once the plane showed up. It was late, as usual. When I got home, went over to Nick's and then we went over to the Half Shell for dinner."

She looked at him, her eyes probing.

"He sure did check on me a lot, him and Terry both. You didn't say anything to them, did you?"

He was glad to see a glimpse of her former confidence and independence. He shrugged. "I may have mentioned something about keeping an eye on you while I was gone."

She playfully slapped his arm. "I figured." Her eyes flashed serious for a moment. "Thank you," she said, kissing him.

"How was dinner Wednesday night?" he asked. Molly had told him she was going to dinner at Seth and Lee's house.

"Awesome. Lee is a wonderful cook. He showed me a new recipe for grouper. I can't wait to try it for you. He made it look so easy."

"What did he cook?"

"Baked mahimahi. It was scrumptious. And, stone crab claws for an appetizer. You'll love Seth and Lee. They can't wait for you to come over." She had told him they were invited over for dinner Monday night.

After a cup of coffee, he went up to the bathhouse to shower. When he returned, Molly wasn't outside. The companionway door was shut, and he heard the air conditioning on the boat running, pumping water out the stern opening. Puzzled, he opened the door and went down the steps into the cabin, closing the door behind him.

"Molly?" he called out, not seeing her in the main cabin.

"In here," she answered. Her voice came from the forward berth where they slept.

He walked that direction and was shocked to see her reclining on their berth against the pillows, wearing nothing but a smile and a sheer, green negligee. She patted the bed next to her.

"You're overdressed," she said.

Watching her and admiring her body as he moved closer, he replied, "I've only got on a pair of shorts."

"My point, exactly." She licked her lips, her eyes fastened on his midsection.

As he stood next to the berth, she turned on her side and undid his shorts, letting them fall to his feet. He moved to sit, but she stopped him. "Don't move. Stand right where you are," she said, moving her head toward him.

His eyes closed and he drew in a breath as he felt her tongue on him. She teased him at first, making him beg her to finish what she'd started. She toyed with him for another minute, then complied.

"My God," he said afterward, lying on his back next to her, her head lying on his shoulder. "That was incredible."

He felt her smile and turned to look at her.

"You liked it, huh?" She said, "I love doing that to you."

"Whew. Any time. I should go out of town more often."

"Don't even think about it," she said, nipping his nose.

After he caught his breath, he pushed her over on her back. He straddled her and traced his hands lightly over her body. "Have I told you lately how much I love your body?" he asked, pulling the negligee over her head and tossing it aside.

Smiling, she shook her head as she put her hands on his legs.

"Let me show you," he said, kissing her lips and then slowly moving his tongue down her body, determined to return the favor.

"Convinced?" he asked afterward.

Her face still flushed, she nodded. "Oh yes, totally." After a few minutes, she raised up on one elbow. "That earned you breakfast. I'm cooking."

They eventually made their way to the galley. Molly started coffee while Jack looked in the basket where they usually kept the bread. It was empty.

"Are we out of bread?" he asked.

"Crap," she answered. "I was going to get some this morning, but you distracted me."

"I'll give up bread anytime for that," he replied, still grinning. "I'll just walk over to the market and get some for breakfast. Be right back."

There was a little market at the base of the marina, convenient for quick necessities. On his way back to the boat, as he passed the fuel dock, he noticed a twin engine center console boat approaching. The captain waited a little too late to reverse the engines and the bow of the boat slammed into the piling. Jack ran out and caught the line the captain tossed.

Jack chuckled to himself. Everyone had been in that position, but it was still humorous to watch the newbies handle their boats. What made it funnier is that A&B sold only diesel fuel, which was of no help to a boat powered by outboards, which required gasoline.

The man at the helm switched off the engines. "I just needed to gas up," he said.

Jack looked closely, recognizing him. "Randy?"

About that time, Randy looked up and smiled. "Hey, Jack. Sorry, didn't recognize you. Too busy trying to dock this thing in one piece."

Jack chuckled. "We've all been there. Sometimes the current and wind in here can make it a little tricky." He was trying to be gracious, remembering that he'd banged up his share of docks, although it had been a while. Jack had been driving boats since he was twelve and sometimes took it for granted.

Jack pointed across the water to the Chevron sign on another dock thirty yards away. "To get gas, you'll have to go over Key West Bight Marina." Seeing Randy's puzzled look, he laughed. "They don't sell gas here, only diesel. Over there, they sell both."

"Damn. All that for nothing. I didn't realize. Still learning my way around. You have a boat here, right?"

"Yeah, on the other side." Jack pointed in the general direction of *Left Behind,* further out at the end of the main dock.

"The sailboat?"

Jack nodded.

"Nice. What is it?"

"Thirty-eight Island Packet."

"Oh, so that's what an Island Packet looks like. I've never sailed before. Good looking boat."

"We like it. It's home." He nodded toward Randy's boat. "Nice fishing boat you have here."

"Yeah, I like it. Just starting to learn my way around the waters here. You fish?"

"Not as much as I used to. Kind of hard to fish off of a sailboat."

Randy laughed. "I guess so. Maybe you can go out with me one day, show me the ropes?"

"Sure. Give me a call sometime. You know where I am. Did you ever find a slip?"

"Yeah, but not here. A&B didn't have anything open."

Jesse, one of the dockhands who worked at A&B, walked up. She looked at Jack as if to say *You know this dipshit?* Turning back to Randy, she said, "We don't sell gasoline here."

"Jack just told me the news. Sorry," he said, reaching down and starting the engines.

"Be careful, Randy," Jack said.

"Sure. See you around."

Jesse tossed him the line, and Randy put the engines in reverse, backing away from the fuel dock without incident. She watched until he was clear and moving across the water to the other marina.

Still shaking her head, she walked over to where Jack was standing. "A friend of yours?" she asked, derisively.

"I've met him, that's it. New to the area."

"Really? I would've never guessed. I'd be careful going out with him in a boat."

Jack laughed and walked away.

15

Molly was up early Monday morning, getting ready for work. The hospital had called yesterday afternoon and asked her to work 7a to 3p today. She was putting the final touches on her hair before leaving.

"I refused at first—I wanted us to spend the day together—but they couldn't find anyone and practically begged me."

"I understand. We'll do something tomorrow."

She put her hand over his. "What are you doing today?"

"Thinking about taking the boat out with Nick. It needs the exercise."

She frowned and pouted her lip out. "I want to go sailing."

He laughed. "We can go out tomorrow, I promise. Nick suggested going today, and I just want to make sure everything's working." He started to say, "we haven't been out since we left with Kenny and Val," but kept quiet.

She kissed him, then turned to go up the steps. "Be careful. Don't forget we have dinner tonight."

"I know. We'll probably be back before you get home."

He watched her leave, refilled his coffee, and walked up on deck. A bit of a breeze was stirring, out of the southeast, which was good.

Thursday night at dinner, Nick had suggested they go out on *Left Behind* toward the Marquesas and see if they could attract any company. Jack had tried to figure out how he could go without Molly, but the call from the hospital yesterday solved that problem. He'd sent Nick a text message, and told him to come over at seven, ready to go.

A few minutes early, Nick came walking up, carrying a sizeable duffel bag, speargun, and bang stick.

"You planning on spending the night?" Jack asked, laughing.

Nick smiled. "Just a few necessities. Plus, thought we might get to do a little fishing if we're bored."

The plan had been for Jack to broadcast his intentions to go out as widely as possible, hoping to stir up some interest. Every opportunity, he'd made a point of advertising that he was taking *Left Behind* out for the day, toward the Marquesas.

Onboard, Nick went below to stow his bag and reemerged back on deck with a cup of coffee. "You ready?" he asked.

Jack pulled up his t-shirt just enough for Nick to see the grip of the SIG.

The plan was for Nick to stay below in the cabin, giving the impression to anyone watching that Jack was going out alone.

They finished their coffee, and Jack started the diesel, letting it warm up. Nick went below while Jack released the dock lines. Satisfied all was clear, he went back to the helm, put the transmission in gear, and eased the throttle forward.

He picked up the microphone on the VHF radio. "A&B, this is *Left Behind*, over."

In a minute, he heard Jesse's familiar voice. "*Left Behind*, switch and answer six eight."

He switched the frequency over to channel sixty-eight and keyed the mic. "Hey, Jesse."

"Hello, Jack."

"Just wanted to let you know I'm going out for a few hours. Meant to tell you before I left, but forgot. Headed out the Southwest Channel toward Satan Shoal and back. Molly's working, over."

"10-4. Should be a nice day. Give me a shout when you get back, over."

"Thanks. Over and out."

After leaving the bight, Jack set course southwest, the same route he took when Kenny and Val were along. He saw Nick taking a variety of weapons out of his bag, checking and loading them. It looked like he had an arsenal with him.

"I'm going to put up the sails. Might as well exercise her a little bit," he yelled to Nick, over the sound of the diesel.

"Need any help?"

"No, thanks." Jack had single-handed *Left Behind* before. With all of the latest equipment and in light breezes, it wasn't that difficult. Once in the clear, he turned into the wind, throttled back, and raised the mainsail. Once it was all the way up, he fell off to starboard and felt the power of the wind start to move the boat.

He switched off the engine, then released the jib. It was like shifting gears, as the headsail also filled with wind and the boat picked up speed.

Nick stuck his head out the companionway. "Much better."

"I agree," Jack said, looking up at the telltales on both sails streaming aft. He adjusted the sails to maximize their efficiency, then sat back, enjoying the ride.

"You really think this'll work?" he asked Nick.

"Beats sitting around the marina wearing a bullseye, wondering if every person that walks by is the one."

The time went by as they got closer to Satan Shoal. Boats of all types passed by at a distance, but no one seemed interested.

Jack looked at the time, decided to tack, and head home. There was a steady ten-knot breeze out of the southeast, which meant they'd be running a little closer to the wind on the return.

An hour later, as Key West was getting taller on the horizon, Jack was scanning the surrounding waters less frequently. Clouds were building on the western horizon, but nothing near them.

"I think this was a bust," he said to Nick, who was sitting on the deck, his back against the bulkhead, his eyes almost closed. They'd eaten sandwiches and chips after they'd tacked.

The breeze had died and their speed had slowed to half what they were doing earlier. "At this rate, it'll take us forever to get back. I'm going to take the sails down and motor the rest of the way," Jack said.

"If you're going to do that, let's swing by Satan Shoal. I might do a little spearfishing, see if we can get some fresh fish for dinner," Nick said.

"You sure? There were a lot of jellyfish the other day when Molly and I came out."

Nick shrugged. "Always jellyfish. Long as there're no box jellies, I'm not worried."

Box jellyfish were one of the most deadly animals in the ocean. Just last year, a special ops soldier in the water a couple of miles from Key West was almost killed by one.

Jack started the engine, engaged the transmission, and turned into the wind, idling along. He furled the headsail, then dropped the main. Once everything was secure, he turned toward Satan Shoal and moved the throttle forward.

Nick had brought his snorkel gear and speargun up from the cabin and was seated, checking it out.

A few minutes later, Jack looked around and saw a powerboat directly behind them, on the same course, but still a couple of miles away.

"See something?" Nick asked.

"Maybe. There's a powerboat maybe two miles behind us. Looks like it's on the same course as us."

Nick eased down into the cabin, leaving his gear on the seat.

"They can't see you from where they are," Jack said.

"They can if they're using binoculars."

Jack nodded, not considering that. The powerboat was closing, fast. He could tell it was a center console, riding up on plane, probably at a good thirty knots, which was five times faster than *Left Behind*. There appeared to be two people at the console.

"How close?" Nick asked. He was barely visible in the shadows of the cabin.

Jack did the quick calculation in his head. "Five minutes, maybe."

"Put your pistol up on the table, under your towel. Make sure one's in the chamber, and keep your hand on it the entire time."

Jack did as he was told, and the boat was clearly coming straight for them. He peered into the cabin, and could barely see Nick. He was scrunched up against the bulkhead on the port settee.

"They're closer, looks like they're coming to us," Jack said, the adrenalin starting to kick in.

"Make them come alongside to starboard. And you stay on the port side of the helm."

The powerboat, a twenty-six Mako center console with twin outboards, closed to within thirty yards of Jack's stern. Jack turned the wheel slightly to starboard, forcing the other boat to the right side of *Left Behind*.

"Hey, captain," the driver said, cutting his speed back to match the much slower sailboat.

"Howdy," Jack answered. Taking a small step to his left, he kept one hand on the wheel, and the other under the towel. He could feel the handle of the pistol, and he tightened his fingers around the grip.

There were two men on board, both standing at the console. The driver was about Jack's size, wearing a cap. His friend, a bigger, heavier guy, grunted, took a swallow from a can of beer wrapped in a red foam Koozie and gave a half-wave.

"I'm Bobby Tarver. This is my friend, Mike," the captain said, waving his hand toward his companion. "We've been out fishing all day, and was wondering if you're familiar with the area?"

"Some. You from this area?"

"Nah, we're from Georgia. Heard the fishing was good and thought we come down and give it a try."

Jack saw the other guy reach down under the console. He squeezed the grip on the SIG and started to pull it out from under the towel. The other guy stood up, holding a piece of paper.

"We're looking for a spot called Satan Shoal. I can't read the coordinates, and was wondering if you could tell us where that is."

Jack tensed, and the captain of the powerboat said, "Somebody in town told us about it, said it was a good spot to fish. He wrote it down. I just assumed it'd be above water, and we'd be able to spot it."

"We've been looking around for an hour," his friend added. "Ain't seen nothing."

Jack didn't take his eyes off the two men. "It's not far, but it's just shallower there over the shoal. I don't think I've ever seen it above water."

"You mind giving us the numbers?" the captain asked, referring to the map coordinates.

Jack had the coordinates stored on his GPS, but there was no way he was turning loose of the pistol to punch it in. He put his leg up against the wheel to hold it and engaged the autopilot, keeping a close eye on the two men as he did. The autopilot beeped, indicating it was engaged. Still clutching the pistol, he punched in the name, and the coordinates appeared.

"You got something to write with?" Jack asked. The heavy guy rummaged around in the cabinet and pulled out something black and shiny. Jack slid the pistol out from under the towel, but before he could raise it, the man held up a black notebook.

"Yeah, go ahead."

Jack reached over and slid the towel back over the pistol as he called out the latitude and longitude of Satan Shoal.

"Much appreciated," the captain said. "Sorry to bother you. Have a good day," he said as he eased the throttles forward and turned the powerboat back toward Satan Shoal.

Breathing a sigh of relief, Jack watched as the boat gained speed, quickly getting back up on plane and putting distance between them. He took his hand off the pistol, and flexed his fingers, realizing for the first time how sweaty his palms were.

Nick appeared in the companionway, an AR15 cradled in his arms.

"I was ready to shoot the son-of-a-bitch when he reached down under the console," Jack said.

Nick smiled. "You did good. Sounded like just a couple of good old boys out on the water. You recognize them?"

Jack shook his head. "Never seen them before."

Nick started packing up his gear.

"No sense going there if that's where they're headed. The fishing will be ruined by the time we get there. Might as well head home."

Later, as they motored past Mallory pier, a huge cruise ship had moored there since they left. Jack called Molly on her cell to let her know they were almost to the dock. She was over on Doug and Lisa's boat and said she'd be there by the time they got back.

"Thanks for going out with me," Jack said to Nick, as he stuck the phone in his pocket.

"Hey, you never know. Maybe they were watching or had something else to do. We should try it again. Unless you get more information, we're going to have to try and flush them out."

Molly was standing on the end of the dock when they pulled into the marina. Nick and Molly secured the dock lines as Jack backed the boat into the slip.

"Have fun?" Molly asked, her hands on her hips. "While I was working."

Jack laughed. "Always nice to go out on the water. Everything's ready to go for tomorrow."

Nick stepped up into the cockpit lugging his duffel bag in one hand, speargun and bang stick in the other.

"Geez, Nick, you moving in?" Molly said, laughing.

"Just some dive gear, but didn't even get a chance to use it." He glanced at Jack. "Maybe next time."

After Nick walked off, Molly stepped on board and hugged Jack. "I missed you," she said.

Jack smiled and laughed. "Yeah, you just missed sailing."

She grinned. "Well . . ."

16

A bottle of wine in one hand and Molly's hand in the other, Jack walked down William Street toward the Key West Cemetery, looking for the address Molly had given him. On the way, she'd told him the story about meeting Lee and Seth in the fish market.

"Apparently, Lee was a chef in some fancy New York restaurant," she said.

"Well, I'm expecting a gourmet dinner, then." He held up the wine. "I don't want to waste a good wine on fish and chips." They'd stopped at Fausto's Market on Fleming Street and bought a nice Sancerre.

Molly shook her head and squeezed his hand. "Try to behave. I know it's hard," she said, smiling.

They arrived at an older, two-story white house with dark blue shutters, and Molly verified the address as being correct. Like many of the older homes in this area of Key West, this one had been painstakingly renovated. Both the main and second-floor porches had beautiful iron railings with gingerbread trim along the edge of the roof.

They walked up the steps to the front door and pressed the buzzer alongside.

"Coming," they heard someone say and in a minute, a trim, impeccably dressed man in his thirties opened the door.

"Molly," he said, greeting her with open arms and a kiss on each cheek. He stepped back and gave her the once over. "You look marvelous."

He turned toward Jack with his hand extended. "And this must be hubby, who goes by Jack. I'm Seth."

Jack shook his hand and offered Seth the wine. "Thank you for having us. I hope this is satisfactory."

Seth took it, eyed the label, and nodded. "Very nice. Thank you. I'll chill this, and we'll have it for dinner. Speaking of dinner . . ."

Seth led them deeper into the house, back toward the kitchen. "Lee is slaving away on some fabulous dish, so please forgive his dress."

The house was decorated nicely, not ostentatious, but comfortable. The pastel colors and nautical accents combined to give it a Key West flair.

They walked into the kitchen, where a short, heavy-set man was leaning over a commercial gas stove. He wore a white, short-sleeved chef jacket over traditional black and white checked pants, a towel slung over his shoulder. The only thing missing, Jack thought, was a toque.

"Our guests have arrived, Lee," Seth said. Lee kept stirring the sauce, ignoring everyone. He stopped to ladle a spoonful and brought it to his mouth, blowing on it to cool it. Carefully, he sipped the contents into his mustachioed mouth. He closed his eyes, savoring it, then with a flourish, nodded his approval. He opened his eyes and then turned to greet them.

Introductions complete, he turned his attention back to the prep area.

Seth shook his head. "When he's cooking, he ignores everyone, so don't take offense. Let's go back up front, and we'll have a glass of champagne and some munchies."

Twenty minutes later, Lee appeared with a flute of champagne. He'd changed into teal shorts and a flowery print silk shirt. "Dinner in fifteen minutes," he announced, as he sat.

Contrary to Jack's initial impression, Lee was quite sociable. He and Seth were a fascinating couple, widely traveled, and good company. Precisely fifteen minutes later, Lee's phone buzzed and he stood. "If you'll be seated in the dining room, I'll serve dinner."

Seth showed them next door and indicated where Jack and Molly were to sit. "I'll go help Lee," he said, laughing. "He does allow me to serve and clean up."

The first course was a poached pear with goat cheese, sprinkled with sprigs of arugula, and drizzled with Tupelo honey. It was mouth-watering.

"My God," Jack said after the first mouthful. "This is so good."

Her mouth full, all Molly could manage was closing her eyes and murmuring "Mmmm."

The main course was snapper en papillote, and even more impressive than the first course. The Sancerre complimented it nicely, and Lee thanked them for an excellent choice in the wine. Lee beamed at the accolades, glad his guests were pleased.

It was a convivial dinner, with the four of them hitting it off well. Molly was radiant in their company, and Jack could see why she enjoyed them.

As they readied to leave, Jack said, "We'd love to have you over, but I can't come close to matching a dinner like we had. I'd be embarrassed."

Seth held up his hand and waved it at Jack. "Don't be intimidated. Lee enjoys burgers, beer, and oysters as much as anyone."

"In that case, we may be alright, then," Jack said, laughing.

"As you can tell, I love food," Lee said, patting his ample stomach. "We'd be delighted to come over, and I promise to stay out of the way in your kitchen. Besides, I've already seen your wife's ability in the kitchen, and you are a lucky man."

That brought another round of laughter, as they headed toward the front door. Seth and Lee followed them out on the porch to see them off.

After Jack and Molly stepped down the sidewalk, they looked over their shoulder and gave a final wave. Before they turned toward the bight, Jack noticed a lone figure on the sidewalk almost a block behind them. As they started toward home, he heard the door shut behind them.

It was early, and barely dark. The temperature had cooled down some, and with the sun down, it was bearable. Across the street, a couple was holding hands, laughing, walking the opposite direction from Jack and Molly.

"That was wonderful. I really enjoyed meeting them, and the food was absolutely fabulous," Jack said, holding Molly's hand as they walked.

"You've got big shoes to fill," she said, patting his arm. "I'm glad you'll be cooking when we have them over."

"I don't know about that. Lee seemed pretty impressed with your skills in the kitchen. I'd get takeout from Seven

Fish," he said, referring to one of their favorite restaurants on the island.

They passed an alley on the left, and Jack unconsciously steered them closer to the street. He thought he saw a figure in the shadows. A few steps later, he was aware of someone behind them.

He glanced over at Molly and caught movement on the edges of his vision. The person behind them was closer than he realized. He was suddenly aware that his holster and pistol were inside his shorts on his right hip, the same side as Molly. As they approached the corner, he tugged on Molly's hand and turned right. He wanted a view of the person behind them, and a chance to put himself between Molly and the stranger.

By now, the person behind them was only ten feet away, but slowed, as if unsure what to do. He was a few inches taller than Jack, probably six-foot-three, compared to Jack's six foot, and twenty pounds heavier. He wore a grungy blue t-shirt, baggy jeans, and a ball cap tugged low over his head. Both hands were in his pockets.

No cars were coming from either direction, so Jack moved over to Molly's right side, grabbed her hand and kept walking, crossing William Street. He turned his head to the right and saw the guy following them across the street. There was no one on the other sidewalk in either direction.

He put his right hand under his shirt and on the grip of the pistol, easing it out of the holster. When they got to the opposite sidewalk, he did a quick about-face, hanging on to Molly's hand, and putting himself between her and the person following.

"What—"

He squeezed her hand tighter and pulled the pistol completely out of the holster while keeping it under his shirt.

"Are you following us?" Jack asked the stranger in a loud and irritated voice. He kept his eyes on the man's hands, and he felt Molly squeeze his hand harder.

The man stopped, almost tripping, not expecting Jack's abrupt halt. He started to pull his hands out of his pockets.

"Stop," Jack yelled. "Don't move," he said, as he pulled the pistol out from underneath his shirt and aimed it at the younger man. His trigger finger was still alongside the barrel of the gun, but he was prepared to move it inside the trigger guard at an instant.

The man froze, his eyes widened, then darted around, looking up and down the street.

"Hey, man, I wasn't doing nothing," he said, his voice squeaky and unsteady. He took a tentative step backward but kept his hands in his pockets as instructed.

Jack heard voices to his left but didn't dare take his eyes off the man. The man in the street heard them too and glanced to his right.

"Molly," Jack said, lowering his voice. "Take my phone out of my left pocket and call 911."

The voices on Jack's left got louder, indicating the group was getting closer.

The man in the street took one more step backward, then quickly turned and ran the opposite direction.

Jack took a deep breath and lowered the pistol. Convinced the would-be attacker was gone, he turned his head to the left. Two couples were approaching, and from the way they were laughing and talking, had not seen a thing.

Carefully, he placed it back in the holster, pulling his shirt over it just as the group got there.

He turned to face Molly and before she could speak, he shook his head once.

The couples passed, giving them a curious look, and kept walking. When they were out of earshot, Molly said, "What the hell just happened?"

Jack shrugged. "I think he was going to rob us."

"Since when did you start carrying a pistol down here?"

He had deliberately not let Molly see him put the holster in his shorts before they left the boat. "That thing with Kenny and Val got me to thinking—too much probably." He tried to keep his tone casual.

She eyed him suspiciously, wondering whether to believe him or not. Her voice was still shaky. "I've never seen you so jumpy. I guess it was a good thing you had it with you." She grabbed his hand and squeezed it. "I don't like all of this, Jack. It scares me. I thought we came down here to get away from this kind of thing."

"We did, and I probably overreacted. For all we know, he was just going to hit us up for a handout."

"You scared the shit out of him. Me, too."

"I'm sorry. I didn't mean to frighten you." He squeezed her hand and started walking. He felt his hand shaking. He couldn't believe he was that close to shooting someone, someone whose intentions weren't clear.

Maybe carrying a pistol wasn't such a good idea after all.

17

As Jack was readying the boat the next morning, he looked up at the western sky, then south. Most of the weather in Key West usually came from that quadrant, unless there was the rare storm coming from the east. Nothing today but a few puffy cumulus clouds. There was a light breeze out of the southeast, which was perfect. It appeared to be another good day for sailing.

Molly was in the cabin, making lunch. Last night, after they returned to the boat, he couldn't sleep. The incident with the would-be robber weighed on his mind.

By all accounts, it appeared to be nothing more than an ordinary street robbery, not unheard of in Key West. Although the man certainly appeared to be targeting them, he said nothing threatening and brandished no weapon. He appeared to be down on his luck, like many on the tiny island. As soon as Jack confronted him, he turned and ran. But something about it bothered Jack and he couldn't get it out of his mind.

Satisfied everything was ready, Jack disconnected the power and water, then started the diesel. Molly came out, flashed Jack a big grin, and made her way forward to the bow. Her face was shaded by her trademark floppy straw hat, and he stared at her back. Underneath the sheer white cover-up, he could see the outline of a black bikini.

The light southeast breeze kept *Left Behind* against the dock on her starboard side, so Jack had already cast off all of the dock lines except the stern. Molly was standing on the bow, holding on to the forestay. She turned and gave him a thumbs up, so he threw the stern line on the dock, shifted the transmission into gear, and moved the throttle forward, easing the boat out of her slip.

As they motored past the Galleon, Molly waved to her left. Jack saw Nick sitting out on the deck of his boat with his coffee and newspaper, waving as they passed. Jack returned the wave and motored out of the bight.

Once clear, they turned southwest, passing between Sunset Key and Mallory Square. After they had gotten out of the crowded harbor area, Jack turned into the wind and pulled the throttle back, preparing to raise the sails.

He no longer needed to tell Molly what to do. They worked quickly and efficiently as a team. In a few minutes, she'd raised the main, and came back to the cockpit to release the jib as Jack turned back to the southwest. With both sails out and catching the breeze, he felt the heavy boat start to accelerate. He switched the engine off as Molly removed her cover-up.

"I needed this," she said, stretching her arms. She moved next to him and wrapped them around his neck. "I love you," she said.

He snaked his arm around her bare waist. "I love you, too."

She nudged him out of the way with her hip and took the helm. "My turn. You were out yesterday," she said, smiling.

He stood behind her, his arms encircling her, and holding her close to him. "This is much nicer than yesterday," he said, nuzzling her neck.

She leaned her head back against his. "Careful. I might run over someone with you doing that."

He laughed, kissed her neck, and moved away. He adjusted the sails and then sat on her left, looking out on the water. There were boats in every direction, but no one near them. He saw a parasailer up north of them, on the other side of Sunset Key. He gazed back at Molly, and the expression on her face was priceless. She enjoyed sailing as much as he did, which was one of the reasons he was crazy about her.

Being on the water was the best therapy of all. There was nothing more relaxing than the rhythmic sound of the hull slicing through the seas, smelling the salt air, and feeling the ocean breeze on your bare skin. It was salve for the soul and satisfied a primeval need.

They spent the next two hours sailing. Molly was content to steer while Jack piddled around on deck. He occasionally tweaked the sails, more for something to do than anything else. The boat traffic had thinned out, with only a few boats visible on the horizon.

"You want to anchor for lunch? Maybe go for a swim?" Jack asked as they neared Satan Shoal.

"Sure." She stood behind the wheel. "Ready?"

Jack nodded. This time, they switched roles, with Molly steering and him handling the sails. He smiled as he knew she would do it without the engine. She turned the boat into the wind, slowing the boat. The sails started luffing, and he cranked the headsail in first, then dropped the main. "How much water?" he asked.

Molly looked at the depth sounder on the pedestal and said, "Ten feet."

He went forward and released the anchor. He could see Woman Key up ahead. The boat started drifting backward, paying out anchor line. When he spotted the desired mark on the line, he cleated the line and watched as it stretched taught. The boat strained as the anchor caught. Convinced it would hold, at least for lunch, he made his way back to the cockpit.

"You want to go for a swim first, then some lunch?"

Molly nodded and took off her hat. "That would be good."

He looked behind them and saw the current wasn't too bad, the water moving past the boat. He opened the stern locker, took out a coiled yellow line, and tied one end to a stern cleat. Then, he threw the line out, watching it uncoil and stream out behind the boat, floating on top of the water.

He normally liked to keep one person on the boat when anchored out in the open water like this, in case the anchor slipped. But with only two onboard, it wasn't as much fun. By throwing out a floating line, the risk of the boat drifting away was reduced, as long as the people in the water stayed near the line.

Molly scanned the water in every direction, then looked at Jack. "Remember when we used to go skinny-dipping up at Cabbage Key?" she asked.

Before he could answer, she reached behind her back and undid her top, taking it off and tossing it on the seat. He stared at her breasts, her nipples starting to poke out.

"Well?" she continued, hooking her thumbs inside her bikini bottom and pulling it down. She stepped out of it and tossed it over where her top lay, then stood up, facing him. "Hello?"

Seeing Molly completely naked, outside, in the middle of the day on their boat, was incredibly exciting. When his eyes finally made their way back up to her face, she was smiling from ear to ear. "Does he speak?"

He took a step toward her, and she held up her hand. "Not dressed like that."

He grinned, then took off his bathing suit, kicking it aside while not taking his eyes off of her.

Her eyes moved down his body, then back up. She nodded. "Much better."

They made love on the deck. Not the most comfortable of accommodations for that activity, but it didn't matter. Afterward, sitting on the side, with his arm around her, he said, "I don't remember doing that *before* we went into the water that first time at Cabbage Key."

She pinched him. "You were more patient then."

"Me? Patient? I've never been accused of that before. As you recall, we made up for it when we got back onboard."

She lifted her head off his shoulder and patted his leg. "No complaints, love. Let's go for a swim, then have some lunch."

The water felt good, and by the time they got back aboard and rinsed off, they were hungry. They sat at the little table in the cockpit, not bothering to put their swimsuits back on.

Molly had prepared baguettes with mozzarella, tomatoes, and fresh basil, drizzled with olive oil. Munching on macaroons for dessert, Jack noticed a boat coming toward them.

"I guess we better put some clothes on," he said, nodding in the direction of the approaching boat. Molly looked, then moved to pick up her swimsuit and get dressed. She tossed Jack his bathing suit and he slipped it on, not bothering with a shirt.

As the boat got closer, Jack could see it was a center console fishing boat with a white hull, mid twenty-foot range. There were two people at the helm, and the boat slowed as it got closer. He could see fishing rods sticking up from the back of the T-top.

He stood for a better view, looking over the stern. It looked like the identical boat he and Nick saw yesterday. As they closed in, he recognized the same two guys. The boat pulled up on their starboard side, five or six feet away. Jack tried to remember their names.

"Hey, captain, I thought that was you," the man said. He stole a quick glance at Molly, then turned his attention back to Jack. "We just wanted to say 'thanks' for yesterday. We went back over to the shoal, and caught fish till we got tired."

"Great. Glad it worked out." *Bobby and Mike,* Jack remembered. "Bobby, this is my wife, Molly," he said, looking over to Molly, who waved and said, "Hi."

When he turned back, both men were holding pistols pointed toward him and Molly.

"Easy does it, Davis," the man behind the wheel of the powerboat said, pointing his gun at Jack. "No sudden moves." His partner nodded, his weapon aimed at Molly.

"What's going on?" Jack said. His eyes glanced beyond the men, and he saw a large boat not too far away. It appeared to be headed toward them, but he wasn't sure and didn't want to stare. He shot a quick glance at the radio on the helm pedestal, a few feet away.

Bobby caught his look at the radio. "We're not here to hurt anyone, so don't do anything foolish, like reach for that radio." He patted the barrel of his gun. "Hard to miss at this range."

"What do you want?" Jack said. He slid a step closer to Molly, still seated in front of the table.

"Uh, uh, uh." Bobby raised the gun pointed at Jack. "Both of you, stay right where you are. You've got something on your boat that belongs to me. You can get it for me, or Mike here can board you and find it. He's stubborn, so believe me when I tell you he'll find it, one way or the other."

A thin smile crossed Mike's lips.

Jack took a quick glance at the open water beyond the visitors. The boat was getting larger, headed straight for them. It was a big boat, fifty feet long, pushing a huge bow wave, and moving fast for something that size.

"Tell me what it is you want, and I'll get it for you," Jack said.

"A big bag of cash," Bobby said, grinning.

Jack swallowed, trying to keep his poker face, but he knew Bobby didn't miss his look of surprise.

Bobby laughed. "You know what I'm talking about. I can tell by your face."

Jack looked over at Molly. She had a puzzled expression, and he gave her a slight shake of his head.

He turned back to Bobby. "Who are you?"

"Not important. Let's just say I was in the business with Peabo and leave it at that."

At the mention of Peabo's name, Molly gasped, and Jack looked at her, dreading her thoughts. Her eyes bore a strange combination of fear, mistrust, and anger. He wished he could wipe that look away.

"I'll get it for you. It's down below," Jack said.

Molly gave him a glower of utter incredulousness. He had to turn away, unable to meet her stare. He took a step toward the companionway.

"Whoa, hoss," Bobby said, waving the gun at him. "You think I'm just another dumb hillbilly? Gonna let you go down into the cabin by yourself, call on the radio or cellphone, get a gun while you're at it?"

Jack froze. He looked to the horizon and the huge boat was still coming, right at them. He hoped the hell it would get there in time.

"Here's what we gonna do, so listen carefully. Missy's going to move back to where you are and you're both going to put your hands up on your head and keep em there. Mike here is going to get on your boat and fix your radios. You're going to tell him where your cell phones are, and he's going to take care of them, too. When that's done, Davis, you're going to very slowly walk past him and down the steps into your cabin, making sure Mike can see you. With me so far?"

Jack and Molly nodded.

"Good. I'm keeping my gun pointed at her. You even belch, I'm pulling the trigger, got it?"

Another nod.

"You're going to put the bag up on the deck while you stand at the bottom of the steps, not moving a muscle. Mike's going to take the bag and hand it to me, then you're going to come back up on deck and stand there where we can see you. Mike's coming back over here, then we're going to count the money, make sure you haven't forgotten any. If it's all there, then we'll be on our way."

Mike heard the boat approaching and glanced over his shoulder. "Company, boss," he said, tossing his head that direction.

Now everyone could hear the boat. It looked to be fifty feet long, a sportfisherman with a white hull, throwing up huge amounts of water to each side as it bore down on them. Sitting in the path of a boat that size doing thirty knots is not a comfortable feeling. Jack was beginning to wonder if the boat was going to ram them. It would be more like splitting them in half, he thought.

Bobby turned his head for a second, then looked at Jack, undecided. "Fuck," he screamed, the roar of the boat getting louder. It was only fifty yards away and showed no sign of slowing down. "Hold on," he yelled to Mike.

Bobby grabbed the wheel of the powerboat and shoved the throttles forward. The boat hesitated, and for a second looked as if it were frozen in the sights of the mammoth boat closing in. Then, as the engines spun up to maximum rpm the props bit into the water and the boat lurched as if a rocket had been lit. In seconds, it was up on plane speeding away and turning toward the Marquesas, on the other side of *Left Behind*.

Relieved the men were gone, Jack looked up to see the tremendous bow of Nick's boat headed straight for them. He processed the options, but there were none. He couldn't move *Left Behind* in time, and even if they jumped, they were dead. There was nowhere to go.

Suddenly, the big boat turned sharply to the right, squatting down into the water as Nick cut the throttles full back. A wall of water was headed toward *Left Behind*. Jack yelled to Molly to hang on, and the wake caught them broadside, rolling the sailboat from one side to the other, the mast going from ten o'clock to two o'clock and back before starting to center as the wake dissipated.

Nick had made a circle and pulled up as close as he dared. High up on the bridge, he shouted down at them, "Y'all okay?"

"We're fine," Jack yelled as he pulled Molly up and held her close to him. "You going after him?"

"No can do," Nick said, shaking his head. "He's got a head start and fifteen knots on me. Plus, there's some awful shallow water up there for this old barge. I could radio it in, but my guess is he'll be long gone before anyone gets here. Let's go home."

Molly shot Jack a look, then went down below. He started the engine, wondering if he needed to try to get the anchor up alone. When she came back up, she had on a t-shirt and shorts. She walked back to the helm.

"I've got it. Go get the anchor up," she said, her voice hard. She was careful not to touch him as he passed.

After the anchor was up and stowed, he came back to the helm. Without a word, she let go of the wheel and walked away on the opposite side of the helm from Jack. She went to the bulkhead and sat with her arms folded, refusing to make eye contact with him.

"I'm sorry, Molly."

She looked at him, hurt and anger duel daggers from her eyes. She shook her head once, then she stared back out over the open water.

He engaged the transmission and advanced the throttle, heading back toward Key West with Nick trailing behind. Jack told her everything, starting with taking the money from Peabo. He told her about talking to Tony to get his friend's advice. He talked the entire time, and Molly didn't say a word. At times, he wasn't even sure she was listening to him.

When they got to the bight, Molly helped him dock *Left Behind,* making sure all of the lines were secure. As soon as he shut the engine off and connected the water and power, she went down below.

He heard her talking on her phone, and fifteen minutes later, she emerged carrying a small overnight bag and her sandals.

"Molly . . . what—"

"I can't stay here with you." She studied him for a few seconds, her eyes showing nothing but contempt. "How could you?" she screamed. "You lied to me." She spat the words out.

"I apologize, Molly. I made a mistake. I want to make things right."

She held up her hand, shaking her head. Her voice was harsh and flat. "You want to make things right? Then leave me the hell alone." Her words were as cold as steel and pierced his heart. If she had wanted to cut him, she'd succeeded.

"Molly," he said, his voice softer. "I know I hurt you, and I'm sorry. I was just trying to protect you."

Her eyes blazed, and she leaned forward. "Protect me?" she hissed. "You don't protect me by keeping secrets from me. How could you do that? We promised each other, Jack, remember?" She shook her head and looked away.

He dropped his head. He couldn't answer her.

She turned back and locked her gaze on him, her eyes still hot as coals. "Stay away from me. I'm leaving," she said as she stepped off of the boat.

He watched as she walked up the dock. He'd let her down, and it was breaking his heart.

18

Molly walked past Nick as he was coming toward the boat. She gave him a dirty look and didn't speak. He glanced down at her bag in passing.

"Molly okay?" he asked as he stepped aboard.

Jack shook his head. "No. She's going to stay with Lisa, I guess. She said she can't stay here."

He ran both of his hands through his hair and let them rest on his neck behind his head. "I don't know what would've happened if you hadn't been there. I've never been so glad to see a big-ass boat bearing down on me at full speed."

"Yeah, I mighta cut it a little close, but I wanted to make my point. You got any cold beer left?"

Jack stared at Nick, thinking for a moment the Texan was joking. Jack and Molly had almost been killed, she'd just walked out on him, and he's looking for beer?

"What? I'm thirsty."

Shaking his head, Jack retrieved two beers from the icebox, handing one to Nick. They drank in silence for a few minutes, then Nick asked, "The two guys today, the same ones from yesterday?"

Jack nodded.

"Fuck. That's what I figured. You want to tell me about it?"

Jack told him what happened, leaving out the intimate details of his and Molly's lovemaking.

"The son of a bitch said he was 'in the business' with Peabo. I knew it. At least now I've got two faces with names." He shook his head and took a deep swallow of beer. "Why didn't they try anything yesterday, with us?"

Nick drained his beer and pulled two fresh ones out of the icebox next to Jack. He opened them both and handed one to Jack. "Hard to know. Maybe they caught a glimpse of me. Maybe they just felt something wasn't right. Scum like that, sometimes they've got a sixth sense."

Jack squeezed his cheeks and shook his head. "The hardest part was telling Molly. From the start, we swore we wouldn't keep things from each other. I blew it."

"It'll pass. It wasn't like you were running around or anything."

Jack snorted. "You don't understand. She didn't say a word to me all the way in. She's more upset about me keeping this from her than she is about us almost getting killed out there."

"Well, that was a rather significant omission, I'd say."

"You've never been married, have you?"

Nick stroked his chin. "Not exactly."

"Not exactly?" Jack was in no mood for riddles. "What kind of answer is that? Either you have or you haven't?"

"Not always that simple, my friend." He paused. "I was in Lake Tahoe once. Decided to get married, don't ask me why. Sobered up two days later, got back to Texas, and talked a judge into annulling it. In the eyes of the law, I've never been married, but most people wouldn't see it that way."

Jack shook his head. "You are one interesting character, I'll say that."

"Tell me the story again about you taking the money from Peabo, including timeframes."

After Jack had related it once again, Nick shook his head. "There are more than three people that might know something, Jack." He held up his fingers, ticking off the first two. "You left out the two runners in Peabo's SUV when you took the bag." He ticked off the third finger. "Three, the manager at the McDonald's where you left the money. How do you know he didn't peek? Most people would. Plus, Peabo had plenty of time to tell someone else. Remember that Ben Franklin quote? 'Three can keep a secret if two of them are dead?' You got more possibilities than you know."

Jack thought for a minute, then exhaled. "Thanks, that's encouraging. Now what?"

Nick finished his beer. Jack fished him out another and his friend continued.

"People like that go after anyone who has stolen from them. They don't tolerate stealing. It costs them money, and sets a bad example."

Jack was reminded of a conversation he'd had with Tony in Fort Myers. Before he and Molly had moved to Key West, Tony had said the same thing to him, almost word for word. He opened his mouth to ask a question, but Nick silenced him.

"I can't go into details, but I've been involved in more than my share of undercover drug operations. The good news is that whoever it is probably doesn't want to kill you—well, at least until they get their money. If they could get it all back, they'd probably take it and disappear. But, it doesn't sound like that's an option at this point.

"The bad news is that they're serious, and more than willing to hurt you or someone close to you in order to get the money."

Jack's first thought was *Molly*. Whoever was behind this was willing to murder innocent people like Kenny and Valerie.

He thought back to his friend Richard, who had been killed by a corporation trying to protect billions of dollars invested in a new cardiac drug. Once again, Jack was the common link. If it hadn't been for Jack, Richard and Kenny and Valerie would be alive. It must have showed on his face.

"And yes, they are willing to kill," Nick said. "You and Molly are in considerable danger."

19

A re you fucking stupid?" Randy said, trying to keep his voice down. Bobby and Mike cowered across the table from him in the bar where they usually met. *That's a stupid question,* he thought, and almost laughed out loud. He shook his head and lowered his voice. "Who else saw you besides the couple on the sailboat?"

"Nobody," Bobby said. "We got the hell outta there when that big boat came blasting toward us."

Randy closed his eyes, frustrated. He opened them and asked, "What about anyone on that boat? Did they see you?"

"No, we were outta there before they could see us, I swear," Bobby said.

"I thought that son of a bitch was going to run slap over us," Mike added. "I was just about to go aboard and get the money."

Randy glanced around the dark bar which was mostly empty this early in the evening.

"Keep your voices down. Did he say where it was?"

Both of them shook their heads. "He said he was going to have to go down in the cabin to get it," Bobby volunteered. "But then that other boat—"

"You got your boat hidden?"

They looked at each other, then Mike said, "We took it up to that dock on Stock Island, where you told us to."

Randy took a deep breath. He needed these two clowns until he could replace them. The chance of them running into Jack and Molly were pretty slim and it was a chance he'd have to take.

"Don't go anywhere near A&B or the bight, understand? You go to the pier and do your job, then back out to Stock Island. I'll be in touch. Now get out of here."

They almost knocked each other down trying to get up from the table and leave, glad to be dismissed. Randy rubbed his temples, feeling a headache coming on.

It was his fault, not realizing the Texan had gone out to cover Davis. He slammed his fist on the table, shaking the beer in front of him. That was the perfect opportunity, and he knew he wouldn't get another chance like that.

But, he did learn that the money was on Davis's boat, inside the cabin. In the morning, he'd have to take a little boat ride to Key West Bight and check things out from the water. Maybe there was a way to get on the boat at the dock.

"What's the matter?" Mysterie asked. She and Evens were sitting at the table in the small apartment, having dinner. "You haven't been yourself for the past week."

"Nothin," the big man said, refusing to meet her eyes.

She looked at him, wondering what was bothering him. She knew her brother well enough to know that something was troubling him. Lowering her voice and speaking in a softer tone, she said, "Whatever it is, it's okay." She paused for a minute, then said, "What happened?"

He raised his head and looked up at her, his eyes wet with tears. "It was bad," he said, shaking his head.

Now she was worried. He'd been this way since Saturday a week ago. Although he was kind-hearted, he was like a little child in some ways. A genius with mechanical things, his social skills were not fully developed. His physical presence was intimidating, but she knew he wouldn't hurt anything or anybody. She tried to keep her voice calm and quiet.

"Did you do something?"

He shook his head, slowly. "I din't do nothing. I couldn't . . ." The tears started flowing down his cheeks. "I don want to go to prison."

She took a deep breath. This was worse than what she'd imagined. Whatever it was, it was serious.

She reached out her hand and put it on his muscular arm. "You're not going to prison, Evens. But, you got to tell me what happened. I can't help you if you don't tell me."

His sad and fearful eyes looked up at her. "I tole you, I din't do anyting." He started sniffling like a small child.

She tried to remain patient. "If you didn't do anything, you're not going to prison. It doesn't work that way over here."

He startled her by slamming his fist on the table, rattling the dishes. "But I saw what happened. And I din't do anyting."

She nodded, beginning to understand. He had witnessed something terrible and felt guilty that he didn't do anything to stop it. A dreadful thought entered her head.

"Where were you last Friday night? I thought you—"

He pulled away from her and pushed back from the table, still shaking his head. His face flashed anger as if caught with his hand in the cookie jar. "You can't help me. I got to fix tings," he said as he rose and walked out, slamming the door behind him.

She sat back and tried to remember when he started acting this way. It was last Saturday morning, at breakfast. He'd come in late the night before, unusual for Evens. She remembered hearing the door and looking at the clock. It was after midnight.

He had been quiet and aloof the next morning at breakfast. She'd asked him about his evening, but he refused to talk about it. He left for work at the usual time, and she chalked it up to his being tired. Now she wondered what had happened.

Friday night was when that couple had disappeared from their boat out in the Marquesas.

20

Early Wednesday morning, Jack yawned and rolled over in bed, reaching out to touch Molly. His hand found the space next to him cold and empty. Startled, he opened his eyes. The bedding hadn't been occupied. Shaking the cobwebs out, he looked around, then remembered her leaving yesterday afternoon.

He lay his head back on the pillow, wondering if she went over to Lisa's. Last night, he considered walking over there to check but figured she needed some time. He'd called, but it went straight to voice mail and he fell asleep, thinking about how to make up to her.

Based on the limited light outside, leaking through the hatch above, Jack guessed it was around seven. He got up, stopped by the head, then padded into the main cabin. The companionway door was closed, and there was a distinct feeling of emptiness on the boat. He started to put coffee on but decided he needed a run first.

He went to their cabin, retrieved his phone and pushed the button to see if he'd missed any calls or texts. Nothing. Disappointed, he slipped on a pair of running shorts and t-shirt and made his way up on deck.

There wasn't much activity in the marina this morning. Fishermen had already left before daylight, and the tourists wouldn't be stirring until later. Key West was not a morning kind of place.

He tried to get his runs in early while the temperature was bearable. He plugged in the earbuds, switched on the iPod, and walked up to the boardwalk to stretch. The opening riff of "Whipping Post" by the Allman Brothers filled his ears. *Appropriate song to start the day,* he thought.

He was still analyzing the events of yesterday as he set out down Front Street. After a few blocks, he turned left on Whitehead, passing the Hemingway House. Ernest was one of his favorite authors, and some of his best works were written in the house.

His thoughts turned back to Bobby, or Peabo Junior, which is what he was calling the guy driving the boat yesterday. He doubted that either one of them gave their real names. Obviously, Bobby knew that Jack had the money. *Maybe he worked with Peabo?*

That would make sense, he thought when he got to the iconic red, black, and yellow buoy marking the southernmost point of the continental United States. A few early risers were already there, taking pictures.

Bobby's accent did sound a lot like Peabo. Bobby had said he was "in the business" with Peabo, which would also point to someone from Kentucky. *Wren,* he thought, *she might know.*

The haunting solo of Duane Allman on "Memory of Elizabeth Reed" came on as he approached George Street, where he made the slight jog and over to First Street. Before long, he was on the causeway over Garrison Bight and headed home.

He smiled when he walked past the bike rack at the base of Front Street. Molly's bike was there, which meant she was still in the marina.

Back at the boat, he craned his neck, trying to see Lisa and Doug's boat over at Key West Bight Marina as he called Wren. No answer. He hung up and sent her a text, asking her to call him as soon as she could.

He went down, switched the coffee pot on and got a towel and his shaving kit. Taking his phone with him, he went up to the bathhouse and took a quick shower.

When he got back, the coffee was ready. He poured a cup, went up to the cockpit and sat, thinking about what else he needed to do. A large pelican sat on the piling next to the boat, not even stirring at Jack's presence.

He picked up his phone and called Molly. After it rang several times, her voice mail picked up. He disconnected and called Doug's number.

"Hey, Jack."

"Doug. I'm betting you have a guest at your place?"

"Uh, yeah." Doug was silent, but Jack heard voices in the background. He figured Molly and Lisa were there and Doug wasn't able to talk.

"Would you do me a big favor?" He continued before waiting on an answer from Doug. "I don't want Molly going to and from the hospital by herself. Would you—"

"Are you calling to check up on me?" Molly's angry voice interrupted. Apparently, she'd figured out who Doug was talking to and commandeered the phone.

He didn't answer and tried to remain calm. "I just called to say I was worried about you going back and forth to the hospital by yourself. Would you at least let Nick drive you to and from the hospital? Please?"

"Nick? He knew all about it, didn't he? That's why he showed up."

"No, Molly, I swear I didn't know he was going to be out there." He started to add, *I'm glad he was,* but thought better of it.

"But he did know about the money, right?"

Fuck. He was in a corner and knew it. He wasn't going to lie to her anymore. "Yes. I told him a few days ago, hoping he could help me figure out what was going on."

When he didn't hear a reply, he said, "Molly?"

"Hey, it's me." Doug was back on the line. "Sorry, she snatched the phone from me, and I wasn't about to try to stop her."

"I was just calling to say I was concerned about her riding her bike out to the hospital and back by herself. I suggested Nick drive her, but you can see how well that went over."

Doug snickered. "Uh, yeah, roger that. Don't worry, we'll figure something out."

"Thanks, buddy. Call when you can."

He clicked off and called Tony's number.

"Hey, where are you?" Tony asked when he answered the phone.

"In Key West. You got a few minutes?"

"I'm retired. Time is all I've got. What's up?"

Jack told him about yesterday, describing in detail the two characters on the boat. "The one named 'Bobby' said he was 'with Peabo in the business.' He had another guy with him named 'Mike,' but I doubt those were the real names for either of them. Bobby seemed to be the leader."

"What did the cops say?"

He hesitated too long, which gave Tony the answer to his question.

"Listen to me, Jack. This has escalated and you need to go to the cops. These are not people you want to screw around with. I'm assuming you could give them a description of the boat and the two men. Key West is a small place. Having the cops looking out for you and Molly would be a good thing."

"He knew about the money," Jack said. "Do you know anyone in eastern Kentucky you could call and see if Peabo had a lieutenant up there, someone who may still be in the business?"

"Hello? You're not listening. Maybe Molly can talk some sense into you."

Jack paused. "She left me."

"What do you mean left?"

"Left, as in moved out."

"Jesus, Jack. You never told her?"

"I was going to. Then all of this happened. I tried to explain it to her, but she wasn't in the mood to listen."

He heard a long sigh on the other end of the line.

After a minute, Tony asked, "What was the name of that town again, the one Peabo was from?"

"Harlan. Harlan, Kentucky. Way down in the southeast corner."

"I've got a buddy that works for TBI—Tennessee Bureau of Investigation. I'll give him a call, see if he knows anything."

"Thanks, Tony. I appreciate it."

"And Jack?"

"Yeah?"

"Get things straight with Molly. And be careful, will you?"

21

Molly had stormed off of Lisa and Doug's boat to go for a walk to calm down. They lived at the Key West Bight Marina, around the corner from A&B. Home for them was a Catalina 355, *N B Breeze,* named for Jesse Winchester's song "Nothing But a Breeze."

She knew she was welcome to stay there, but it was too close to Jack as evidenced by the phone call. If she'd had a car, she would've left the damn island and gone somewhere else.

She was furious with Jack. When he'd told her that Nick knew about the money, she slammed the phone down on the table and walked out. Doug had picked it up and was talking to Jack when she left.

What she didn't want to show was that she was also hurt, wounded by the fact that Jack had kept something so important from her. From the beginning, they'd both sworn to not keep secrets from each other.

She sat on a bench next to the boardwalk and watched as Jack sat out on their boat, drinking his coffee and talking on the phone. He disappeared below, then locked up the boat and left, leaving with a small bag. She needed to pick up a few things but didn't want to risk running into him.

After giving him another ten minutes, she decided he wouldn't be back for a while, so she walked over.

Although she'd been by herself before on the boat, it seemed different. As she unlocked the companionway door and stepped down inside, it seemed emptier than normal. There was a noticeable vacuum in his absence.

She took a deep breath and swore she could smell him. She grabbed the toiletries she'd forgotten and a few other clothes, putting them into another tote bag. Anxious to leave, she hurried back out, not wanting to spend any more time onboard than necessary.

Since she didn't have to work until seven tonight, she decided to get breakfast and walked over to the Cuban Coffee Queen. The money wasn't the main issue, and Jack knew it. Surprisingly, the incident yesterday didn't leave her as upset as she would've thought. She felt like he had betrayed her, and maybe that had overshadowed what happened out on the water.

She got coffee and toast, then sat on a bench to consider her options. She thought about calling for an appointment to see her therapist.

As she was finishing her coffee, Lisa walked up.

"You okay?" Lisa asked.

Molly shrugged.

Lisa nodded down toward the bag next to Molly. "Been shopping."

Molly shook her head. "Just needed to pick up a couple of things from the boat."

"Mind if I get a cup and join you?"

She didn't respond, which Lisa took as permission. She walked over, bought a cup of coffee, came back and sat next to Molly.

"Sorry about that scene on the boat," Lisa said. She took a sip of her coffee.

"Not your problem."

"I don't think I've ever seen you and Jack have a fight." She laughed. "Of course, Doug and I fight all the time. Two Italians, what do you expect?"

"Don't know, don't care."

Lisa raised her eyebrows. "Wow. You're really pissed, aren't you?"

Molly shot her a glance and stood. "You feel like going for a walk?"

"Sure."

They walked back over to Lisa's boat and dropped off the bag, then headed up Margaret Street.

"You'd be mad, too," Molly said. She'd told Lisa what happened yesterday, leaving out the exact amount of money involved.

"Weren't you scared? What did the cops say?"

Molly snorted. "We didn't report it. Jack is concerned about the fact that technically, he stole the money from a drug dealer. He thinks he may be in trouble for not mentioning that little tidbit to the cops."

Lisa crossed her arms. "You're welcome to stay with us as long as you need, you know that."

She nodded. "Thanks, I appreciate it. Right now, I'm too angry to think straight."

As they crossed Duval, Molly said, "Did I tell you I went to Mysterie's?"

"No, again? When? What did she say?"

Molly told her about the last visit and some of the things she'd learned. "You were right, she's the real deal. I want to go back, but . . ." She told Lisa about Yvonne's caution. "What do you think that was about?"

Lisa shrugged. "Mysterie is kind of eccentric. Some people are frightened of her."

"Why?"

"I don't know. I guess because she's so accurate with her predictions. That kind of spooks some people. They think they want to know, but they really don't, you know what I mean? What does Jack think?"

Molly looked sheepish and hesitated. "Uh, he doesn't exactly know about it."

Lisa laughed. "Let me get this right. You're mad at him for keeping secrets, but you didn't tell him you went to back to see her?"

"There's a big damn difference, and you know it."

Lisa's eyes widened, and she held up her hand. "Whoa, sorry. I'm not excusing him, okay? Just saying. Boy, you are pissed, aren't you?"

Molly tried to explain how she felt, that it was a breach of trust about something important, not just spending fifty bucks to get your palm read. That was more like buying a pair of shoes and hiding them in the closet.

"This must be your first big fight?" Lisa asked.

Molly cocked her head, thought about it, then nodded. "I guess so."

At the Green Parrot, they turned right on Whitehead Street, heading back toward the bight. "I thought what we had was different," Molly said.

Lisa chuckled. "And I still think it is. You and Jack do have *it,* no doubt in my mind. Just seeing you two together, you can tell. But any relationship worth having is work."

Molly nodded. "I hear what you're saying, but . . ."

"You can make up when he gets back. That's always fun. That may be a good time to tell him about Mysterie, so it evens things out."

"You're sick, you know that?"

Lisa grabbed her arm and grinned. "But, I'm your friend. And, I'm right, aren't I?"

When they got back to the bight, Molly said, "Crap. I forgot to get that Gillian Flynn book you wanted to read. Let's go by the boat and get it." She and Lisa were always swapping paperbacks. Their tastes were similar, and they saved money and precious space by sharing books since both of them preferred real books instead of e-books.

When they boarded *Left Behind,* Molly pulled her key out and stopped in her tracks.

"What's the matter?" Lisa asked. Molly pointed to the lock on the companionway door. It was hanging on the hasp but unlocked.

"Oh my God," Lisa said. Then she whispered, "Let's go get someone."

Molly took a step back, studied the lock, then shook her head. "Wait a minute. There's not anyone inside."

"How do you know?" Lisa asked, still keeping her voice down.

Molly started laughing. "Because, silly. Think about it. The lock is through the hasp. How could someone inside do that?"

Lisa scowled, then grinned, and started laughing. "I guess you're right, that would be kind of hard. But why is it unlocked? Did someone break in while you were out?"

She reached over, removed the lock, and opened the companionway door. "I was just over here. I was in a hurry and probably just forgot to lock it. Besides, I don't think anyone would be breaking in during the middle of the morning."

She stepped down into the cabin and looked around. Lisa was right behind her on the steps, her hand on Molly's back.

"Nothing looks disturbed," Molly said. She went over and grabbed the book off the shelf and handed it to Lisa. She took two bottles of water out of the refrigerator and they went back up on deck to sit for a few minutes.

"That scared the shit outta me," Lisa said after taking a swallow of water.

"Me, too, for a second."

Lisa was facing the dock and got a funny look on her face. "Stay calm," she whispered to Molly.

Molly turned to see Nick standing beside the boat.

"Good morning, ladies."

"Jack's not here," Molly said, her voice cold and hard. She didn't invite Nick on board.

Nick held up both his hands, petitioning for a truce. "I know, I just loaned him my car." He dropped his hands, putting one into his pocket and withdrawing a set of car keys. He held them up toward Molly.

"I wanted to offer the use of my car to go back and forth to work. I won't be using it, and—"

"I don't need it. You've done enough, already," Molly said, bristling for a fight.

"Molly . . ." Lisa said.

Molly turned on her. "I don't need it, I said."

Lisa looked at Nick and raised her eyebrows as if to say, *I tried.*

Nick started to say something, then put the keys back in his pocket. "I'll be around if you need anything." Without waiting for an answer, he turned and walked away.

Once he was out of earshot, Lisa said, "Molly, maybe you—"

"Don't start, Lisa. Nobody's after me, they just want the damn money. I've a mind to find it and set it out on here on the deck with a fucking note—'Here it is.'"

Lisa held up her hands in surrender. "Okay, but I think you should be careful, just the same. What are you going to do?"

"I don't know."

Randy stood on the dock at the waterfront in Key West Bight, next to his boat. He was trying to make sense of what he'd witnessed so far.

He'd come over earlier by boat to check out Davis's sailboat from the water and decided to get some breakfast and hang out for a while. He was glad he did since there was a lot happening so far this morning.

Sitting in his spot at the restaurant, he had watched earlier as Davis had left his boat with a small bag. Then, a few minutes later, his wife walked over to the boat and went down below into the cabin. Twenty minutes later, she emerged carrying a duffel bag. He'd hastily paid his check and followed her to the Cuban Coffee Queen, where another woman he didn't recognize joined her on a nearby bench.

They chatted for a few minutes, then walked over to another sailboat docked at the Key West Bight Marina. They left the bag there, then the two of them went for a walk, heading out Margaret Street. He'd followed them as they made a loop around several blocks, then walked back to A&B where they now sat in the cockpit on *Left Behind*.

He drank his coffee, wondering how much longer he should hang out. As he stood there, Molly and the other woman left A&B and walked back over to the sailboat at the Bight Marina and boarded, joining a man sitting on the deck.

Interesting. It appeared Davis was gone and his wife was staying with another couple on a sailboat named *N B Breeze*. Maybe Davis was going somewhere. He needed to find out what was going on.

He boarded his boat and idled out the channel in the bight as he approached the outermost dock at A&B. No boats were docked on the outside of it, so he had a good view of *Left Behind*, which was in the slip immediately adjacent to the inside of the outermost dock. The back end of the sailboat was facing him and the main dock that connected the top of the T to the boardwalk. Directly across the main dock was the fuel dock, which was unoccupied at the time.

As he motored past A&B, he came to the Galleon Marina and spotted the big sportfisherman belonging to the Texan. Its stern was facing A&B, but without a clear line of sight to the sailboat's companionway.

Not impossible, he thought as he left the bight and headed back toward Stock Island and his dock. He needed to find out where Jack was.

22

Jack got in Nick's car and checked his phone. No calls from anyone. *Screw it.* He lowered the convertible top and thumbed through the music on his iPhone. He wanted rock and roll, something to pound away the worries. He grinned when he got to the Rolling Stones classic album, *Hot Rocks*. Perfect. Cranking up the volume, he put the car in gear and pulled out of the garage at the Galleon Marina.

He was headed to the shooting range on Big Coppitt Key. He'd called Nick to see if he wanted to go, but he had an appointment and was unable to leave today. When Nick offered his car, Jack decided to go alone. He was looking forward to blasting away at some targets to take out his frustration.

Thirty minutes later, at Mile Marker 10, he slowed and turned in to the parking lot at the gun club. He parked, grabbed his gun bag and phone and went inside.

"Morning. Can I help you?" the man behind the counter said. He was heavy-set, but not overweight, with thinning gray hair. He wore a shirt with the gun club name emblazoned on it.

"Hi, I'm Jack Davis. Nick Campbell sent me, said to ask for Kyle."

The man grinned and stuck out his hand. "I'm Kyle, pleased to meet you. How's that old cowboy doing?"

Jack laughed. "Fine, he's a neighbor of mine in Key West. I live at the marina next door."

Kyle shook his head. "Sorry to hear that. Must be a bad neighborhood. What could I do for you?"

Jack opened his bag and removed the SIG, explaining that while he loved the pistol, he was in the market for something a little more concealable.

Kyle nodded. "Nice gun, but yeah, a little bulky for shorts and t-shirts. You looking for anything in particular?"

"No, Nick mentioned a few different guns, but I'm not wedded to anything in particular. I just want something reliable and easy to carry without spending a small fortune."

Kyle walked over to the case, pulled out a gun and walked back. He pulled the slide back, confirmed it wasn't loaded, and handed it to Jack.

"Ruger LC9S, just came in yesterday. Nine millimeter. A guy bought it new, last week. Changed his mind. Not a thing wrong with it."

Jack took the gun, wrapping his hand around it and aiming it at the wall. It was considerably smaller and lighter than the SIG. He released the slide, then pulled it back again, locking it open.

"Nice feel to it. Mind if I shoot it?"

Kyle shook his head, reached down and brought out a small box of ammo and the magazine. He slid a clipboard holding a release form over to Jack.

"Not at all. Fill this out, then you can go back and try it out. If you like it, I'll make you a good deal."

"Thanks."

Jack filled out the form, signed it, and handed it back. He gathered everything and walked to the door leading to the range, handing a copy to the person at the desk. He glanced at it, nodded, and handed him a paper target. "Lane 4. Don't forget your eye and ear protection before you go in."

Fifteen minutes later, Jack came out and found Kyle.

"What do you think?" Kyle asked.

Jack showed him the target. Most of the shots had landed within a 5-inch circle.

"I liked it. What can you do?"

An hour later, Jack walked out, the proud owner of a new pistol. He'd shot another hundred rounds with it and really liked it. After buying a holster and ammo, he was ready to leave, the gun inside the waistband of his shorts, covered by his Hawaiian shirt.

On his way to the car, his phone buzzed. It was Wren.

"Hey, Wren. How are you?"

"I'm good, Jack. Sorry I took so long to get back to you. I had a test this morning."

"No problem, how did you do?"

"Good. I'm really enjoying nursing school. Still making As and Bs, so I think I'll make it."

He laughed. "I know you will. Molly and I never had any doubts."

"Thanks. How's she doing?"

He hesitated. "Right now, she's mad at me, but we'll get it sorted out," he said, downplaying the rift between him and Molly. Wren laughed, and he continued.

"Listen, I hate to dredge up bad memories, but I need to ask you something about Peabo."

There was a silence on the other end of the line.

"Okay," she said, her tone guarded.

"Did you ever know anybody that worked for him named Bobby or Mike?"

After a few seconds, she said, "Yes, why?"

"Which one?"

"Both. There was a Bobby and a Mike."

Bingo, Jack thought as he got his pen ready.

"What were their last names?"

"Bobby Wilson," she said, "but he was killed in a car wreck right after I first met you and Molly. Mike was . . . Mike Lowe. Why are you asking?"

Jack swore under his breath. Bobby was out, so that left Mike still a possibility.

"What does Mike look like?"

She chuckled. "Like a bowling ball. About five-four and almost as big around. What's going on, Jack?"

He threw his pen down. The Mike he encountered was pushing six foot tall. Maybe Mike had lost a lot of weight, but he doubted the man had grown half a foot taller.

"Nothing," he replied. "A couple of strangers showed up asking around and I was just wondering if there might be some connection. Obviously not. Sorry, I didn't mean to upset you."

"That's okay, you had me worried for a minute."

"Hey, we need to plan a time for you to come visit," he said, trying to lighten the conversation. "You'd like it down here."

"I'd love to," she said, her voice back to normal. "Maybe when this semester's over. By the way, I love living on a boat. It's awesome. Thank y'all so much."

"Glad you like it. Everything else going okay?"

"Yeah, just busy. I've been doing some volunteer work at the shelter—you remember it?"

Jack's thoughts flashed back to the shelter where Wren had briefly stayed.

"Yes, I do and I think that's great you're helping."

"Listen, I've got to run, but talk to y'all soon, okay? Tell Molly 'Hello.'"

"Will do."

He put the phone in the console and shook his head. For a minute, he'd thought he had something. He started the car and dialed up some Joe Bonamassa for the ride home.

Outside Key West, when he got to College Road, he turned right and pulled over as soon as he got past the intersection. He turned the music down and called Doug.

"Hey, Molly around?" he asked Doug when he answered.

"No, the hospital called and she had to go in early."

"Thanks, gotta run. Talk to you later."

He drove down to Lower Keys Medical Center and parked. Inside, the same lady was at the reception desk who had been there when he had surprised Molly for lunch a few weeks ago. He was hoping that was a good omen.

"May I help you?" she asked.

He fought to remember her name, then glanced down at her badge. *Rhonda.*

"Hey, Rhonda. I'm Jack Davis, Molly's husband? I met you a few weeks ago when I came out and surprised her—"

"—for lunch. I remember," she said, grinning broadly. "Y'all are such a cute couple. Are you here to see her?"

He nodded. Leaning over the counter, he whispered, "I wanted to surprise her. Is she working?"

Rhonda nodded. "I saw her earlier. Want me to get her down here?"

"Yes, but I don't want her to know. Come up with something good." He stood up and saw the flowers out front of the little gift shop. "I've got an idea."

He walked over and found an arrangement of fresh flowers. He bought them and headed back over to Rhonda.

She was still grinning. "I told her someone was down here with a delivery for her and she had to sign for it."

Now, Jack grinned. "Thanks, Rhonda. I'll wait over there," he said, pointing to the gift shop.

He walked over and sat in an inconspicuous spot, where he could see Molly, but she wouldn't see him.

In a few minutes, Molly walked past, over to the reception desk where Rhonda sat. Before she could speak, he stood and walked over, his outstretched hand holding the flowers.

"Hello, Molly." He saw her stiffen, then turn around. "These are for you."

She just stared at him, and it was getting awkward. "What are you doing here?" she said, folding her arms across her chest.

He smiled, trying to gain her good favor. "I wanted to surprise you." He held out the flowers.

She glanced at them but kept her arms folded. "Thanks, but I'm really busy." She lowered her arms and stomped off.

He watched as she disappeared around the corner. He turned back to Rhonda, who wore a look of complete and utter astonishment.

"I guess she's still mad," Jack said.

He handed Rhonda the flowers. "Thanks," he said as he turned and walked out the front door.

23

When he got back to the Galleon Marina, Jack parked and then walked out to Nick's boat to give him the keys. The sportfisherman was locked and Nick was nowhere to be seen, so he headed back over to *Left Behind*. At A&B Marina, he ran into Detective Stevens coming out of the dockmaster's office.

Now what? he thought. "Detective," he said, walking up to her.

"Mr. Davis. Got a few minutes?"

"Always for you." She had more questions, and the conversation almost deteriorated into an argument.

Jack shook his head. "Look, you're missing something. I'm telling you, it's connected to what happened up the coast."

"Why are you so convinced it's related? You say no one has threatened you. There's no indication, at least that we're aware of, that anyone is 'out to get you.' Is there something else we should know?"

He sighed, thinking back to what happened Wednesday out on the water and remembering Tony's advice.

"You're telling me that until something else happens, there is nothing you can do?" Jack said.

"Look, I'm frustrated, too. What we *do* know strongly suggests that what happened to your friends was an encounter with smugglers—the unfortunate result of being in the wrong place at the wrong time."

She cleared her throat. "I wish we had a crystal ball, Mr. Davis, but we don't. If you see anything suspicious, let me know immediately, and we'll check it out. I'm afraid that's all we can do at this point."

She turned and walked away, leaving Jack shaking his head. He had to know who was stalking him.

He walked out to *Left Behind,* glad to see his sailboat in spite of the fact that he knew he would be spending the night on it alone. The attachment to a boat was hard to understand for a non-boater, but undeniable. At least *she* was there for him.

He unlocked the companionway door and stepped down into the cabin. Looking over at the settee above the locker where the money was stashed, he decided the money had to go. It was the root of his problems and a curse.

He called Walter Dobbs's cell phone and was surprised when the attorney in Fort Myers answered.

"Jack, how are you?" Walter's deep voice resonated over the phone.

"Good, Walter. And you?"

"Not getting to play enough golf or go sailing."

After a few minutes of pleasantries, Jack said, "I wanted to run something by you if you've got a few minutes."

"Sure, what's on your mind?"

Jack cleared his throat. "You're still my attorney and anything we discuss is covered by attorney-client privilege, right?"

"Um, correct."

He lowered his voice. "It's about the money I took from Peabo Watson, the drug dealer? I want to do something with the balance of it, around $400,000. Cash."

"I'm listening."

"I want it to go to help abused young girls, like maybe a foundation or something."

There was a hesitation on the line before Walter spoke. "There's a couple of problems right off the bat. First, while I could set up the legal mechanism for you, that amount of money isn't going to really do a lot. You need seven or eight figures to do a foundation properly. An even bigger problem, which I won't help you with, is how to get that kind of cash into the foundation. You know you can't just waltz in with a big bag of money. The feds will be all over you. People go to prison for that, Jack."

"But I want the money to go to help people, not end up in the government coffers, which is what will happen if I go to the authorities."

"I understand what you're saying, but legally, you don't want to go there."

"So what do I do? Go drop it off on some charity's doorstep?"

"Maybe that's not such a bad idea."

There was another long silence on the line before Walter continued.

"Sorry, Jack, but I can't help you with this one. You asked my advice as your attorney and that's as much as I can say. Tread carefully. I don't do criminal law."

"I understand. Thanks, Walter. Take care."

After he hung up, he opened the locker and dug around until he found the blue sail bag. He set it on the table and unzipped it. The money was still there, unmarked and most of it neatly wrapped in mustard-colored currency straps. Each strap contained 100 bills, worth $10,000 each, and was less than half an inch thick.

He stood there, staring at it and considering his options. He took a picture of the contents, zipped it back up, and returned it to its place in the locker.

Jack stepped back up to the cockpit and sat, looking around the bight. There were hundreds, if not thousands of people out and about, any of who could be a threat. He thought about Walter's words and knew what he had to do. He picked up his phone and called Hertz to reserve a car for in the morning.

Thirty minutes after he finished his call, Nick walked up and stepped on board. "You got anything cold to drink?"

Jack stared at him, then shook his head. "My day sucked, thanks for asking." He went below, got a couple of beers and came back up, handing one to Nick along with the car keys. "Thanks for letting me use your car. It was fun driving a convertible."

"What happened?" Nick asked.

"The day started out good. Top down, nice drive. I spent a few hours at the range, bought a new gun." He pulled it out, dropped the magazine, and cleared the chamber before handing it to Nick.

"Nice," Nick said, looking it over and getting a feel for it. "How's it shoot?" he asked, handing it back to him.

"Good. I put a hundred rounds through it. Most of them landed in the five-inch circle."

"Not bad. You talk to Molly?"

Jack grimaced and took a long swig from his beer before answering. "Now we get to the part that sucked. It was a short conversation. On the way into town, I stopped by the hospital to surprise her. I did, alright. She basically told me what to do with the flowers, and it wasn't to put them in a vase."

"Ouch."

"Put it this way, the lady at the reception desk gave me a big smile when I gave her the flowers."

"Sorry, my friend."

"I think it's going to take her a while. After driving your car, I've decided to rent a car and take a little road trip, heading out first thing in the morning. Probably do me good to get off this island for a few days."

Nick eyed him suspiciously. "You're welcome to take mine. Anywhere in particular?"

Jack shook his head. "Thanks, but not sure how long I'll be and don't want you without wheels."

He ignored Nick's question about the destination and Nick didn't pursue it. That was another reason for renting a car.

"I would appreciate it if you'd keep an eye on Molly."

"Sure thing." Nick finished his beer and stood. "I've got to go to a Galleon Marina meeting. Somehow I ended up on the board. You need a ride to the airport in the morning?"

"No thanks. I'll be in touch."

"Be safe."

24

Molly was tired and irritable as she left her therapist's office Thursday morning. Since she had an appointment that morning after work, she had breakfast first and then went straight there on her way back to Lisa's boat.

It had been a long shift. One of her patients died last night, and Molly was already upset about Jack stopping by the hospital unannounced. She was hoping that her session with Diane would help her feel better, instead, it left her more frustrated.

Molly had told her about what happened with Jack and how she felt betrayed. When she'd mentioned moving out, Diane had asked if she thought that might be running away from the problem instead of confronting it. Not what she'd wanted to hear.

What Molly really wanted to know was what happened that night in the motel on Clearwater Beach. When she'd told Diane that, all she got was a lot of mumbo jumbo about traumatic stress and the mind working to keep memories buried and how some things were better left undisturbed. Apparently, no one, including Diane, could help her learn that information.

She wasn't ready to go back to Lisa and Doug's. They were very kind to put her up and she appreciated it, but three people on a boat were too many. As she pedaled past Seth's shop on Duval, she noticed he was at work already, so she turned around and parked her bike.

The door was locked, but he was inside, puttering about. She tapped on the glass, and when he saw her, he smiled and walked over. He unlocked the door, let her in, and locked it back.

"What are you doing out and about so early?" he asked, greeting her with a perfunctory hug and kiss on each cheek.

"Just getting off work, and saw you inside."

Holding her at arm's length, he studied her face. "Why so glum, today, love?"

"Am I that transparent, or are you just that perceptive?"

He smiled. "Stay away from playing poker, dear. What's the matter?"

"Have you got a few minutes?"

"Always, for you. I came in early to rearrange a few pieces, but that can wait." He led her to his desk, patted the chair next to it, and sat in his chair. Without asking, he swiveled around and made her a cappuccino.

"Now," he said, sliding the cup toward her. "Tell me why you have such a sad face."

She started with her and Jack having a fight but then had to backtrack and tell him about the incident Tuesday on the sailboat. She finished with telling him about her staying on Lisa and Doug's boat.

Seeing the shocked look on Seth's face, she said, "I told Jack that I was not staying on the boat with him."

"Have you talked with him since he left?"

She shook her head. "Not exactly. He calls, but I won't answer. He did come to the hospital yesterday to surprise me and I blew him off. I'm thinking about going back to our boat. Lisa called me last night and told me he left for a few days to sort things out. Doug and Lisa are wonderful, but their boat's getting a little crowded and I know Doug's keeping Jack posted on my whereabouts."

Seth shook his head. "You do not need to be on that boat by yourself, not until this *thing* with these hoodlums is settled." He thought for a moment. "Why don't you come stay with us at our house? We've plenty of room, and we won't be spying on you. You can even use one of our cars to get to work. We don't need two vehicles. In fact, we've been talking about selling one since we use it so infrequently."

Molly shook her head. "I didn't come by here to ask—"

"Nonsense," Seth said, holding up his hand. "I know that, and you're staying with us. Case closed."

"Are you sure?"

"What did I just say? Case closed. Do you need any help getting your things?"

Molly left Seth's store in much better spirits than when she first came in. She'd told Seth she get her things and come by later. She loved the eccentric couple and would feel more comfortable at their place. It wasn't a long-term solution, but this would give her a safe place to stay and time to sort things out.

She got on her bike and headed down Duval Street. As she approached Petronia, she hesitated. *Screw Diane,* she thought. She turned and then parked her bike next to the door to Mysterie's shop.

She stepped inside and Mysterie was sitting behind the counter. The tattooed girl was nowhere to be seen.

"Good morning, Molly. How are you?"

Molly shrugged. "Are you busy now, or could you do a reading?"

Mysterie smiled, slid off the stool, and stepped out from behind the counter. She was wearing a turban and the single, gold hoop earring.

"Of course. I'll have to close the front door. Cassie won't be in until later, and I don't like to leave the shop unattended."

"That's fine," Molly said.

Mysterie closed the front door and flipped over the OPEN sign so that the CLOSED side was showing. She led Molly back to the same room as before. "Would you like some tea?"

"That would be nice. That tea, do you sell it? It was exceptional."

Mysterie smiled and shook her head. "No, though I probably should. It's my own blend of tropical flowers, a recipe given to me by my late aunt."

Molly watched as she heated the water in a clear glass teapot. Then, she removed a small box from underneath the table and opened it. Taking a teaspoon, she carefully measured loose tea out of the box and dumped it into the infuser. Once the water was hot, she inserted the infuser and put the lid on the teapot.

"What's the matter?" Mysterie asked. "Husband problems?"

Amazed, Molly looked at her and nodded. "How did you—"

"Tell me about it."

She was hesitant to go into the details of what happened Sunday. "He was keeping things from me. When we got married, we vowed we wouldn't do that."

"What kinds of things? He's not seeing someone else."

Before Molly could answer, Mysterie picked up the teapot and held it up to the light, looking at the tea. She took a teacup and saucer from the shelf, set it on the small table, and filled it. Molly could see wisps of steam rising from the cup as Mysterie slid it toward her.

She picked it up and noticed the same tropical scent as before. She took a small sip, then set the cup back in the saucer. The warm liquid eased down her throat, the vapors almost intoxicating. She closed her eyes for a few seconds, savoring the taste.

"Is it okay?" Mysterie asked.

Molly nodded. "Very nice. Thank you."

She gave Mysterie a brief summary of what happened Tuesday, which led to a discussion of exactly what information Jack had withheld. As they chatted, she sipped the fragrant tea. She found herself relaxing and almost feeling sleepy.

Mysterie held out her hand and asked for Molly's. "Close your eyes, and empty your mind. In your heart, you know Jack's not a bad person. He loves you very much."

Molly felt herself drifting as Mysterie continued talking.

"There's a darkness casting its shadow over you and Jack."

Mysterie was quiet and Molly opened her eyes. Mysterie was looking at her and a tear rolled down her cheek.

"What is it?" Molly asked, alarmed.

"I see much sadness."

A shiver went down Molly's spine. "Tell me what you see. Please."

Mysterie gave a slight shake of her head and rose. "We need to stop for today, Molly."

"You're scaring me. You've got to tell me what you see."

Mysterie took Molly's hand. "Nothing more than what I said. I'm sorry. I can't always see things clearly or in detail. Come back tomorrow, and we'll try again. I promise."

Confused, Molly left and headed toward the bight to get her things from Lisa's boat.

* * *

The next morning, daylight streaming through the bedroom window woke Molly. She rubbed her eyes and looked around, trying to get her bearings. The room was tastefully decorated with high ceilings and French doors opening out onto a second-floor balcony. She remembered she was in an upstairs bedroom in Seth's house.

Getting out of bed, she pulled the tail of the long-sleeved shirt down and opened the doors to the balcony. She stood there, wrapping her arms around herself, feeling the warmth of the well-worn dress shirt, one of Jack's.

This was the first one she'd taken and her favorite to sleep in. Often, it was the only thing she wore on the boat. It was a way of surrounding herself with him and gave her solace.

Absentmindedly, she fingered the buttons between her breasts. She smiled as she thought of Jack slowly unbuttoning them. When he undid the last one, he'd move back up to her chest. Then, he'd open the shirt and slide it off her shoulders, letting it fall to the floor as if unwrapping a gift.

She shuddered, walked out on the balcony, and leaned against the railing, studying the well-manicured backyard. She figured it was around seven, based on the temperature and the angle at which the sunlight was just beginning to spill through the canopy of trees.

She recognized her hosts' voices out on their patio below. "Good morning, guys," she said.

"Good morning, Molly," they replied in unison.

"Come on down and join us for coffee," Seth said.

She smiled. "On my way."

Back inside the bedroom, she slipped on one of Jack's old sweatshirts and a pair of shorts. She checked herself in the mirror, ran a brush through her hair, and decided she was fine for coffee.

She walked downstairs to the kitchen and next to the coffee pot was a fresh mug sitting on a hot plate. *Lee,* she thought, smiling. She filled it with steaming coffee, took a whiff, then walked out on the patio. A basket of fresh croissants and a carafe sat on the table set for three.

"Sleep well?" Seth asked.

"Yes, I did, thank you." She took a sip of her coffee before sitting. "Great coffee, Lee."

He smiled and gave a slight nod. "Life's too short to drink cheap coffee or wine."

She looked down and noticed a set of car keys next to her plate.

"Those are for the green Smart car parked out front," Seth said. "Yours to use as long as you want."

"I don't need it. I have a bicycle, which is fine."

"We have two cars too many as it is," Lee said.

Seth added, "You'd be doing us a favor. It doesn't get used enough just sitting out there."

She wondered if Jack was behind this offer, but the looks on their faces appeared genuine. "Thank you."

They chatted for a while as she ate a croissant. When Seth finished his coffee, he rose.

"I suppose I should go open the shop this morning." He turned to address Molly. "I'm usually home by five thirty. Chef Lee can discuss the dinner menu with you since I'm not usually allowed in the kitchen."

Lee waved his hand at Seth and turned to Molly. "Is because he cannot cook," he said. "You, on the other hand . . ." He raised his eyebrows, smiled, and nodded.

She couldn't help but laugh.

After breakfast, she started clearing the table, but Lee shooed her away, telling her she was a guest. With nothing to do, she went back upstairs and showered.

In the bedroom, as she was deciding what to wear, her phone beeped, indicating a voice mail. Jack had called while she was in the shower. She held the phone against her chest, then listened to the message.

He wanted to see her this weekend. He said he had to go to the mainland for a couple of days and would call again on his drive back.

She played the message again, just to hear his voice. Even though she was still hurt and angry, she did want to see him.

She set the phone down, deciding she'd deal with that later.

25

Jack stopped for the first time since he'd left Key West earlier this morning. He refueled, then pulled the car over to the end of the building housing the convenience store and fast-food restaurant. McDonald's wasn't his first choice, but he didn't feel like making another stop before he got back on I-75 for the section known as Alligator Alley.

He checked his phone, hoping but figuring he'd not missed any calls while driving through the Keys with the top down. He'd called Molly earlier, but she didn't answer. Not surprised, he'd left her a voice mail, asking if they could meet somewhere this weekend and talk.

He reached over to the gym bag on the seat next to him, unzipped it, and pulled out the hard plastic case with a lock securing it. He glanced around to make sure no one was watching, then unlocked the case and removed his new pistol.

Bringing his gun had posed a problem since he picked up the rental car at the airport. In Florida, concealed weapons were very much illegal anywhere in an airport, even in the unsecured areas. The last thing he needed was to get stopped with a gun and $400,000 in cash. To be safe, he'd been careful to lock his unloaded pistol in the hard-sided case and pack it in the bottom of his bag along with a loaded magazine. Now, he intended to put the loaded gun in its holster and inside his shorts before going inside.

It was a long eight hours of driving to get to Clearwater from Key West and he was about halfway there. Jack had told no one where he was going, telling Nick and Doug that he was taking a couple of days to think about everything. This was something he had to do alone. If he ever got the chance, he'd tell Molly. Regardless of what happened with them, he was determined to give the money away.

After he got everything comfortable, he locked the bag in the trunk and went in for a quick lunch and restroom break.

Before he got back on the interstate, he saw a thrift shop and wheeled in for a quick stop.

Two hours later, he drove past Fort Myers on I-75 without stopping. He thought about the people, past and present, he knew there. He smiled as he thought first of the good memories: Molly, Tony and Connie, Walter, and Peter. Peter was the one who'd left him the Island Packet, much to Jack's surprise.

His smile faded as his thoughts turned to Richard, his close friend who'd been murdered. He would always feel responsible for getting Richard involved. Now, he was also bearing the burden of Kenny and Valerie.

Farther up the coast, he turned north off of 275. It felt strange going back to Clearwater and in a car, no less. Although it had been less than a year, it seemed like it had been much longer. He regretted not being able to see Tina and Wren, but it was better if they knew nothing about his brief visit.

He pulled over and parked a couple of blocks away from his destination. He looked at his watch. 3:10. Perfect. He wanted to get in and out before five, ahead of the afternoon traffic.

He looked in the mirror. He was wearing a tattered Atlanta Braves ball cap, cheap sunglasses, and a baggy, well-worn long-sleeved shirt. He'd purchased his outfit for cash at the thrift shop when he'd stopped earlier this morning. The entire outfit was going in a dumpster as soon as he left town.

His pistol was still tucked in a holster inside his waistband. He wasn't expecting trouble, but he'd be damned if he had come this far to be robbed of the burden that had caused him so much grief.

He walked a block east, to a corner he remembered was usually frequented by the homeless. This was the riskiest part of the plan. He'd wrapped the money in a plain cardboard box, tucked underneath his arm.

He approached the skinny fellow standing on the corner, who was smoking what was left of a cigarette. With streetwise eyes, the man eyed him as he approached.

"I need a favor," Jack said, his eyes glancing around the area to make sure nothing looked suspicious or no one was paying attention.

The man nodded, staring at the box under Jack's arm.

"I'll give you a hundred dollars to take this package to the shelter on the next block. It's for my girlfriend who's staying there. I'm not supposed to come around there—they'll call the cops if they see me, but it's stuff she left. Nothing illegal, I just wanted to make sure she gets it."

Jack looked down at his hand where he held a folded hundred-dollar bill, the corner sticking out. The man followed his gaze and his eyes lit up when he saw the money.

"Okay," he said, reaching his hand out for the money.

"Just so we're clear," Jack said. "I'll be watching. Soon as I see you walk back out the door without the package, I'm gone. If you still have it, I *will* catch you. Understand?"

Jack held out the hundred dollar bill. "Take it, it's yours. All you got to do is deliver this package to the person at the front desk, right inside the door. I'll be watching. You come out empty handed, and you'll never see me again."

The man hesitated, but the lure of the money was too tempting. Jack gave him the money and the box, watching as the man ambled down the street toward the shelter. When he got there, he turned and looked at Jack. Jack nodded and the man walked up to the door and rang the bell.

As soon as he went inside and the door closed, Jack turned and walked halfway down the block toward his car. He stopped and stood next to a tree where he could see the front steps at the shelter.

A few minutes later, the skinny man stepped outside on the porch, empty handed. He looked around, but couldn't see Jack, then walked down the steps to the sidewalk.

Jack turned and walked to his car, nervously looking around to see if anyone was following him. When he turned the corner, he stopped in his tracks. A police car, with blue lights flashing, was parked behind his rental. The cop was standing beside his car looking at the back of Jack's convertible.

Jack's hand immediately fell to the loaded gun in his waistband. There was nothing illegal about it, he reassured himself. He had a valid Florida license to carry a concealed weapon.

He swiveled his head around to see if anyone was behind him, half expecting to see the homeless man running up holding a badge. An older woman was walking her dog down the other side of the street, but that was it.

A smile crossed his face, as he realized with relief that at least he didn't have the cash on him. The smile quickly disappeared when he also realized the homeless man could easily identify him.

He took a deep breath and walked toward the policeman.

"This your vehicle, sir?" the policeman said as he saw Jack approaching.

"Yes, uh, well it's a rental, but I'm driving it. The papers are in the glove compartment."

"May I see some identification, please?"

"Sure." Jack reached for his wallet in a slow, deliberate fashion. The policeman was an older man and appeared to be relaxed, which in turn made Jack a tad more comfortable. He read the name on the badge: Martin.

Jack opened his wallet and was then faced with another decision. He knew Florida was not a "duty to inform" state. Duty to inform meant you were required to disclose your concealed weapon license whenever stopped by a law enforcement officer. But, if Officer Martin suspected Jack was carrying, he might ask and then wonder why Jack hadn't mentioned it.

Jack pulled out his driver's license and handed it to the policeman. He left his concealed weapon license in his wallet and held his breath.

"Your vehicle is illegally parked," the officer said, pointing to a No Parking sign in front of Jack's car. The hours were listed in small print.

"I'm sorry, officer. I used to live around here and was in the area. I just wanted to stop by and check it out, see what's changed."

The officer studied the license.

"Key West, huh? This address correct?"

"Yes, sir. My wife and I live there now."

"Would you mind getting the rental agreement, please?"

"Oh, yeah. It's in the glove box."

Jack heard the officer call in his driver's license as he clicked the key fob to unlock the car. After opening the door, he reached inside, opened the glove box, and removed the folder containing the rental agreement. He handed it to Officer Martin.

Martin unfolded the paperwork and glanced at it. He nodded and handed it back.

"I'm not going to give you a ticket, Mr. Davis, but you have to move your car."

"Yes sir," Jack replied. "Thank you."

Jack got in the car and left, leaving Officer Martin still parked on the street. He was anxious to get out of Clearwater. Checking his rearview mirror every few minutes, he made his way back across the Courtney Campbell Causeway to 275 and drove south, the rush of adrenalin still fueling him. He felt like a burden had been lifted.

By the time he'd reached Fort Lauderdale, four hours later, the excitement had faded. He was exhausted. Convinced no one was following him, he stopped at a cheap motel next door to a truck stop and paid cash for a room.

As soon as his head hit the pillow, he was asleep.

26

Randy slowed the boat down to idle as he and Bobby entered Key West Bight that afternoon. He glanced at his watch. 5:47.

As he passed A&B Marina, he noticed the fuel dock was unoccupied. A young man was working on the dock coiling up lines and getting ready to close. Randy turned the boat and pulled in next to the dock.

The dockhand stopped what he was doing and turned to greet Randy. At first, he seemed disappointed that someone would want fuel this close to closing time, then he smiled as he looked at the boat.

"Sorry, sir. We only sell diesel here. You can refuel over there." He pointed across the way to Key West Bight Marina.

Randy smiled. "Thanks, but I was looking for a friend of mine—Jack Davis, *Left Behind.*" He pointed over to the sailboat. "I've tried to call him a couple of times today and stopped by, but he's not around. Do you know by any chance where he might be?"

The kid grinned and nodded. "Yeah, he's out for a few days. Not sure when he'll be back."

"Okay, thanks. I'll just have to catch him when he returns. Have a good evening." Randy reversed the engines and backed away from the dock. He pointed the boat further into the bight where he found an empty slip on the waterfront where he could tie up for a few hours.

He and Bobby would split up and go to different bars. A&B closed at six and a few hours later, once it was completely dark, Randy would walk over to Davis's sailboat. Provided the coast was clear, he'd pop the latch on the companionway, go in, and get the money.

He debated whether or not to send Bobby to break in, but since Randy was somewhat known at the marina and knew Jack, he had the better story should someone question him being there.

It was a risk having Bobby in the marina area since Jack and Molly would recognize him. With Jack out of town, Molly was still unaccounted for, but Randy had seen her with some guy taking her belongings out of the sailboat at the Bight Marina and loading them into a small green car. Still, he'd had Bobby shave his beard and not wear a cap. It was amazing how much that changed his appearance.

Once Randy had the money, he would call Bobby, who would bring the boat over to the fuel dock, pick him up, and head back to Stock Island. Randy would've preferred having Evens pick him up, but he wasn't answering Randy's calls. That bothered him, but he'd deal with that later.

About quarter of eight, Randy settled his tab and texted Bobby to tell him he was leaving. He picked up the small bag containing his tools and headed over to the A&B dock. He felt a little conspicuous carrying a bag, but he'd found an old sail bag with a faded North Sails logo on it, so he figured it would fit in.

He glanced around, scanning the area as he walked over to A&B Marina and out their dock. Halfway down, a man stepped off a large powerboat in a slip and walked toward him. The man seemed to be checking him out.

Randy nodded and said, "Evening."

The man, noticing the sail bag with the logo prominently displayed, smiled, and returned the greeting as he kept walking.

When Randy got to the end of the dock, he took another quick look around before boarding. The man from the powerboat was already on the boardwalk and headed the opposite direction. Randy stepped onto *Left Behind* and crouched down in the cockpit in front of the companionway.

He looked up at the lock securing the door and tried to figure out the best approach. The lock looked more substantial than he had realized. Bolt cutters weren't going to do the job. That meant using the pry bar to break the latch loose. Effective, but that would be noisy and take longer. He didn't see any other option.

He pulled the pry bar out of the bag and stuck it between the latch and the fiberglass bulkhead. Pressing down on the other end, he felt the resistance and heard the groaning of fiberglass as he pressed harder. He let off when he realize it was going to crack the fiberglass and make a considerable racket.

"Shit," he said under his breath. He wished he'd thought to bring a block of wood to place underneath the bar, between it and the fiberglass. He wiped the sweat from his brow and snuck a look around. Nobody seemed to be paying attention.

He swore and put the tool back in place, pressing harder this time. It was working, but making a lot of noise.

Craaack. The fiberglass splintered and he almost lost his balance. He looked around again, but with the music coming from different venues around the water, it apparently didn't attract any undue attention.

He turned around and tugged on the latch. "Fuck," he said, a little louder than he intended. That had broken loose only half of the screws securing the latch. He'd have to repeat the process over again for the top side.

At last, he got the companionway door open and stepped inside. He quickly made a first pass through the main cabin, lifting seat cushions and opening cabinets and lockers. He moved to the forward cabin, where he found a safe in the wardrobe.

He shook his head. If it was in there, there was nothing he could do. He went through every conceivable hiding place but found no money. He looked at his watch. He'd been in there for twenty minutes.

Time to leave. He texted Bobby that it was time to go.

He had a few minutes before Bobby would get there, so he hurried back to the rear cabin and ransacked it. Still no money. Bobby had sworn it was inside and not in one of the outside lockers. Either it was in the safe or Davis had moved it.

Randy froze when he heard footsteps on the dock, right behind the boat. Even though it was fairly dark, the companionway door was open and it was obvious someone had busted the latch. He listened closely, but the person had stopped moving. The sound of music and voices from around the waterfront drifted in through the open companionway. Randy quietly reached into his pocket and pulled out his gun.

He took two small steps toward the doorway leading to the main cabin and stopped. The stairs were on the other side of the thin wall. He strained to hear. Nothing. He raised the pistol and waited.

"Hey, you in there?" a voice whispered from outside.

What the hell? Randy cocked his head and didn't move.

"Randy, you in there?" Another whisper. This time, he recognized the voice.

He put the gun back in his pocket and climbed up the steps to see Bobby standing on the dock, leaning over and grinning.

Randy shook his head. If there weren't so many people around, he would've shot him.

27

Mysterie was in her reading room, meditating when her concentration was disturbed. She heard the door chime, signifying someone had walked in. Cassie was out front and Mysterie cocked her head to hear.

A familiar male voice said, "I need to see Mysterie."

"She's busy right now," Cassie said.

Before the man could say anything, Mysterie pushed the beaded curtain aside and stepped into the shop. "It's okay, Cassie. Why don't you take a break?"

Cassie nodded and grabbed her wallet. Stepping out the front door, she said, "I'm going to grab a coffee. Want anything?"

"No, thanks," Mysterie said. She watched Cassie walk away, then turned to face Randy Jenkins. "What are you doing here?" she said, her voice sharp.

Jenkins looked around to make sure they were alone.

"Where's Evens?"

"He went to work this morning. Afterward, he was going fishing."

Randy shook his head. "Bullshit. I checked. He didn't show at work today and he's not answering his phone."

Mysterie was confused. Evens had left at his normal time this morning and she assumed he was going to work as usual.

"You sure he's not here?" Randy said, looking over her shoulder at the curtain.

"I told you, he left at the usual time for work. You can go back there if you want to check."

"Call him."

She hesitated, then said she'd have to get her phone in the reading room. Randy followed her past the beaded curtain, watching as she picked up her phone and called her brother. It went to voice mail and she disconnected.

"It went to his voice mail," she said.

Randy stepped toward her. "Find him and tell him I want to see him—now," he hissed. He turned, swept the beads aside, and walked out, Mysterie at his heels. Before he made it to the front door, he stopped and turned around.

"I need to see the redhead."

"I can't make her—"

"You're not listening to me. Figure it out. Get her in here. Understand?"

She stared at him, motionless, for several beats, then nodded.

"Let me know when she's going to be here." Randy turned and walked out of the shop.

Mysterie went over to the doorway of her shop and gazed toward Duval Street, watching the tourists crowding the busy street tonight. Another cruise ship had docked in Key West that afternoon, disgorging thousands of passengers now wandering throughout the downtown area. Several had stopped in earlier, wanting their future predicted, and she was glad for the break.

Randy's visit had rattled her. There was no way she was going to deliver Molly to him. She had warned Evens about hanging around Randy, but he still did odd jobs for the man from time to time. Evens had broken down and told her what had happened.

Randy had talked him into taking him out on a boat late Friday a few weeks ago. He said he needed to ride out to the Marquesas Keys and check on something.

They had stopped to talk to a couple on a sailboat, anchored there for the evening. Randy had pulled a gun and before Evens could do anything, Randy had shot the man, seriously wounding him. When the woman reached for the radio, Randy shot her, killing her instantly.

Evens had insisted on calling for help, but Randy told him he'd end up spending the rest of his life in prison if he said a word to anyone.

Mysterie didn't understand what that had to do with Molly but knew that Jenkins could easily pin the murders on her brother. She also knew Evens would never survive in prison, and she was determined to avoid that.

Cassie walked back up the street, holding a cup of coffee. She was used to strange requests from customers, so Mysterie asking her to take a break was nothing out of the ordinary. The tattooed girl smiled and walked past her, reclaiming her usual spot behind the counter.

Mysterie's phone buzzed. Evens. She stepped outside to answer.

"Evens? Where are you?"

"It's better you doan know."

"*He* came by here earlier, looking for you. He seemed upset and wants to see you, as soon as possible. What's going on, Evens? Talk to me."

"I'm gonna make tings right," he said and hung up.

Mysterie exhaled and shook her head. She was afraid to guess what her brother was up to, but if it involved Randy, it wasn't good.

28

Friday morning, Jack awoke, refreshed after a good night's sleep. He showered, then got a large coffee and breakfast sandwich at the truck stop before heading home.

He'd just pulled out when the sound of "Clocks" came from his cell phone. Nick. He started not to answer but decided it must be important.

"Hey Nick," he answered.

"I hate to bother you. I wanted to let you know that someone broke into *Left Behind* last night."

Jack almost laughed out loud at the irony. "Molly wasn't there, I take it."

"No. She's okay. Terry called me first thing this morning, right after he called the cops. Doesn't appear they took anything, but pretty well trashed it. They pried the door, kinda messed it up. I'll put something over it to secure everything until you get back."

"Don't worry about it. I should be back in three or four hours."

He set the phone back in the console and chuckled as he headed south.

In Marathon, he stopped to use the bathroom. When he got back to the car, he called Molly.

"Hello," she said, surprising him by answering. He'd been composing his message and stumbled to reply.

"Hey. You doing okay?"

"I'm fine."

"I had some business up the coast and I'm on my way back home. I was . . . I was hoping maybe we could get together this weekend, maybe dinner?"

There was a long pause, then she said, "How about lunch?"

He tried to hide his disappointment. "Sure, lunch would be good. What about Blue Heaven? Tomorrow?" Blue Heaven was one of their favorite restaurants on the island.

Another pause. "Let's just go to Eaton Street, around noon. We can sit outside and talk."

He shook his head. Lunch at the seafood market. She wasn't going to make it easy.

"Okay, I'll see you there." She disconnected and was gone.

He was back in Key West by lunchtime. He turned in the car, got his bike, and rode to the marina. Nick's was his first stop.

"Quick trip," Nick said. He was sitting on the back of his boat when Jack walked up carrying his bag, now lighter.

"Long enough. You had lunch yet?"

Nick shook his head.

"Good. Give me ten minutes and I'll meet you at Alonzo's. I'll even buy."

Jack stepped onboard *Left Behind* and cringed when he saw the cracks in the fiberglass next to the companionway door. That pissed him off more than the person breaking in.

The lock was hanging securely on the hasp, dangling from the door.

So much for the high-security lock, he thought. He looked at the alarm decal and chuckled. He'd never activated the monitoring, counting on the sticker to deter would-be thieves.

Somebody knew he was gone and Molly wasn't on the boat. He glanced around the small harbor and thought about Bobby and Mike. They had been watching.

As he opened the door, he thought about it. It would be risky for them to be hanging around the area since he or Molly could identify them. Maybe they had accomplices.

It would be a lot easier to keep track of a thirty-eight-foot sailboat than two people going different directions, especially if you knew where the boat was most of the time. They were watching the boat, not him. It didn't matter where he or Molly went, as long as the boat was where it belonged.

He set his bag down in the cabin and looked around. Whoever it was had made a mess. Contents of drawers, cabinets, and lockers were strewn all over the floor. They had been in a hurry. He walked through his home, doing a quick mental inventory. Nothing seemed to be missing. He'd straighten up later.

He went back outside, climbed up on the cabin roof, and stood next to the mast. There were dozens of vantage points where someone could keep an eye on his boat. Too many people out and about, and too many places for them to hide out in the open. It could be a hired "watcher," for that matter, someone who would just call when *Left Behind* was getting ready to leave. With a top speed of seven knots, it wasn't like someone couldn't easily catch up.

They knew the money was on the boat, so keep up with the boat. But why would you have someone watching a boat that didn't move ninety-five percent of the time? That didn't make sense. Then it dawned on him. *What if you put a tracking device on the boat?* Then, you could monitor it electronically and, more importantly, remotely.

His phone chirped, indicating a text message from Tony.

Talked to TN - no help. Sorry.

Jack shook his head, disappointed. Tony had talked to his friend in Tennessee, and he wasn't any help on coming up with names of Peabo Watson's known accomplices. Jack knew it was a long shot but had hoped for something.

Still holding his phone, Jack turned back to the question of a tracking device. He wouldn't know how to go about finding it, but he knew just the person to ask. He called Doug. No answer. *Damn,* he thought, *does anybody answer their phone anymore?* He texted Doug a quick message and not bothering to close the damaged companionway door, he walked up to Alonzo's.

"I think I figured out who's watching us," he said as he sat across the table from Nick, who was there waiting with two beers on the table.

Nick raised his, took a deep swallow, and stared at him. "Who?"

Jack grabbed the other bottle and took a drink. He shook his head, "Sorry, not *who,* but *how.* I think I know how they're keeping track of me."

"I'm listening."

"It's so obvious, I don't know why you didn't think of it earlier. There's nobody standing around the bight, watching us all the time. Not necessary. We've been looking for some*one* instead of some*thing*."

He grabbed his cell phone and held it up. "Probably smaller than this. A tracking device, there's a tracking device on the boat."

"I thought about that, it's what I would've done."

Jack sat back and frowned, shocked at his friend's admission. "Why the hell didn't you say something before?"

Nick shrugged. "I didn't think we were dealing with rocket scientists here, only good ole boys. My experience has been with more sophisticated criminals."

"Thanks. You probably know what to look for, too. I don't, so I called Doug. I'm betting he can help me find it."

"Is he coming over?"

Jack shook his head. "He didn't answer. I texted him, so we'll see." He had barely got the words out of his mouth when he saw Doug and Lisa walked along the boardwalk.

"Hey," Jack hollered. They turned around and came over to the table.

"I got your message and we were just going to stop by. Computer problems?" Doug asked.

Jack shook his head. "Something else. You got a few minutes?"

They joined them at the table and Jack gave them the abridged version. "I think the guys that stopped us the other day have some sort of tracking device on our boat." He looked at Doug. "Can you help me find it?"

"Wow, this is cool," Doug said, delighted at the challenge.

Lisa rolled her eyes. "This is not cool, Doug. This is creepy."

He looked at Lisa, then back at Jack. "I guess not. Sorry."

Jack chuckled. "No problem. Can you help?"

Happy to talk tech, Doug nodded. "Sure. All of those things transmit some kind of radio signal. I've got a portable scanner I use to . . ." He hesitated and looked at Lisa. ". . . to check for transmissions from various electronic devices. It doesn't matter if it uses audio, video, GPS—anything."

Nick laughed. "We've got our own version of NSA right here in the bight."

Lisa shook her head. "I don't even want to know what you're talking about, just help them find the damn thing."

"That's no problem. When do you want to do it?"

"Right now," Jack answered.

Ten minutes later, Doug met Jack and Nick at *Left Behind,* holding a black box about the size of a paperback book, only half as thick and with two stubby antennae sticking out the top.

"That's it?" Jack asked.

Doug handed it to him. "Yep. This is a professional, multi-channel detector. Picks up Bluetooth, Wi-Fi, GPS, cellular—everything."

Jack was surprised at how little it weighed, probably five or six ounces. He looked at the front which had rows of LED indicators and acronyms, none of which he understood. "What does something like that cost?"

Doug glanced around. "Don't tell Lisa. You can get a cheapo model for a little over a hundred bucks. A professional model like this one, well, that's going to run close to a thousand."

"The man does it right," Nick offered. "Gotta give him credit."

Jack handed it back to Doug, and he switched the power on. It beeped, all of the lights lit, then blinked, with most of them going out. Several remained on.

Doug nodded, tweaked several switches and knobs on the device, and looked up at Jack. "You don't have any of the boat's electronics on, do you?"

"No, that's all switched off at the panel."

Doug nodded again, then stood and turned in a complete circle, holding the device out in front of him. He frowned, then turned back to his left and stepped toward the aft locker.

"Here," he announced. "There's something transmitting in this locker. What's in there?"

"That's where the propane tank is located," Jack said. He bent over, unlocked the padlock, and lifted the lid. He kneeled down and stuck his head inside. "I don't see anything. What am I looking for?"

"Move," Doug said, kneeling down next to Jack. "Let me look." He stuck his head in the locker. After a few minutes of rattling around inside, he emerged, grinning. "Found it. It's on the inside, near me. You'd never see it from just looking inside the locker at a normal angle."

Doug moved aside while Jack stuck his head in and searched. "Son of a bitch," he said, pulling his head out and closing the locker.

"How far does this thing transmit?" Jack asked.

"Anywhere you've got cell service, I'm guessing," Nick said.

Doug laughed. "You got it. Anywhere it has cell service."

Jack had a puzzled look on his face.

Doug continued. "It transmits through a cell network to another device, which could be a phone, computer, anything connected to the Internet, basically."

"How long does the battery last?"

Doug contorted his face, doing the math in his head. "This one's probably got a motion-sensing feature—it goes to sleep if it's not moving, perfect for a sailboat sitting at a dock. Probably six weeks or so."

Jack looked at the locker and held up the padlock. "This stays locked. Unless someone broke—"

"When's the last time somebody was in that locker?" Doug asked.

Jack shook his head and thought. "Nobody's been in that locker that I know of."

"What about the refrigerator guy?" Nick asked. "He would've had to turn off the propane before he worked on the refrigerator. When he was done, he would've had to go back into the locker again and turn it on before he left."

"Of course," Jack said. "I wasn't here, but you're right. He would've had to access this locker."

Nick stroked his chin, thinking. "Pretty clever, actually. My guess is that somebody nearby is monitoring your boat. When it moves, they send someone to check it out. That would only work in a small place and with a sailboat. It's not like it's going to get too far away before someone can catch you."

"Could we take the tracking device and put it on another boat? Or work backward to see who's monitoring it?" Jack asked.

"No," Nick answered, "on both counts. First, they are probably visually verifying the boat, and it would have different speed characteristics. For example, if we put it on a powerboat, it would move a lot faster. Second, this thing is just transmitting through the cell network to the Internet and then to a server God-knows-where. The monitoring person just signs in to the server to track the movements. Given enough time and resources, somebody like Doug could probably track it back, but this is way beyond this group."

Doug nodded in agreement, impressed with Nick's explanation. "This dude knows his shit."

Jack noticed that Nick seemed to understand a lot more of what Doug was saying than he did.

"How do we lure them out? Just keep taking the boat out, and hope that someone shows?" Jack said. "Maybe I should plan another sailing trip?"

"Maybe so, but first I think we need to find the guy who worked on your refrigerator," Nick said.

29

After Doug and Nick left, Jack walked down to the dockmaster's office to talk with Terry. On the way, he passed Jesse, one of the few bona fide "conchs" or natives of Key West Jack knew.

"Afternoon, Jack."

"Afternoon, Jesse. Terry in?"

She laughed. "He's on the phone. What's new?"

He thanked her and walked up to the office. He pushed the door open, seeing Terry on the phone as Jesse had described. Terry held up a finger as he finished the conversation.

"Hey, Jack. What's up?" he asked, as he hung up the phone.

"The guy who fixed our refrigerator—Evens. How much do you know about him?"

Terry gave him a concerned look. "Why? Is there a problem?"

Jack smiled and shook his head. "No, no. I just had a question about boat refrigerators and wanted to get in touch with him. I misplaced his card. Does he live on the island?"

Terry relaxed as he reached over and flipped through an ancient Rolodex on his desk.

"He works for Keys Marine, so he lives somewhere close by. Here," he said, grabbing a pen and scrap of paper. "I'll write down their number."

Disappointed in the scarcity of information, Jack took the slip of paper and stuck it in his pocket. "Thanks, Terry."

He was hoping for more. He already had the number for Keys Marine and was hoping for personal information. He walked back to the boat, passing Jesse at the fuel dock. She had finished filling up a boat and was helping them leave.

"Hey, Jesse," he said, as the boat pulled away from the dock. "Do you know Evens, the boat mechanic from Keys Marine?"

"Sure." She frowned. "Why? Got a problem?"

"No, not at all. He worked on our refrigerator a few weeks ago. It's working like a charm. I just wanted to ask him a question about something else on the boat. That's all." He pulled out the piece of paper Terry had given him.

"Terry gave me his work number, but I didn't want to go through them, know what I mean?"

She nodded, giving Jack an understanding look. Most repair shops didn't like their valued technicians giving out advice, especially when it pertained to things they could charge for. A lot of good mechanics moonlighted on the side to supplement their income.

"He lives on the island. With his sister." She grinned and whispered in a conspiratorial voice. "She's a palm reader. Owns that shop just off Duval, on Petronia. Mysterie is her name."

"Evens is Mysterie's brother?"

Jesse nodded.

He thanked Jesse for the information and walked back to his boat, pondering the connection. Obviously, Evens was working with Bobby and Mike, but what was Mysterie's relationship?

He got back to the boat and started cleaning. Doug and Nick had both offered to help Jack clean up, but he declined, saying it was a good excuse to do a little housecleaning. They had agreed to reconvene later on Nick's boat.

Several hours later, Jack stood at the bottom of the stairs in the main cabin, appraising the results of his efforts. It looked almost back to normal. The damage wasn't as bad as he'd initially thought. The safe hadn't been opened and other than a few broken items, everything was there. Mostly, the burglar had rifled through draws and lockers, spilling the contents on the floor.

He'd found the empty sail bag where he had stashed the money, along with the other bags in the locker. He wondered if they realized the money was not on the boat.

He finished putting things he wanted to throw away into garbage bags and was about to take them up to the dumpster when he heard a female voice calling his name.

"Mr. Davis? Is that you?"

He stepped up on deck to see Detective Stevens standing by his boat.

"Afternoon, Detective. Come aboard."

She took off her shoes and stepped onto the boat. "I was down this way and thought I'd stop by and see how you were doing."

"Just trying to get things straightened up."

"Anything missing?"

"Not that I know of." He was surprised to see her and it apparently showed.

"I caught the call this morning," she explained.

"I thought you were homicide?"

She shrugged. "Robbery and homicide are done by the same detectives here."

He nodded. "Nobody was hurt and everything was still in the safe."

"I figured they were looking for cash or jewelry. When they couldn't get into the safe, they bailed. Not unusual. I understand your wife's not staying here at present." She stared at him, and he wondered where she was headed with this.

He shook his head. "We're having some . . . some marital issues. She's staying with friends." He had the distinct feeling she already knew that.

"Where were you last night?" she asked.

He held her gaze as he debated what to say.

"I was in a motel at the intersection of 75 and 595 outside of Fort Lauderdale. Molly and I are trying to work through some problems. I needed to get away and drove up to the mainland to do some thinking. I've got the receipt if you'd like to see it."

After a few seconds, she shook her head. "Just doing my job, Mr. Davis."

He rose from his seat. "If you don't have anything else, then, I need to fix the lock on my door," he said as he pointed to the padlock still dangling from the hasp.

"Sorry to hear about you and your wife. I hope you get things patched up," she said as she stepped off the boat and put her shoes on. "Have a good evening."

Jack took a deep breath as he watched her walk down the dock. He turned his attention to fixing the latch so he could lock his cabin again.

At six, he locked the cabin and walked over to Nick's. He'd showered after he finished working, and was glad to get the grime off.

Doug was already there, and the two had started without him.

"Lisa must be working," he said to Doug as he stepped onto the big sportfisherman.

"She and Molly both."

Jack helped himself to a beer and sat. "Well, I got everything put back together. Not as bad as I thought. Fixing the latch, on the other hand . . ."

"You get it where you could lock up?" Doug asked.

Jack nodded. "It needs some cosmetic work, but it'll do for now."

"Did you find out anything from Terry on your mechanic?" Nick said.

"His name is Evens. Works out at Keys Marine. Guess where he lives?" He paused to have a drink and pique their interest.

"Where?" Doug asked, unable to stand it any longer.

"Petronia Street. He's the brother of the palm reader Mysterie."

"That's an interesting connection," Nick said. "Didn't Molly go to see her?"

Jack nodded.

"Mysterie's spying on you?" Doug asked.

"I don't know. It's starting to get confusing. What's your take, Nick?"

"Hard to tell, but we need to find Evens."

After they finished their beers, they walked downtown to DJ's for dinner. They discussed who should go to the palm reader's shop. Everyone agreed that Mysterie didn't know any of them on sight, so that wasn't a factor.

"No reason I can't go. After all, it's my problem," Jack said as they found a table in the back and sat. "I'm just going to see if he's there and try to find out if he put that bug on my boat and who he's working for."

"I think Nick's probably better at this sort of thing," Doug argued.

Nick shrugged. "I don't think it really matters. If Evens is there, I don't really think he's going to do anything. And, I seriously doubt he'll say anything to any of us. The best we can hope for is that he'll help us flush out the others."

"I'm going," Jack said, settling the discussion. "It's only a block away, so go ahead and order for me. It shouldn't take long."

He walked the short distance to the shop and stepped inside. A tattooed girl sat behind the counter, her head propped on her hands, reading a magazine.

"Could I help you?" she asked, looking up when he entered.

"Is Mysterie around?"

"No, she's out. I'm not sure when she'll be back. Could I give her a message?"

Jack shook his head. Everyone had agreed that whoever went, it would be better not to tip their hand.

"I'm really looking for Evens? Is he here?"

The girl sat up at the mention of Mysterie's brother. "Is there something I could help you with? "

He smiled, trying to put the girl at ease. "No, he did some work on my boat and I just had a few questions." He asked again, "Is he here?"

"No, he's not. Did you check at Keys Marine?"

"They were closed already, and I thought maybe I could catch him at home."

"Sorry," she said. She folded her arms across her chest, ending the conversation.

When Jack returned to DJ's, Nick and Doug were sitting out back, waiting for their food.

"That was quick," Doug said.

"Nobody home." He relayed the details of the short visit.

"Sounds like there's no doubt he lives there, though," Nick said. "I'm sure the clerk will pass along the message that someone was looking for him. It'll be interesting to see what that triggers."

"Let's talk about a sailing trip," Jack said.

30

Early the next morning, Jack's phone rang, waking him up.

"Hello," he answered, wondering who was calling.

"Jack? This is Connie Budzinski."

He heard her voice catch, and before he could say anything, she continued. "Tony's had a stroke," she said in a hurried voice as if to get the words out before she lost her composure.

"Jesus, Connie, when? How is he?"

"He's still at Rivers." She choked back a sniffle. "He's not doing good, Jack, not at all."

He could hear her muffled crying.

"I'll be there as soon as I can, Connie. Is someone with you?"

Between sobs, she got it out that her neighbor was there with her at the hospital, and her sister was on her way down from Atlanta.

"I'll call as soon as I figure out how I'm getting there. Tell him I'm on my way."

He called Silver Airways. They were booked and didn't have a seat available until in the morning. Delta and United had a seat this afternoon, but it was going to be $800 and involve a connection, which meant it would take hours.

He could drive it in five hours. He washed his face, threw on some clothes, and packed enough for a couple of days. He called Hertz and reserved a car, then locked up and walked over to Nick's.

His friend was sitting out on the deck of his boat, reading the paper and drinking his coffee.

"You're up early," Nick said. He noticed Jack's bag and asked, "You going somewhere again?"

"I'm headed to Fort Myers. My friend Tony's had a stroke. His wife just called."

"Jesus, sorry to hear that. You flying?"

Jack shook his head. "Nothing available today. I've got a rental car reserved."

Nick reached into his pocket, pulled out his car keys and handed them to Jack. "Take mine."

Jack hesitated. "I'm not sure how long I'll be. I hate to—"

"Doesn't matter. Take it."

He took the keys. "Thanks, Nick. I'll give you a call when I know what's going on."

Five and a half hours later, he pulled into the parking lot at Rivers Community Hospital in Fort Myers.

As he went through the front doors of the hospital, Jack looked around. The lobby was the same, but he saw no familiar faces. He smiled as he remembered this was where he'd first met Molly.

The smile faded as he looked up and saw the sign pointing to the Pharmacy, reminded that not all of the memories were good ones.

Richard had been the Pharmacy director at Rivers when Jack and Molly worked there. He had also been Jack's closest friend. The trio had stumbled on a scheme to cover up the poor results of an expensive cardiac drug. That discovery had ultimately cost Richard his life.

He went to the fifth floor, exited the elevator and turned right, looking for 520A.

The door was open a few inches, and Jack saw the name A. BUDZINSKI next to the opening.

Jack rapped softly on the door.

"Come in," said a female voice he recognized as Connie.

He pushed the door opened, then stepped inside. Connie was seated by the bed, looking to see who was there.

When she recognized him, she smiled and then burst into tears. She came over and hugged him and he felt her tears on his neck. Over her shoulder, he peeked at Tony.

His friend was lying on his back, his mouth open slightly and his eyes closed. An oxygen tube was stuck in his nose, the elastic strap behind his head. Wires snaked from his chest to a monitor, sounding a rhythmic *beep, beep, beep*. Plastic tubes connected him to multiple IV pumps. Various size bags half-full of liquids—one clear, one with a yellow tint—hung above his head. Another tube led from under the sheet down to a plastic bag hanging low on the bed rail. His chest rose and fell at an almost imperceptible rate, just enough to tell he was alive if you could call it that.

"Thank you for coming." She went over and sat back down

Jack followed her and sat in the chair next to hers, his eyes on Tony.

"What's the doctor say?" he asked, his voice thick with emotion.

Connie wiped her eyes with the handkerchief she was clutching and shrugged. "Dr. Powell says he needs to get all of the test results in." She sniffled and blew her nose. "I'm sorry. He did say it was a serious stroke. He doesn't know . . . what the prognosis is."

She told him when it had happened. "It was so sudden. We'd gone out to eat and he said he wasn't feeling good. When we got home, he didn't look good and said he was going to get ready for bed. I was reading and I told him I'd be along soon." Her voice caught, and she paused for a moment to regain her composure.

"I heard him fall. I jumped up and ran into the bathroom. He . . . he was lying there, on the floor, not moving. I called 911 and the ambulance got there in a few minutes, but it seemed like forever." She looked over at her husband, the tears flowing. "He's been that way since he came in."

After an hour or so, Jack convinced Connie to go with him to the cafeteria for a quick bite to eat since she couldn't remember the last time she'd eaten.

At the table, she rearranged the salad in front of her, occasionally eating a mouthful.

"He was supposed to take Vasotec daily, but he cut them in half to save money since it was so expensive. I told him he shouldn't be doing that, but you know how stubborn . . ." She broke down and started crying.

Jack didn't say anything, waiting for her to gather herself. When he put his hand on her arm, she patted it and said, "I'm sorry, Jack."

"Connie, you don't have to apologize," he said in a soft voice.

She nodded, blew her nose and continued. "Then, his insurance wouldn't pay for Vasotec, only the generic version, but Dr. Powell wouldn't prescribe the generic. He said he'd contact the insurance company, but nothing happened."

She took a deep breath. "His drugs alone are over a thousand dollars a month. Dr. Powell has him on Aricept, which is half of that. Tony is terrified of Alzheimer's, so he wasn't going to cut back on that one."

Jack shook his head. He knew how expensive drugs were. He'd assumed Tony's retirement included decent health care coverage.

"They keep cutting back on benefits for retirees," Connie said as if reading his mind.

They went back upstairs, where Connie resumed her vigil. Dr. Powell came by to talk with Connie, and she had insisted that Jack be included in on the conversation.

Tony had suffered a severe ischemic stroke. The good news was that they had got him to the hospital within an hour and were able to start tissue plasminogen activator shortly after. That greatly improved his chances of recovery.

"What about surgically removing the clot?" Jack asked.

Dr. Powell shook his head. "Unfortunately, he's not a candidate for mechanical thrombectomy." He went on to say that tPA was very effective at dissolving clots, trying to stay optimistic. When Connie asked how much ability Tony would regain, he said that it was impossible to predict at this point. The immediate plan was to continue tPA and closely monitor him for twenty-four hours. They would re-assess things at that time.

Jack looked over at Tony and kept silent. He knew it was impossible to predict, but he also knew that the more ability a patient had immediately after a stroke was a big indicator of how much recovery to expect. The prognosis was not good at all.

After the doctor left, Jack excused himself to call Nick. He needed some fresh air, so took the elevator down to the ground floor.

As he walked outside, he pulled out his phone and turned off airplane mode. *Shit,* he thought. He just remembered his lunch date with Molly. Five hours ago.

"How's he doing?" Nick asked as soon as he answered.

"Not good. Not good at all." He told Nick what was going on and his opinion of Tony's condition.

"Sorry to hear that, Jack."

"Thanks. Nothing else to do right now. I'll spend the night and see where things stand in the morning and let you know. Listen, I need a huge favor. I was supposed to have lunch with Molly. With everything going on, I forgot all about it. Could you please try to find her and let her know what's happening?"

"I'll do my best."

Jack stayed at the hospital all afternoon. When Connie's sister arrived that evening and said she'd stay with Connie, Jack left to get something to eat.

He drove over to Ray's On the River, thinking it would be nice to sit outside overlooking the water. Ray's had been one of their favorite restaurants in Fort Myers, located between the marina where Jack lived and Molly's condo. Jack, Molly, and Richard had spent many fond evenings there.

He turned the corner and was surprised to see an empty lot where Ray's once stood. He pulled over to the side of the street and stopped. It was fenced in and appeared some construction project was just getting started. Ray's was gone, probably demolished for another hotel or condo complex. Maybe Thomas Wolfe was right.

He turned around and drove downtown, not wanting fast food, but not willing to go too far from the hospital. He crossed under Cleveland Avenue and passed the convention center. A half dozen food trucks were parked on Edwards Drive, next to Centennial Park where a small crowd milled about. Apparently, there was some sort of event going on.

He found a parking spot, got out and walked over to the first food truck he found that served seafood. Ordering a grouper sandwich, he asked the woman in the truck what was happening.

"First Friday," she said. "It's a local deal, entertainment and eats the first Friday of every month."

He paid for his sandwich and found a spot to sit and eat, listening to a duo perform on the small stage that had been set up. *Not bad,* he thought, referring to both the meal and the music.

He finished his sandwich and headed back to the hospital.

When he got to the lobby, his phone rang. It was Molly.

"Hey," she said when he answered. "Nick told me. How's he doing?"

He turned around and walked back out, not wanting to talk inside.

"Sorry, I forgot about our lunch meeting."

"It's okay, I understand."

He told her what he knew and also about his conversation with Connie regarding Tony's drugs.

"That's sad," she said. "He spent his whole life working his tail off, then can't afford the meds. Now, he's in the hospital, and they'll pay for that, but wouldn't pay for his drugs? What kind of sense does that make?"

"No money, no care," Jack said. "You know how it works."

"Call me in the morning and let me know what the doctor says."

"I will. Thanks for calling."

He was angry, angry that it was preventable and caused by nothing but greed. Here was a good person, someone who had worked hard all of his life, serving the public and putting his life on the line. Now, through no fault of his own, he had suffered a catastrophic health event.

Molly had agreed that the outcome didn't look good. More than half of stroke victims died or suffered severe impairment.

He hoped Tony wasn't one of the latter.

31

Jack was there the next morning when Doctor Powell made his rounds. There wasn't much change in Tony's condition. The doctor suggested they give it another day and he'd be back in the morning.

Connie seemed calmer. Having her sister there helped, and Jack figured she was exhausted as well. There wasn't anything he could do. Now that her sister was with her, Connie was in good hands. Jack excused himself to call Molly.

"No change," he said when she answered her phone on the second ring. He told her Connie's sister had arrived and he was considering coming home. "Nothing I can do, other than hang around and wait."

"There's nothing you can do. There's no way of telling . . . how long," she said. She didn't have to say more. They both knew how this was going to end.

"Maybe we can have lunch tomorrow?" he asked.

"Got to work. How about Tuesday?"

"Tuesday it is. I'll try not to forget."

He heard a chuckle on the other end. "Be careful driving home."

He went back to Tony's room and asked Connie if she needed anything before he left.

She stood and hugged him. "No, now that Edith's here I'm okay. Thank you so much for coming. It means a lot to me, and to Tony."

"Keep me posted, and call if you need anything at all."

Edith hugged him and also thanked him for coming

He stepped over to Tony's bedside, reached out and put his hand on Tony's arm. "Take care, my friend. Try not to give everyone any trouble. See you soon."

He turned and walked out, not letting Connie and her sister see the tear rolling down his cheek.

Out in the hall, he stopped to take a deep breath. He knew he'd never see Tony again.

Downstairs, he got in the car and called Nick. His friend didn't answer, so he left a message saying he'd be back this afternoon.

Jack had a message from Paula, his accountant friend in Miami, so he called her before he left the hospital.

"Hey, I was returning your call," he said when she answered.

"I just found out something I thought you'd be interested in. It's regarding 1AAA."

She proceeded to tell Jack that the mystery purchaser of the medical equipment company was none other than Manuel Torres, the alleged head of the Cuban mafia in south Florida.

"*The* Manuel Torres?"

"The one and only. Apparently the offer was twice what the company was worth. Trying to 'clean up' some of his funds is the rumor."

Now Jack understood why Frankie Crispino was so anxious to buy Tony out at the actual book value of 1AAA. As soon as he owned all of the shares, he was going to turn around and sell it for twice what it was worth.

"Thanks, Paula. I owe you one."

As soon as he hung up, he Googled the address for 1AAA and plugged it into the GPS on the car.

He lowered the convertible top and thumbed through the music on his iPhone. He wanted rock and roll, something to pound away the worries. He smiled when he got to the Allman Brothers classic album, *Live at Fillmore East*. Perfect. He cranked up the volume, put the car in gear, and headed south toward home.

When he got to the east coast, Jack threaded his way through Miami, over toward the docks. It was a sketchy neighborhood, part industrial, part shady retail. The area was littered with pawn shops, payday loan places, and massage parlors, scattered amongst plumbing supply, heating and air contractors, and a few garages.

He finally saw a huge, shiny sign for 1AAA Medical Supply and turned in. There was a huge paved parking area clearly marked for customers and with lots of handicapped spaces. It was nearly full. Jack parked the rental car and locked it, heading for the sign designating the office.

Opening the door, he was greeted by an attractive young woman sitting behind a desk. He looked around the waiting room and was surprised. The interior was several notches above the neighborhood.

"May I help you?" she asked. She was wearing a tight, low-cut top that showed plenty of her ample cleavage. Jack wondered if that was part of the uniform.

"Yes. My name is Jack Davis. I'd like to see Mr. Crispino, please."

She flashed him a megawatt smile. "Did you have an appointment?"

He returned the smile, trying his best to match hers. "No, I'm sorry, I didn't. I was in Miami and wanted to talk to him about a mutual friend, Tony Budzinski. It'll only take a few minutes."

"Certainly. I'll check and see if he's in."

She picked up the phone as Jack stood there waiting. He knew Frankie was in since he'd called on his way over.

She hung up the phone and flashed him another phony smile. "He's busy at the moment, but if you don't mind waiting a few minutes? He shouldn't be long. Would you like something to drink while you wait?"

"Thank you, a black coffee would be wonderful."

He sat in a chair close to the reception desk and looked around the waiting room. It was packed with people exhibiting all kinds of problems, from oxygen bottles to wheelchairs to crutches and God knows what else that he couldn't see. He picked up a dated, well-worn copy of *People* and flipped through the pages, amazed at the content or more specifically, the lack thereof.

Halfway through the magazine, another young, big bosomed woman wearing a short, tight skirt, walked toward him with a cup of coffee. When she leaned over to hand him the coffee and introduce herself, he was afraid the scantily clad contents of her top were going to tumble out. *What a dress code*, he thought.

"I'm Sofia—Frankie's assistant," she said. She handed him the coffee with one hand and extended the other for a handshake.

"Thank you, Sofia. A pleasure to meet you."

"If you'll follow me, you can wait in his office. It'll be a little quieter there," she said.

He followed her past the reception desk and into the back offices. It was hard not to notice her hips, twisting from side to side as she walked on six-inch heels. She led him into a large, nicely furnished office and asked him to sit at the conference table.

A few minutes later, he heard the door open and looked over to see a man in a wheelchair entering the room.

"Mr. Davis. Thanks for waiting. So glad to meet you."

The man wheeled over and extended his hand. Jack tried not to stare.

"I'm Frankie. Frankie Crispino. My friends call me Frankie Crip. My enemies just call me Crip. Heh, heh, heh." His laugh was a big, belly-shaking laugh of exactly three beats.

Jack hesitated and shook his hand.

"What's a matter? Tony didn't tell you, huh? Never seen anyone in a wheelchair before? Who better to sell medical equipment? Heh, heh, heh."

"Sure." was all Jack could manage to say.

"How's Tony? What could I do for you?"

The man was irritating, to say the least. Jack politely waited for him to take a breath so he could state his business.

"Tony's not doing well at all. I just came from the hospital this morning, and between me and you, I don't think he's going to make it."

The news seemed to slow Frankie's motor for a heartbeat.

"Why? Tell me what's going on?"

Jack shook his head. "He's had a massive stroke and I'm not convinced he's going to recover. Which leads me to what I wanted to discuss. I understand you recently bought out Tony and Connie's interest in 1AAA?"

Frankie's mouth opened, then closed before speaking, which told Jack that his antennae were up.

"To put it bluntly, the check seems to be short," Jack said.

Frankie's expression turned suddenly darker. He folded his hands together and put them on the table before speaking.

"Mr. Davis, if you have any questions regarding that transaction, you need to speak with my attorney, assuming you have any right to do so."

Frankie's reaction was expected, so Jack plunged ahead.

"I don't think that's necessary." Jack leaned forward to emphasize his point. "All I am asking is that you give them their fair share."

Frankie sat up straighter, his confidence returning. "Based on the accountant's report, which I'm assuming you've examined, you should know that not only is what I paid them fair, but it also included a ten percent bonus in light of our relationship."

Jack smiled and shook his head. "I'm not protesting the financial condition of 1AAA. From what I know, it was fairly stated by a reputable accounting firm."

Frankie interrupted and pushed back from the table. "Well, then, I really must get back to work. Sorry, I don't have time to chat with you, but I think we're done here."

About that time, the office door opened, and a beefy guy with no neck walked in, wearing a sports coat that looked to be two sizes too small. He walked over to Frankie's side and turned to face Jack, puffing out his chest.

"Lorenzo will be happy to escort you to the front door," Frankie said.

Jack held up his hand. "I'm not done yet. Lorenzo may want to go get a cup of coffee first." Lorenzo bristled at the suggestion and Jack continued.

"I know who you sold the company to and for how much."

The color drained from Frankie's face. His eyes searched Jack's, trying to gauge how much Jack knew. Convinced there was more, he turned to Lorenzo. "Take a smoke break."

Lorenzo looked down at his boss, confused.

"Take a break. I'm okay."

Lorenzo hesitated, then nodded. He mustered the dirtiest look he could to give Jack on his way out the door.

As soon as the door closed, Frankie tried to regain the advantage. "Look, Davis, I'm not sure what your game is, but my financial records here at 1AAA are squeaky clean. You've seen the statements. If you or anyone else want to contest them, then knock yourself out."

He sat back, a smug grin on his face. Jack was about to wipe that off.

"Not arguing about that at all. You almost got away with it. I know Manuel Torres bought it and I know he paid you twice what it was worth. It's called 'money laundering' and it's highly illegal."

He watched as Frankie started to squirm, and then he delivered the knock-out punch.

"I'm going to give you a lifeline, Frankie. You write Connie Budzinski a check for half a million dollars. That's for what you screwed her husband—your friend—out of. She gets the check, you never see me again."

Frankie's face flushed red with anger. "You're fucking crazy. There's no way—"

Jack held up his hand. "Special Agent Dan Cox, with the FBI over in Miramar, is a personal friend. If Connie doesn't receive that check by the end of the week, then he's going to get an anonymous tip stating that a Frankie Crispino is going around complaining that Torres is laundering money. What do you think Torres will think of that?"

"You can't get away with this." Frankie's resolve was fading fast.

"Try me."

"How do I know you won't turn me in any way? Or, come back asking for more?"

Jack shook his head. "*I* don't intend to screw my friend. If I turn you in after you pay, they'll take the money away from Connie. As for coming back? I don't want your blood money. All I want is to see Connie taken care of. That's it."

Jack rose to leave. When he got to the door, he turned to face a shaken Frankie Crispino. "By this Friday. And . . . make it a cashier's check."

Three hours later, he was in Marathon. When he got to Mile Marker 50, just before the Seven Mile Bridge, he pulled over and shut the car off, getting out to stretch his legs. He stood, looking out over the expanse of water ahead encompassing the Atlantic Ocean on one side and the Gulf of Mexico on the other. He took a deep breath, inhaling the sweet aroma of salt air.

He had to admit, despite the hassles of traffic, the Overseas Highway was still one of the most beautiful drives in the world, a bucket-list trip. But it was even better to be on a sailboat on the water, with the love of your life.

He got back in the car and headed home, resolved that he was going to do everything in his power to see that he and Molly would be back together on *Left Behind*.

32

Randy smiled as he watched the Texan load his bicycle with a beach mat, small cooler, and tote bag. After he was satisfied everything was secure, he mounted the bicycle and pedaled away from the marina.

Randy turned and strolled back to his car. He was betting that the Texan was going out to Fort Taylor for some beach time. He'd followed him on a couple of occasions and knew that's where he liked to go, always alone. If previous trips were any indication, the man would go up to the far end of the beach where it was less crowded and take a nap on the sand.

In no particular hurry, Randy drove the short distance to the state park, paid his entrance fee, and went over to the parking lot next to the beach.

He found a parking spot close to the end and pulled in. He waited until a couple next to him left, then got out. From the trunk of his car, he removed a small cooler and a bag about four feet long, then locked the car. He pulled a rolled up beach mat halfway out of the bag and left the mat sticking out of the end. He picked up the cooler, slung the bag over his shoulder, and headed toward the trees next to the far end of the beach.

Once he knew where the Texan liked to go, Randy had come out here and scouted the area, looking for a good spot. He'd found the perfect location at the edge of the trees. It was within range of where the Texan usually went but somewhat isolated.

As he got closer, he saw a young woman with a little girl headed toward his spot. He picked up his pace and managed to arrive there first. Quickly, he set the cooler and bag on the picnic table, claiming it for himself. She stopped about fifteen feet away, giving him a dirty look. He shrugged and said, "Sorry." As she turned around and walked away he heard her mutter "asshole."

As he opened his bag and removed the contents, Randy looked toward the beach and saw Tex in his usual spot. He was stretched out on his back on a towel spread out over his mat. Randy shifted his gaze and saw Tex's bicycle propped up against a tree about forty feet away. About the same distance from Tex, farther down the beach, was an older couple, the nearest people to him or Tex.

Randy made a note of the slight breeze, coming from left to right. He removed a towel, potato chips, and a sandwich from the bag. Then, he took out a small, clear plastic tube containing three darts. Last, he removed a four-foot-long blowgun and laid it on the table next to the darts.

Most people didn't realize how accurate blowguns could be in experienced hands. He could routinely put a dart inside a two-inch circle forty feet away. They were cheap, silent, and completely legal in most states, including Florida.

The darts were tipped with curare, a plant-based poison. Over the years, Randy had perfected his recipe. It was fast-acting and more importantly, caused progressive paralysis. By the time the victim figured out what was happening, he was unable to verbalize or control his movements before losing consciousness.

He checked, and the Texan was still on his back. Randy pulled a beer out of his cooler, stuck it in a Koozie, and sat on the picnic table facing the water, eating his sandwich. When he finished, he unscrewed the tube containing the darts and pulled out a small bottle. Carefully, he opened the bottle and dipped the tip of the each dart inside, coating the point with the gooey substance. After giving it a minute to further congeal, he loaded one inside the blowgun and waited.

Soon, the Texan turned over on his stomach. As Randy waited for him to get settled and turn his face toward the water, he glanced around to make sure no one was coming toward them. Satisfied, he picked up the blowgun, held it down by his leg, and walked over to the spot near some brush surrounding a tree. He knelt down and checked around once more before raising the tube. He filled his lungs, held his breath, and put his mouth up to the mouthpiece as he aimed the gun. Holding both hands steady, he blew out, emptying his lungs.

The Texan jumped as if stung by an insect. Without moving his head, he moved his arm to his side to swat the bug. When his arm started moving slower, Randy stood, walked back to the picnic table, and calmly packed up to leave.

After he parked, Jack walked over to Nick's boat to return his car keys, but Nick wasn't there. He stuck them in his pocket and walked over to *Left Behind* to drop off his bag.

He called Nick and again, got no answer. He pressed Doug's number.

"Hey, are you back?" Doug asked.

"Just got here. Do you know where Nick is? I've tried calling and stopped by to give him his keys. He's nowhere to be found."

"Nope, haven't talked to him today. We still on for in the morning?"

"Absolutely."

"You sure about this, Jack?"

The three of them had hatched a plan the other night at DJ's. Jack was going out on his boat Sunday morning, to the same area where he and Molly had almost been hijacked by the two thugs. Doug and Nick were renting a go-fast boat and would hide in the Marquesas until Jack called them on the radio. They had agreed to lay low this evening and not be seen together, knowing someone was probably watching.

"Certain. See you out there. Don't be late."

"Okay. Be careful."

33

Early Sunday morning, Jack's alarm went off, but he was already awake, lying in his berth and staring at the sky through the hatch above. He shut the alarm off and got up.

After his customary morning pilgrimage to the head, he padded to the main cabin to get a bagel and coffee before he left. He turned the coffee maker on and sliced a bagel, smearing it with cream cheese. He stopped, staring at the pictures displayed on the digital photo frame. Molly had surprised him with it on his birthday and loaded it with hundreds of their favorite pictures.

He watched as the pictures flipped by, pausing for ten seconds or so on each one. A picture of Molly, Richard, and Jack popped up on the small screen. It was a picture they'd taken up on the beach at Cayo Costa State Park, just north of Captiva. The three of them had been the best of friends in Fort Myers. Richard had discovered that a pharmaceutical firm had changed the recipe for their blockbuster cardiac drug. In return, he'd been murdered.

He swallowed as the next picture replaced it. It was a picture of Jack and Molly, sitting on the back of *Left Behind*, just opposite Cabbage Key. They had their arms around each other and were grinning from ear to ear. It had been taken the morning after the night their relationship had changed forever, crossing the chasm from friendship to lovers.

He turned and poured a cup of coffee. It was time to put Clearwater behind them, completely. This was a wedge between him and Molly and had to be excised, like a cancer. Only then could he concentrate all of his attention on making amends.

He went topside and prepared to leave the dock. He laid the SIG on the helm, underneath a towel. The Ruger was in the pocket of his shorts. Minutes later, alone at the helm, he passed the jetty at the entrance of Key West Bight and turned left, heading out the Southwest Ship Channel.

Nick had insisted on radio communication between the two boats, even though there was a slight risk that Bobby was using a scanner and might pick up such transmissions. Cell phone service could be spotty out there, so Doug had suggested a couple of options which wouldn't show up on a scanner. The first was a UHF radio, but would only provide about a mile or so range. They decided on using Channel 78A on the Marine Band and keeping communications to a bare, as-needed basis. It was a frequency not normally used, and since it was VHF, it would have a range of five or six miles on the open water even from handheld radios.

Jack tried to keep from scanning the horizon more than normal in case anyone was watching him with binoculars. When he got out of the busy harbor traffic, he turned into the breeze and raised the sails. For a thirty-eight foot boat, *Left Behind* was surprisingly easy for one person to handle in normal conditions. All the lines led aft to the cockpit, and with roller-furling rigs, it was a snap to raise and lower the sails.

As agreed, he set course for the same general area south of the Marquesas Keys that he and Molly had gone to for lunch less than a week ago. He'd head out the Southwest Channel, then angle due west, taking him between Woman Key and Satan Shoal, then turn northwest toward the Marquesas.

In the much faster powerboat, Nick and Doug would leave later and loop north, going out the Northwest Channel and coming south on the other side of the Marquesas, using the group of islands as cover.

His phone chimed and he ignored it. A few minutes later, it chimed again, starting to irritate him. The third time, he snatched the phone up and looked at the screen. Three calls from Doug.

He pressed the button to call him back.

"Jack. Where are you? We've got a problem. Nick's not here."

"What do you mean?"

Doug explained that he'd tried to call Nick last night to confirm everything and was unable to reach him. He assumed Nick was out carousing and didn't think any more about it.

"I tried calling him before I picked up the boat this morning and still didn't get him. I didn't want to be late, so I got the boat and now I'm back at the Galleon. Nick's not here."

Jack checked the time. Although they were much faster, they had farther to go. He did a quick calculation and figured Doug needed to leave within the next thirty minutes.

"Keep trying to find him. You've got thirty minutes. I'll call you back."

He disconnected and looked around. As usual, there were lots of boats out on the water, but they were far away and none seemed to be taking any special interest in him.

He wondered what the hell was going on with Nick. It was unlike the Texan to be late and not call.

He turned the radio over to the weather channel and listened to the latest forecast. Last night, when he'd checked, a low was moving in tomorrow from the west, promising to dump lots of wind and rain on the Keys for the next few days.

Doug called back.

"I found him. He's in the hospital."

"What?"

Doug said that Nick had been darted and was in intensive care in Jackson Memorial in Miami.

"Darted? What the hell do you mean by darted?"

"He was shot with a poisonous dart, probably from a blowgun."

Jack slammed his fist against the wheel. The bastards had gotten Nick.

"How's he doing?"

"Not good. He's in a coma. Maybe we need to abort, Jack."

"We're not aborting. Those bastards got Nick and they're out here following me. I know it."

"Jack . . ."

"I'll be on 78 alpha."

He ended the call and switched the radio back to channel 78A. He was tired of screwing around with all of this. It was like a cloud hanging over him and he was ready to put this mess behind him.

A quick scan of the horizon still showed no boats close by, but he knew Bobby and Mike were out there somewhere. He sat at the helm holding the wheel, preferring to steer instead of turning the autopilot on.

He needed tunes. Scanning through the music on his iPhone, he settled on Stevie Ray Vaughan and cranked up the volume. "Shake for Me" filled the speakers on the boat. It was hard to play Stevie Ray softly.

On his right, a few miles away, there was a small island he figured must be Woman Key. He looked down at the GPS and confirmed it. That meant he was between Woman Key and Satan Shoal, about halfway to the Marquesas.

He set the autopilot and checked the SIG, making sure there was a round chambered and the magazine was locked in place. Placing it back underneath the towel, he went down below to get something to drink. After he took a soda out of the refrigerator, he decided to make a sandwich while he was below.

Singing along with Stevie Ray, he got out the ingredients for a turkey sandwich. While rooting around, he discovered an unopened bag of pretzels and a Ziploc bag containing a couple of chocolate chip cookies. Pleased with the additions to the lunch menu, he assembled his sandwich and put it on a paper plate along with the pretzels and cookies.

There was a brief silence between songs and he froze as he thought he heard something outside. He reached into his pocket and put his hand on the loaded gun as he cocked his ear toward the open companionway, straining to hear. All was quiet, then the high-energy opening of "The House is

Rockin'" caused him to jump. *Shit,* he thought, releasing the pistol, glad he didn't have his finger on the trigger.

He took a deep breath, laughing at his nervousness, and started bobbing his head to the beat of the music. He put everything up, grabbed his food, and started up the stairs to the cockpit.

When he stepped out on deck, he was surprised to see a powerboat idling quietly alongside *Left Behind.* Bobby was pointing a black pistol at him and Mike was driving.

"Gotta love these four-strokes," Bobby said, nodding toward the twin outboard engines on his boat. "Really quiet, aren't they?"

Jack looked around. Still no boats to be seen except in the far distance. *Where the hell did they come from?* They had to have been hiding in the mangroves on Woman Key. He cursed himself for letting his guard down. He looked at the radio on the helm and took another step.

"Stop right there, Davis. Another step and I'll shoot."

Jack froze, his mind searching for an out.

"You by yourself?" Bobby said.

Jack hesitated, wondering if it was a question or a statement. It was obvious no one else was on the boat, especially if they'd been watching.

"There's another boat, following me," Jack said.

Bobby looked around. "Must be one of those stealth boats. I don't see anything around, do you, Mike?" Mike shook his head, grinning.

"You're all alone and your buddy won't be driving up to save your ass today. Why don't you go sit down behind the wheel and keep your hands up where I can see them? You even think about touching that radio and I swear I'll shoot you. Stop the boat so I can come aboard."

Jack almost laughed. Clearly, Bobby didn't know anything about sailing. *That might be an advantage,* he thought. He went back to the helm and sat. He looked up at the sails as if evaluating the mechanics of complying with Bobby's request, then shook his head.

"Not that simple on a sailboat. You have to start the engine, then turn into the wind. Then, you have to let the sails down one at a time, starting with the headsail."

Bobby looked over at Mike, who shrugged as if to say, *Hell if I know.*

The truth was Jack was only making about three knots, so it wouldn't have been that difficult to drop the sails, but Bobby and Mike didn't know that.

Bobby looked up and down the length of the sailboat. "Well, just slow it down some."

Jack shook his head. "Well, to do that, I'd have to reduce some sail, probably starting with the big one up front. The problem with that is, then the boat goes too slow and the autopilot starts overcorrecting. When that happens, it starts swinging back and forth, kind of zig-zagging because it can't maintain a straight line."

"Goddammit, I don't give a shit about all the sailing talk. I'll just step over. Mike, pull up next to him." Bobby was getting impatient.

Mike eased the powerboat up alongside while Jack's eyes followed them. It was all he could do to not scan the water, looking for Doug, then he remembered he was supposed to meet him on the other side of the Marquesas, ten miles away.

"Keep your hands up, Davis." Bobby's voice was harder this time. "Don't even sneeze." Mike eased the boat closer until it bumped *Left Behind.*

Bobby put his pistol in his shorts and turned to Mike. "If he as much as twitches, shoot his ass." He checked to make sure his pistol was secure in the pocket of his shorts, then stepped up onto the gunwale of the center console. He held on to the T-top support, trying to time his move.

The powerboat drifted away a bit, leaving a gap of a couple of feet between the boats.

"Dammit, Mike, keep these sons-of-bitches together."

Mike turned the wheel of the powerboat to the left, bumping into the sailboat. This time, he kept the wheel turned into the sailboat, and they bumped along, scraping each other's sides.

Bobby scrambled over the lifeline, and down into the sailboat cockpit. He straightened up and looked at the lumpy towel on the helm table and grinned. He reached over, picked up the pistol, and pointed it at Jack.

"Nice gun. I see you were waiting for us."

Bobby reached into the pocket of his shorts and pulled out a couple of thick, black plastic zip ties that appeared to be a good eighteen inches long.

He eased closer and stuck one out for Jack. "Take this." Once Jack took it, he said, "Now, fasten your right hand to the steering wheel and pull it tight."

Jack risked a peek to each side and saw nothing but open water. A quick glance at the radio brought a rebuke from Bobby.

"Don't even think about it."

Jack got the tie around his wrist and the rim of the stainless wheel, somehow managing to fasten it with his left hand. Bobby pulled it tighter until Jack could feel it cutting into his wrist.

"Put your left hand on top of the wheel." When he had done so, Bobby set the gun down and quickly tied Jack's left wrist to the wheel.

"I think this is a better plan than before, don't you?" Bobby asked.

Jack stared at him, not answering.

"Since you know what I want, we can dispense with the preliminaries and get right down to bidness," he said, deliberately emphasizing the vernacular. "We can do this the easy way or the other way—up to you. The easy way is you just tell me where it is. I'll get it, verify it's all there, and we'll be on our way. Simple, right?"

"Who are you—really?"

"Not important, is it?"

"Why'd you dart my friend?" Jack was desperate to keep the conversation going.

Bobby cocked his head with a puzzled look. "What the hell you talking about?"

"You shot him with a blowgun."

Bobby chuckled. "What you been smoking? Ain't shot nobody with a blowgun."

Jack was surprised. Either the man was a pathological liar or he didn't know about Nick.

"That's right, you prefer a gun. You shot that couple out here, didn't you?" Jack said.

"You jerking my chain? No, you're stalling for time. Back to my question. The hard way or the easy way? In the end, I'm still going to get the money. Like you, I'm not a very patient man, so I'll give you a few seconds to think about it and then we'll start."

Jack's eyes darted around, still looking for the other boat. Hoping. He didn't know how much longer he could stall.

Bobby caught him looking and laughed. "You must be trying to figure out where your friend is?"

Jack's heart sank. He knew about Doug and that wasn't good.

"Right now, he's about ten miles from here. We're guessing he's headed toward the other side of the Marquesas to meet you." Bobby leaned close enough for Jack to smell his cigarette breath. "Like I said, you're all alone."

He leaned back and pointed the gun at Jack. "Time's up. What's it gonna be?"

"It's in the safe. I'll have to open it."

Bobby cackled and shook his head. "Do I really look that dumb? If it's a key, then tell me where the damn key is. If it's a combination, then tell me what it is. And before you tell me it requires your fingerprint, I should point out that I'll cut your fucking finger off if I need to. My patience is running out."

Jack stalled for as long as he could, then stammered, "It's a combination."

"And?" Bobby poked him in the chest with the barrel of the gun.

"24-37-16."

Bobby poked him again.

"Forward berth, behind the closet door."

Bobby grinned, turned, and walked through the companionway to the steps down into the cabin.

Since they already knew he was looking for another boat, Jack swiveled his head as far around as possible in each direction, hoping to see Doug. He knew he had precious little time, but he saw no other boat anywhere near them. The speaker on the radio squawked, and he recognized Doug's voice.

"On schedule. Confirm, over."

A minute later, Doug repeated the message. When Jack didn't answer, Doug would know something was wrong. But even in a boat going sixty miles per hour, he was still ten minutes away, even if he could find him.

Bobby emerged from the companionway, a frown on his face. He walked over and jabbed the pistol under Jack's chin. "You're fucking with me, Davis. That combination's no good, and you know it."

Jack's head was straining under the pressure of the gun barrel, pushing up into his chin. "24-16-37. I told you," he croaked, trying to talk with the gun pressing hard against his jaw.

Bobby pushed the barrel harder, making it difficult to breathe. "You told me 24-37-16. Which is it? And, this time, it better be right." He pulled the gun away and stepped over to the gunwale to talk to Mike. "Hand me the bolt cutters."

Mike reached down and pulled up a set of well-used bolt cutters that looked to be three feet long. He handed them to Bobby. Bobby set the pistol down on the seat, turned around, then opened and closed them in front of Jack's face.

Jack heard the squeak of rusty metal against metal, a thick coat of rust covering the metal jaws. He'd deliberately transposed the middle number of the combination with the last, trying to buy some precious time. He didn't think he could afford to do that again, especially since the money wasn't even in the safe.

Bobby opened the jaws of the tool, reached down and clipped the antenna cable going to the radio. "Damn, they're still pretty sharp." He set the bolt cutters on the seat and picked up the gun, letting it hang by his side. "Last chance for the easy way. You want to repeat that combination one more time?"

Jack swallowed, another bead of sweat running down his forehead and into his eye. He blinked and took one more look out on the water. He thought there was a boat there he hadn't seen before, coming this way, but he didn't want to stare.

"It's not in the safe."

"I ain't got all day, Davis. Where is it?"

34

Jack took a deep breath, knowing he was running out of time. Once Bobby figured out there was no money, he would kill him, just like he did Kenny and Valerie. *Where the hell was Doug?*

"It's in an old blue sail bag. In the locker underneath the port dining room settee."

"Goddammit, Davis. Don't give me that fucking nautical crap. I want English."

Jack hesitated, then said, "Left side, the seat behind the dining table."

"You better be right this time," Bobby said, as he turned and went down into the cabin once more.

Jack turned his head and saw a boat, headed toward them. Mike hadn't seen it yet. Jack knew the bag was jammed underneath several other things in the locker. But now it contained sails and no money. He heard Bobby throwing stuff down in the cabin as he searched.

"About time he found us," Jack said, loud enough for Bobby and Mike to hear. The noise in the cabin stopped. Mike grinned, apparently thinking Jack was trying to distract them. His smile quickly turned into a frown as he heard the boat approaching and turned to see what Jack was watching.

It was another white, center console boat, about the same size as Bobby's, heading straight toward them at high speed. *Doug cut it a little close,* Jack thought. He squinted to see, but there was only one person visible—a large, dark-skinned man driving. The boat slowed as it got closer. Mike looked as surprised as Jack. Whoever it was, it wasn't Doug.

"Bobby," Mike yelled. "We got company."

Bobby stuck his head out through the companionway and looked over at Mike. "Who the hell?"

"I don't know. Some big black dude."

"Shit," Bobby said, as he stepped up in the cockpit, his pistol at the ready. He had the blue sail bag in his other hand, unopened.

Jack closed his eyes for a second. *If he opens the bag, I'm screwed.* Nothing was in it but bundles of newspaper.

Bobby took one look at the boat coming around on the opposite side of *Left Behind* and shook his head. "Son of a bitch. What the fuck are you doing out here, Evens? Checking up on me?"

Evens? Jack thought.

"Ain nobody else dying," Evens said.

Bobby looked confused for a second. "What are you talking about?"

"What I said. You get what you came for, but no more killing."

Bobby laughed. "You got to be kidding me? You don't even have a gun. How the hell are you going to do anything?" He pointed the pistol at him. "I just might shoot you right now and be done."

The man called Evens grinned, the sunlight reflecting off a single gold tooth on the upper side of his mouth. "I don't tink you wanna do dat."

A scowl crossed Bobby's face. His bravado seemed to shrink a bit. "What are you saying?"

"I put everyting in a letter to my sista. I doan come home dis afternoon before she does, she gonna read it and call de law."

Bobby's eyes narrowed as he studied Evens's face, trying to determine if he was bluffing. "You're bullshitting me. You do that, you're going down, too."

Evens held his stare. "Doan care."

Bobby thought, then turned and pointed the gun at Jack. "How's that going to keep me from shooting him?"

Jack's stomach did a flip. This was not the way he wanted to die. He looked at Evens, who was still fixated on Bobby.

"You do dat, I'm comin over to get you. You'll have to shoot me. I done tole you, I doan care."

Jack stared at Evens, looking for a crack in his façade. He didn't appear to be bluffing. Jack looked over at Bobby, who was still trying to decide.

Bobby finally shook his head and lowered the gun. "You're fucked, you know that? Randy's going to have your ass."

Jack swallowed. *Randy?*

Evens shrugged. "Dat's not your business."

Bobby stared at Evens, then held up the blue sail bag in his hand. "Fuck it. This is all I was paid to do." He turned to Jack, pointing the gun at him. "You go running your mouth, we'll meet again." He nodded toward Evens. "He can untie you once we're gone."

Bobby threw the sail bag over into the boat with Mike. Just as he went to step over into the boat, Jack jerked the wheel of the sailboat as far right as he could, contorting his back to get it hard over.

The sudden movement caught Mike and Bobby unawares as the back end of *Left Behind* swung away from the other boat. A three-foot gap opened up between the boats and Bobby stepped off into thin air.

Mike's delayed response was to turn his boat to the right, forgetting that Bobby was now in the water in between them.

"Goddammit, Mike. Turn left, turn left." Bobby said, gasping for air as his head came up out of the water, only to see the two boats about to make a sandwich of him.

Jack looked over his right shoulder to see Bobby's head floating like a cork, starting to fall behind them as the boats continued forward.

"Don't worry about him right now, turn around and come get me, you dumb-ass," Bobby yelled.

Getting his bearings, Mike spun the boat around and headed back toward Bobby. Evens was still running alongside *Left Behind,* but now Jack had a new problem. He was cuffed to the steering wheel and the autopilot was engaged. Evens present or not, Bobby was probably going to kill them both once he got back onboard his boat.

"Evens," Jack yelled. "You've got to get over here and cut me loose." Evens looked at Jack as if he were crazy.

Jack tried to press the autopilot button with his foot to turn it off. If he could do that, the boat would head up into the wind, slowing it down enough for Evens to get on board.

He turned to see where Mike was. He was pulling up next to Bobby. It would only be a minute or two before Bobby was back on board his own boat.

Jack tried again to push the button but failed. *Fuck.* The angle wasn't right for him to get enough pressure on it to depress it.

He turned again to see where Bobby and Mike were. Suddenly, he heard Bobby scream. Although they had only put a few dozen yards between them, he knew by the sound that Bobby was in trouble.

"Evens. Get back here. I need you to help me get Bobby in the boat," Mike yelled.

Jack watched as Evens turned back toward the other boat, moving farther away. When Evens got back to them, Jack heard shouting and more screams from Bobby. He kept trying to figure out what was going on. Then he heard Mike say, "If you leave, I'm shooting your ass."

He watched as Evens's boat turned and started back toward *Left Behind.* Jack held his breath, waiting for the sound of gunfire.

"You get back here, now," Mike yelled.

When Evens pulled up next to him, Jack didn't waste time asking what happened. "Put your radio on Channel 78A and call for Doug. Tell him where we are. He can be here in ten minutes."

He heard Evens talking to Doug on the radio, giving him their location. Relieved, he heard his friend say he'd be there in six minutes.

"What happened back there?" Jack asked, nodding back toward Bobby and Mike.

"Box jelly."

Jack shook his head, at first, trying to understand what Evens was saying. Then, it dawned on him. Box jellyfish.

"Box jellyfish?"

Evens nodded. "Nothin to do."

"Who are you?" Jack asked.

"Jus somebody tryin to make tings right." He looked around the boat, then back at Jack. "You alright?"

"Yes, thanks to you." He heard the roar of a go-fast boat approaching and turned to see one headed toward them at a high speed. Doug.

He looked back at the center console boat and saw Mike shove the throttles forward, quickly getting the boat up on plane, heading toward Woman Key. Bobby was nowhere to be seen.

"I best be goin."

"Bobby said 'Randy.' Randy who?"

The big man stared at him.

"You doan wanna know." He eased his throttles forward until he was clear of Jack, then advanced them. Within seconds, the boat was up on plane and headed toward Key West.

A few minutes later, Doug was idling alongside.

"You okay?"

Jack explained his predicament.

Doug tied the go-fast boat to *Left Behind* and climbed aboard.

"Sorry it took me so long," Doug said, as he cut him free.

"I'm just glad you got here when you did," Jack said, rubbing his wrists and flexing his fingers. "The bad guy is on a twenty-five-foot center console with twin Honda four-strokes, headed toward Woman Key. Don't let him outta sight, but don't get too close. Call the Coast Guard, let them handle it."

"What about the other boat?" Doug asked. "The one headed toward Key West."

Jack shook his head. "If it wasn't for him, I'd be dead. I'll fill you in later, back at the dock."

Doug nodded. "What about you?"

"I'm going home. I've had enough boating for one day."

"Alright."

Doug stepped back onboard the powerboat. He untied and let it drift away from Jack's boat. As soon as it was clear, he pushed the throttles forward. The engine responded with a deafening roar, hesitated for a split-second, then shot out of the water up on a plane, headed northwest toward Woman Key.

Jack sat there and looked down at his hands. They were shaking.

After a few minutes, he turned the music and autopilot off. Setting his course for Key West, he trimmed the sails and settled in for the ride. He needed to evaluate the latest piece of the puzzle; Randy.

As he listened to the sound of *Left Behind* slicing through the water, he thought about it. Based on the conversation he overheard, Randy was the boss and apparently all three guys worked for him. But Randy who? And why wouldn't Evens tell him?

Movement on the water ahead caught his eye. He watched as a Coast Guard Response Boat screamed across the water a couple of miles away, with blue lights flashing, heading the same direction as Mike had gone.

He thought back to anybody he knew named 'Randy' and nothing clicked. He had an idea, picked up his phone and made a call.

"Wren?" he asked when she answered.

"Hey, Jack. How are you?"

He always smiled when he heard her cheerful voice.

"Pretty good, right now, since I'm out on *Left Behind*. How are you?"

"I'm jealous. You guys are out on the water and I'm headed to work."

She thought Molly was with him and he wasn't going to correct her at the moment.

"I won't keep you, I just wanted to ask you a quick question related to our conversation the other day. Do you know anybody named 'Randy' who might have been associated with Peabo?"

It was so quiet on the line that for a moment, Jack thought the call had dropped.

"Wren? You still there?"

"Randy is Peabo's half-brother."

35

Two hours later as he approached Key West, Jack furled the sails and started the diesel. He called Doug on the cell phone.

"Where are you?"

"Home, just got back from returning the go-fast. Damn thing cost me six hundred bucks to refuel it. Lisa will have a cow when she sees the credit card bill."

"Thanks, I'll pay you back, don't worry. I'm coming into the bight. Come on over to A&B."

Doug was waiting for him when he got to the dock. After Jack tied up *Left Behind* in her slip, he waved Doug aboard.

"Any news on Nick?" Jack asked.

"No change. I called Lisa on the way back to the marina."

"What happened out there? I saw the Coast Guard headed your way."

"I called it in, told them some crazy guy in a boat was shooting at people on the water. I didn't hang around, but based on what I heard, there wasn't much left of him or his boat. Guess he didn't recognize that was a machine gun on the front of the Coast Guard boat. I don't think those guys will be bothering you or anyone else."

Jack shook his head.

"They weren't the problem. They were just hired help."

He shared with him what he'd learned from Wren. Randy Jenkins was from Harlan, Kentucky. He was Peabo Watson's younger brother, same mother but different fathers.

Randy had worked with Peabo off and on over the years, learning the illicit drug trade. Not as ambitious as Peabo, he dropped out of the prescription business and started working with plant-based medications. That was why his name wasn't familiar to Jack and hadn't surfaced when Drager got caught.

"According to Wren, he worshiped Peabo."

Doug shook his head. "That's not good. So not only is he after the money, he wants revenge."

"I believe so."

"Where does the other guy fit in, the one in the boat that headed back here?"

"The guy that saved my butt? That was Evens, who worked on my refrigerator, the palm reader's brother. He's the one who planted the tracking device on my boat."

"Now I'm confused. I thought you said all three of them worked for Randy. Whose side is this Evens guy on?"

Jack shook his head. "Not sure, but he saved my life out there and the other two were not pleased with him interfering." He stood, looking at Doug. "There's one way to find out. Let's take a walk."

They walked up Duval to Mysterie's shop. Jack remembered it as the one he and Molly had passed what seemed like months ago. A tattooed young girl sat behind the counter and looked up when they entered.

"May I help you," she asked.

"Is Mysterie in?" Jack said. Doug was busy checking out the strange items on the shelves.

"She's busy right now."

"We'll wait."

He turned and casually looked at stuff on the shelves while he checked out the shop. The only other entrance besides the door to the street was a doorway with beads and a curtain at the rear of the tiny shop.

He made his way toward the door and pulled the curtain aside to peek in.

Tattoo girl jumped up from her seat and went over to Jack. "Hey, you can't go back there."

The curtain concealed a small room which held a round table and only two chairs. There was a closed door on the opposite side marked PRIVATE.

"Where does that go?" Jack asked, nodding toward the door.

She stepped between the door and Jack, crossing her arms. "That goes to her private residence. If you don't leave, I'm calling the cops."

Under different circumstances, Jack would've thought it humorous. He was a good six inches taller and probably a hundred pounds heavier than she was. He could have easily brushed her aside and walked past. However, she did not appear to be bluffing and wore the defiant expression of someone with street smarts beyond her chronological age.

Jack smiled. "You might want to check with your boss before you do that. We'll wait in the shop." He released the curtain, turned and walked back to Doug, standing in the middle of the shop, mouth agape.

Jack shrugged and busied himself looking at various objects on the nearest shelf, giving no hint of leaving.

Tattoo girl made her way back behind the counter, keeping a wary eye on both of them. She picked up her phone and punched in a number.

This is going to be interesting, Jack thought, figuring she was calling the police. She talked quietly on the phone and he made out the words "I think you need to come out front."

Minutes later, Jack heard a door close behind the beaded curtain. A striking lady with mocha-colored skin emerged, parting the curtain like smoke sifting through the openings between the strands. She wore a single, large gold hoop earring in her left ear and a flowing, multi-colored print dress. A bright orange scarf was tied around her head.

"I'm Mysterie," she said. Her voice was sultry and bore the distinct traces of the Caribbean. "Is there something I could help you with?"

"I need to speak to you." He glanced at tattoo girl, then back at Mysterie. "In private."

"I don't think that is—"

"It concerns your brother."

Her expression changed at the mention of her sibling. She turned and glanced at Doug, then looked back at him.

"He's with me," Jack said.

At last, she said, "Follow me." As she turned, she spoke to the wide-eyed girl at the counter. "Cassie, please see that we're not interrupted."

She led them back to a small covered patio facing a tiny courtyard. Out in the middle of the yard, there was a tree-like shrub probably six feet tall, with trumpet-shaped flowers hanging down like bells. The plant appeared to be raining flowers.

Jack noticed scuba gear against the wall. A couple of air tanks, fins, buoyancy vest, weights—even a bang stick. He chuckled. The only people he knew who used those were alligator hunters and ocean divers.

A bang stick was essentially a one-shot firearm designed to work underwater. The powerhead, or business end, was attached to a four or five-foot pole. It required direct contact with the target and relied on the muzzle blast, not the projectile itself, to do the damage. It was effective at short range with large animals like sharks.

"My brother's equipment," she said, noticing him checking it out.

She gestured to a small, round table with four chairs. When they were seated, she looked at Jack and asked, "What about my brother?"

Jack met her eyes and asked, "Evens, who works for Keys Marine, he's your brother?"

She hesitated, then nodded once without speaking, waiting for him to continue.

"Does he work for Randy Jenkins, too?"

Her right eye twitched and she stiffened for a second. He looked at Doug, who gave a slight nod. He'd noticed it too.

Jack looked back at Mysterie and thought about how to proceed. Clearly, she knew the name Randy, but he still wasn't sure whose side she or Evens was on.

"I'm not after Evens," he said, in a measured voice, wanting to gauge her response. Her head tilted ever so slightly, as if interested in what he had to say.

"Your brother saved my life today, out on the water." She was unable to mask her look of surprise. *She didn't know,* he realized.

"You saw Evens?"

"Two thugs, Randy's hired hands, would've killed me if it hadn't been for your brother. I got the impression that his interfering wasn't going to make Randy happy."

Jack watched her for a reaction and she started to say something, then stopped.

He glanced at Doug and saw another slight nod. Looking back at Mysterie, he waited for her to speak.

"What do you want?" she said.

"I need to know where to find Jenkins."

She shifted in her chair. "I can't help you."

"You can't or you won't?" Jack asked.

Mysterie stiffened again, and Jack knew he'd hit pay dirt. She crossed her arms over her chest and shook her head. "I'm sorry. There's nothing I can help you with."

"Look, I know your brother's a good man. I don't want trouble for him. I just want to know where to find Randy. An address, phone number, anything. That's all."

She didn't speak.

"Randy's got something on your brother, doesn't he?" Jack asked.

He upper lip quivered just a fraction, but she kept her arms crossed and didn't speak.

He thought about how much to tell her, still unsure of her allegiance. She was protecting her brother, that much was certain.

The three of them sat there in silence for a minute. When it was obvious she wasn't going to talk to them, Jack looked at Doug and gave a slight nod toward the door.

Jack rose, took out one of his business cards, and handed it to Mysterie. "Jenkins is a very dangerous person. I hope your brother knows what he's doing. If you change your mind, give me a call."

As soon as they stepped out on Petronia Street, Doug said, "You gotta call the cops."

"The thought has occurred to me, but what exactly am I going to tell them? Bobby and Mike are dead. Nick's in the hospital in Miami. Evens is in hiding somewhere and she's protecting her brother. I've got *nada,* zilch."

"What are you going to do?"

"I don't know. We've got to find Jenkins, somehow."

"We?"

36

Mysterie looked down at the business card she was holding. Jack Davis. Evens had rescued him from two of Randy's boys out on the water. She tried to call her brother again, but no answer.

He still wouldn't tell her where he was hiding. She'd talked to him once since Friday and Randy had called twice looking for him. Now, two others were looking for him.

His diving equipment was still on the patio, so she knew he was still on the island. Evens loved to dive, and he wouldn't have left it here if he was gone. She just wished she knew where he was.

She closed her eyes and tried to concentrate.

A storm was coming and she was afraid of what it was bearing. Bad things, but she couldn't see what they were.

She had to find Evens.

Randy was pissed, sitting alone at his usual watering hole in Old Town, trying to keep his temper under control. For the last several hours, he'd been trying to get in touch with Evens, Bobby, and Mike with no success.

Yesterday, when they got the signal that Davis was going out on his sailboat, Randy had sent Bobby and Mike after him to get the money. He'd explicitly told them to do whatever they needed to succeed.

They had agreed to meet Randy back at the Stock Island house before dark. As insurance, he'd called Evens and told him to make sure the pair didn't get any other ideas. He didn't completely trust any of them but figured Evens was the most frightened of the three and less likely to defect.

Several hours before dusk, the tracking app had showed Davis's boat back at A&B, so Randy had waited for them at the house. Night came, but Mike and Bobby were nowhere to be found. Neither had answered their phone when he called.

When he'd called Evens, there was no answer either. Smelling a rat, Randy had gone down to the bight to see if Davis's boat was actually at the marina. Davis was back in his slip, on his boat with the guy from the sailboat over at Key West Bight Marina. It appeared to be business as usual with no indication that anything was amiss.

He tried reaching his crew again, and still no answer. Maybe they'd had boat trouble, but that didn't explain why they wouldn't answer their phones. He was beginning to wonder if they had double-crossed him and taken off with the money. After discreetly asking around, he picked up a rumor that someone on a boat had been shot and killed out near Woman Key that afternoon.

Details were sketchy, but apparently a lone white male in a center console had tried to outrun the Coast Guard and made the fatal mistake of firing shots at them. Either he didn't recognize that the contraption on the front of the Coast Guard boat was a machine gun or he panicked.

Nobody would ever know since he didn't survive the encounter to tell his side.

While the vague description of the boat involved matched Bobby's, something didn't add up. If it was Bobby, where was Mike? All accounts agreed there was only one person on board.

His phone rang and he looked at the screen. It was Evens.

Randy wasted no time in ripping into him. "About damn time. Where the hell have you been?"

"Bobby and Mike are dead."

That wasn't the response Randy was expecting.

"What the fuck you talking about?"

Evens told him that Bobby fell overboard and was stung by a poisonous jellyfish. Mike was shot and killed when he fired on the Coast Guard.

"How do you know all this?"

"I was there."

"There? Where?"

"Out on the water. When dey stopped that sailboat. I tole them dey not going to hurt nobody else."

If what Evens was telling him was true, it meant the whole operation was blown. And Davis still had the money. It couldn't be right. Bobby would've shot Evens.

"You're lying. Why would Bobby listen to you? You don't even have a gun."

"Doan need no gun. Dat sailboat back, ain't it?"

Randy swore under his breath. Evens wasn't smart enough to make up a story like this. He silently counted to five.

"Where are you? We need to talk."

There was a deep chuckle on the other end.

"Dey nothin to talk about. You doan have no friends, no boat, no money. You next," he said, disconnecting.

Randy slammed the phone down so hard, it cracked the screen. He finished his beer and pulled a roll of cash out of his pocket. He peeled off a twenty, threw it down on the table, and stormed out of the bar in a rage.

Out on the sidewalk, he lit a cigarette. He reached down and felt the bulge of the pistol in his pocket as he turned and walked toward Petronia Street.

"You're a dead man, Evens," he muttered to himself.

He walked with purpose, but by the time he got close to Mysterie's shop, he had cooled off enough to realize he needed to think this through. This could be a trap. He was not going to let that black bastard goad him into doing something stupid. No more misfires.

A block away from her shop, he stopped and lit another smoke. He could see her shop. It was tempting, but he forced himself to take a deep breath. He'd deal with Evens and his witchy sister later, but now he needed to stay focused on his priorities. Family first.

He turned around and headed back to his car.

Jack Davis was one lucky son of a bitch, but his luck was about to run out. Randy grinned. Family first can cut both ways.

Jack walked up Duval Street to Seth's shop, but it was closed. He looked in through the glass door. All the lights were off, except for the ones in the window, and there was no sign of anybody inside. He backed away and looked at the door. HOURS 10-6 MON-SAT. He checked his watch. 6:26.

He turned around and stopped to think about how to get to Seth's house from here. He had to talk to Molly. He'd called several times and she wouldn't answer. He walked down to Fleming and turned right. When he got to William Street, he recognized where he was and soon found the house.

When he knocked on the door, Lee, the chef answered.

"Lee? Hi, I'm Jack Davis, Molly's—"

"I know you." He stood there in the door, not inviting Jack in.

"Look, I need to talk to Molly. It's very important."

About that time, Seth walked up behind Lee. "Hello, Jack."

"Hi, Seth. Sorry to drop in unannounced. I stopped by your shop, but you were obviously closed, so I came here."

"What could I do for you?" Neither offered to let Jack in.

"Molly is in danger. I'm worried about her and wanted to let her know."

The two men looked at each other. Seth gave his partner a slight nod, then stepped out on the porch. Lee disappeared inside.

Seth held his hands up. "She's not here."

"Not here? Where—"

"Don't panic. She's at work. They called her in and she left about ten minutes ago."

"Which way did she go? We need to—"

"Please. Jack. Calm down. She took our car, she's okay."

"Your car?"

Seth explained that they had given her use of one of their cars as long as she was staying there. She'd been driving to work and not taking her bicycle.

Jack breathed a sigh of relief. "Thank God."

"You mind telling me what this is all about?"

Unsure of how much he knew, Jack gave him the abbreviated version. The brother of the drug dealer who had kidnapped Molly was in Key West and seeking revenge. Molly was in danger.

"Have you notified the police?"

On the way over, he'd thought about his answer to that question, knowing it was probably forthcoming. He wasn't prepared to go into that with Seth.

"Not yet. I just found out this afternoon. The first thing I wanted to do is alert Molly."

All of that was true.

"I'll let her know, but she's safe here. We have a state-of-the-art alarm system in the house with 24/7 monitoring."

Seeing Jack's skeptical expression, he continued. "Looks can be deceiving. Lee and I both are certified firearms instructors and have won numerous medals for marksmanship. I can assure you we are well-armed and know what to do."

Jack shook his head. "I'm sorry, I didn't mean to imply—"

"No offense taken. We find that the stereotypes work to our advantage on occasion. Don't worry, she'll be fine."

"Thanks, Seth. Would you tell her . . ."

"I will. Have a good evening, Jack. Now, if you'll excuse me, I'll get back to my dinner."

Jack walked back toward the bight, embarrassed by underestimating Seth's and Lee's abilities. They were probably better equipped to protect her than he was.

He realized he now had a slight advantage over Randy: he knew who Randy was. Randy had operated with impunity so far, relying on the fact that neither Jack nor Molly knew him. Maybe he could use that to his advantage somehow.

The marina office was closed when he got back. He'd intended to ask Terry if he had any contact information for Randy, but it would have to wait until morning.

When he got back to the boat, he sat out on deck, watching the people milling about on the boardwalk. Music from several different places drifted across the water, entangled with laughter and bits of conversations.

He wondering if Randy was watching him. He hoped so because he wanted Randy to see that he had survived this afternoon and was still here.

He sat there until midnight, running through different scenarios. He kept returning to notifying the police. That's what Tony and probably Nick would've advised him.

When he went down below, he closed the companionway and rigged a pot as a noise-maker if anyone tried to come in. Before he turned out the light, he checked his pistol to make sure it was locked and loaded. Satisfied, he placed it under the pillow next to his, Molly's pillow.

He was done being on the defensive.

37

As he got ready to go for his morning run, Jack looked up and saw Detective Stevens walking down the dock toward *Left Behind*. She was carrying the worn blue sail bag that Bobby and Mike had taken from him yesterday.

"Detective. Good morning."

"Mr. Davis. You have a few minutes to chat?" Stevens said.

"Sure. I was just going out for my run. You're welcome to come aboard, as long as you don't mind taking off your shoes." He tried not to look at the bag in her hand.

Stevens slipped her flats off and stepped aboard.

"Have a seat. Could I get you anything to drink? Soda, water?"

"Water would be nice, thank you."

Jack went below and returned with two bottles of water. "What could I do for you?"

Stevens hefted the sail bag up and set it on the cockpit table.

"This belongs to you," she said.

"Me? What makes you think—"

She pointed to faded black letters stenciled on the side. *Left Behind.*

"We recovered it from a boat yesterday. Out near Satan Shoal."

There was no denying it belonged to him. The question was *How did it end up on the boat with Mike?* He had to be very careful here.

Jack nodded as if the answer just came to him. "It must have been stolen when they broke into my boat. You found the thief, huh?"

She studied him for a moment, then continued.

"Coast Guard got a call yesterday afternoon. Somebody reported a guy on a boat harassing people at gunpoint. They went out to investigate, the guy started shooting at them. Big mistake. Coasties shot back. We got called out, and found this on the boat."

"Just an old sail bag, guess that's why I didn't realize it was missing. Did you arrest the guy?"

She shook her head. "He didn't survive." She glanced over at the bag, then looked back at him. "Fascinating, the contents. It's full of small bundles of newspaper. Almost the size of paper money."

He feigned disinterest, not saying anything and waiting her out.

She pulled out a form, slid it across the table to Jack, and produced a pen. "We need you to sign this, which shows we gave it back to you."

He signed the form where she indicated and handed it back to Stevens.

"Thanks, but I really haven't missed it."

"Maybe when you went out would, huh? Have you been sailing lately?"

He studied her face, trying to figure out what she knew, but her expression didn't give anything away.

"Actually, I went out for a bit yesterday. By myself. It was a nice day, and with the front coming in this afternoon, figured I'd take advantage of the nice weather while I could."

She nodded. "Yeah, I don't blame you. Where did you go, anywhere in particular?"

He shrugged. "Not really. Out toward Satan Shoal, turned around and came back. Just wanted to get out on the water. Sailing is my therapy."

She laughed. "Maybe I should try it."

He started to mention seeing the Coast Guard boat and then realized he was talking too much. He tried to suppress a smile. Just what the detective wanted. She was good. He hated being disingenuous with the cops, but he wasn't ready to say anything just yet.

Without taking her eyes off of his, she said, "Looks like you got some rope burns on your wrists. You should be more careful."

He felt his face flush and resisted the effort to look down at them.

"Thanks for bringing the bag by," he said.

She watched him for another few seconds, then rose and moved to step off of the boat.

"Thanks for the water."

On the dock, she slipped her shoes back on and looked up at Jack.

"Let me know when you're ready to tell the truth," she said, turning to leave.

Jack watched her walk away. She was halfway down the dock when he called her to come back.

* * *

"You got a little while?" he asked as she stepped aboard. "I think someone is trying to kill me."

Detective Stevens pulled out her notebook and sat across from him, waiting for him to speak.

He started with going out for a sail yesterday. Somewhere near Satan Shoal, he turned around to head back to Key West. He went down below to prepare lunch and with the music blaring, he hadn't heard a boat approach. When he came up on deck, two men in a center console had guns pointed at him.

He recognized them as Bobby and Mike, the same two good ole boys who'd stopped to ask for directions when he and Nick Campbell had been out just a few days ago. Other than that, he'd never seen them before.

"Then what?"

"The one named Bobby boarded my boat and took the pistol I had on the cockpit table."

Stevens interrupted. "You always keep a pistol up on deck?"

He shook his head. "No, but I was out by myself and with what happened to Kenny and Val ... I was being cautious."

She asked for details about the pistol, making more notes, then asked, "What happened next?"

He told her about Bobby tying his wrists to the wheel and cutting the antenna cable to the radio, pointing to the still severed cable in front of them as proof. While Mike kept his gun pointed at him, Bobby went down in the cabin.

"I heard him rummaging through things and assumed he was looking for stuff to steal. Then, another boat approached and Mike called for Bobby."

"Tell me about the other boat."

Jack told her about Evens and described the exchange between the men, careful to portray Evens as a Good Samaritan.

"Bobby had this bag with him and tossed it over to the other boat. When he tried to step over to the powerboat, I jerked the wheel hard over and he fell into the water."

Stevens set her notebook down and stared at him.

"Why did you act like you didn't recognize it a few minutes ago?"

He held her gaze. "I honestly didn't know it was the same one. Yesterday, I was tied to the wheel of my sailboat, two men with guns pointed at me. I really wasn't paying a whole lot of attention to the details of what he took. I was too busy trying to figure out a way to avoid being killed."

She stared for a few seconds longer, then picked up her notebook.

"How did you know this Evans?"

He shook his head. "Evens with an E, not Evans, and I didn't know him. I heard them call him by name and they pronounced it with a long E. That's how I know, but I'd never seen the guy before."

As she wrote, she said, "Bobby's in the water. Then what."

"Mike pulled away in their boat and turned around to go retrieve Bobby. Remember, I was still underway, so they were behind me, drifting farther away. A couple of minutes later, I heard Bobby screaming bloody murder. Evens went to help, then came back and told me that Bobby had been stung by a box jellyfish and there was nothing he could do."

Stevens looked back through her notes.

"If they were going to kill you, why didn't they just shoot you when you came up on deck?"

Jack shook his head. "I don't know. Maybe they were supposed to take me back to Randy."

She nodded, but he wasn't sure if she agreed or not.

"Let me get this straight. Bobby's in the water, Mike went back to get him. Evens is now back at your boat, right?"

Jack nodded.

"Lead me through what followed."

Jack told her that Doug had come by in a go-fast he was renting for the afternoon. He'd spotted what he thought was Jack's boat along with two others and had come over to investigate.

With Doug closing in, Evens left in one direction, and Mike took off in the other, minus Bobby. When he got there, Doug untied him from the steering wheel. Jack had instructed him to call the Coast Guard and go on back to Key West. Doug placed the call anonymously because he didn't want his wife to know about the powerboat.

Jack and Doug had rehearsed this story yesterday evening.

Stevens looked skeptical. She put her notebook down again and studied his face.

"Exactly why didn't you report this yesterday?"

He paused before answering, nodding toward her notebook. "I panicked, I guess. Remember, I'd been told Bobby was dead and I didn't know who any of these people really were. I wanted some time to try and figure things out before I called so I didn't look like a paranoid fool. Don't forget, I tried to tell you earlier that I thought things were related to the episode in Clearwater and nobody believed me then."

He saw her look of disbelief and added, "I was still sorting things out this morning when you walked up and caught me off guard. I apologize." He started to add that it wouldn't have made any difference, but he wanted to make nice.

She retrieved her notebook, apparently deciding to leave that be for the moment.

"Tell me about Randy Jenkins and why you think he's trying to kill you."

He recounted the story about Wren and Molly being kidnapped by Peabo Watson, the notorious drug dealer up in Clearwater.

"When I heard Bobby and Mike mention 'Randy,' I couldn't think of anybody I knew by that name so I called Wren."

He told her what Wren had told him about Peabo's half-brother, Randy Jenkins. He gave her Wren's contact information and encouraged her to call for verification.

"When she said 'Randy Jenkins,' I realized that he was the man I'd met a few weeks ago at the marina. I've seen him around the bight a few times, but I have no idea where he lives or anything else about him other than what I've just told you. I never heard the name before I met him and when I talked to Wren."

"Anything else?"

"Yes, I'm worried about Molly. You know we're separated. She's staying with a couple that has a house over on William Street. I went over there last night to see her.

She was at work, so I explained the situation to Seth, one-half of the couple."

Stevens wrote down the information, then closed her notebook.

"I'll get the word out at roll call so everyone on duty is aware of what's happening. I'll also see what we can find out about Mr. Jenkins, check if he has any outstanding warrants or priors. Absent that, there's not a whole lot we can do other than have a little chat with him, let him know we're watching." She stood to leave.

"If you think of anything else, give me a call. You did the right thing, Mr. Davis."

I hope so, he thought as he watched her walk away.

38

Randy sat in his car in the parking lot at Lower Keys Medical Center. He'd gone by the house where Molly was staying and the tiny green car was missing. On a hunch, he figured she was probably at work.

He knew the nursing staff usually worked twelve-hour shifts, either seven-to-seven or three-to-three. Molly was working seven a.m. to seven p.m. today and he checked to make sure the tiny green car she'd been driving was in the employee lot.

He also knew she had an appointment with Mysterie at eight tonight. He'd got the waitress at the Old Town Bar to call, claiming she was Molly and had misplaced her calendar. The girl who answered the phone was happy to look it up and remind her of the appointment tonight at eight.

He checked his watch. 7:25 *Soon,* he thought.

He lit a cigarette and watched as the security guard for the hospital made his rounds. If asked, Randy was going to say that his sister was visiting a girlfriend and he was just waiting outside.

"Excuse me, sir. There's no smoking allowed on the hospital premises."

Randy started to make a smart-ass remark, then thought better of it.

"Sorry."

He mashed the cigarette out in the console ashtray, then held up an empty hand.

"Thank you. Have a good evening," the guard said as he walked off. He didn't even ask why Randy was sitting in his car.

It was already dark outside when Molly had finished her shift report and was headed to her car. She smiled as she realized she was starting to call the green Smart car 'hers.'" While she enjoyed riding her bike to the hospital, she had to admit it was nice to have a car when it was dark or raining.

She spoke to Allen, the security guard, as she neared her car. After her conversation with Seth last night, she was more alert than usual and was relieved to see Allen close by. He watched as she got in the car, started it, and pulled out of the parking lot. Molly waved to him as she drove by.

Seth had told her about Jack's visit. It had upset her and she'd been tempted to call Jack last night, but decided against it. She knew she couldn't avoid talking to him forever, but she needed to finish getting her thoughts together first.

The name Randy Jenkins sounded vaguely familiar to her, but she couldn't place it. Even though Jack had told Seth that Randy was Peabo's brother, she couldn't place it in the context of what happened up the coast. Probably sounded like the name of a patient she'd had or something along those lines.

As she headed into town, she was excited about her appointment tonight with Mysterie. Molly had formed a bond with the palm reader and was making steady progress in dealing with the ghosts in her past. Mysterie was understanding and patient and seemed to have a sixth sense about how far to go with Molly at each session.

She considered driving directly to Mysterie's, but wanting to respect her hosts' generosity, she went to their house instead. Seth and Lee had been extremely gracious and kind. Besides, it was a pleasant evening and the walk would do her good.

Inside the house, she greeted the two men out on the patio, where she usually found them this time of day.

"Just in time for cocktail hour," Seth said, standing to give her a peck on the cheek. "I just got in myself. How was work?"

Lee started to pour her a glass of wine, and Molly placed her hand over the empty glass.

"I've got an appointment with Mysterie at eight, so I'll pass." She'd been very open about her visits to the palm reader and if they had opinions on the subject, they'd not expressed them to her.

"You should've just gone straight there from the hospital," Lee said.

"Thank you," Molly said, "but it's only a few blocks and the fresh air will do me good."

Seth pushed his chair away from the table and started to rise. "I can walk you—"

Molly placed her hand on his shoulder and pushed him back down into his seat.

"Don't be silly. Enjoy your wine. I'll be fine, I promise."

Seth gave her a frown, then smiled. "Okay, but stay on your toes. And call us if there is the slightest hint of anything that doesn't look right."

She blew them a kiss. "I'm going upstairs to change and I'll let myself out. Later."

Randy watched as Molly walked down the steps of the house on William and headed toward Petronia. He could've easily hit her with the blowgun, but that wasn't what he wanted. She was bait.

He followed her from the hospital, wondering if she would go to the house first or straight to Mysterie's. When he saw her turn toward the house, he kept driving and parked near Petronia and walked over to William.

This was perfect, and he was glad he'd taken the time to come up with a plan.

Mysterie had done a reading earlier that evening. The young woman was recently divorced, in Key West with her girlfriends to celebrate her newfound freedom. Mysterie had trouble concentrating and knew she didn't do as good a job as normal. The woman seemed delighted, though, and was happy for the little information she received at the session.

At five minutes after seven o'clock, Cassie totaled out the register, closed the front door, and hung the closed sign up.

"You need anything else before I leave?" Cassie asked, poking her head through the strands of beads.

"No, thanks, Cassie. Have a good evening."

"You, too."

Mysterie heard the chime sound and the door close. She called Evens again, but it went straight to voice mail. This time, she left a message.

"I'm worried about you. Please call me or come by. The shop is closed, but I have a reading at eight and should be done by nine."

She disconnected and went into the shop where she busied herself checking in several boxes of new inventory and completing sales tax returns for the month.

At ten minutes before eight, the door chime sounded. It was Molly.

"Hello, Molly," Mysterie said as she opened the door.

"Hi. I'm early. Hope that's not a problem."

She smiled. "No, let me finish this last box and we'll get started."

"No problem. Anything I can help you with?"

Mysterie started to say "No," then figured *Why not?* She took out the packing slip and handed the small box to Molly. "Third shelf from the bottom on the far wall. If you'll put them out, I can go ahead and enter this in the computer."

Molly took the box and walked over to the other side of the small shop.

"How have you been?" Mysterie asked.

"Okay. I heard from Jack last night."

Mysterie froze, her fingers over the keyboard in midstroke. "Jack?"

Molly smiled. "Yes, Jack. My husband. I thought I told you his name before?"

Mysterie's mind was racing. "Uh, maybe. If you did, I'm sorry, I'd forgotten it." *Maybe it was another Jack.* "What did he want?"

Molly stopped putting the books on the shelf. "He thinks somebody here on the island may be out to hurt us."

"Why?"

"I told you about what happened up the coast with the drug dealer. Jack is convinced that the dead guy's brother is out for revenge and he's tracked us to Key West."

His phone vibrated and Jack looked at the screen before answering. The number was blocked. He started not to answer, then thought it might be Detective Stevens.

"Hello?"

"Davis. I think you know who this is." There was a pause on the line. Jack's heart sunk. It was Randy Jenkins.

"What do you want?"

Randy laughed. "Time to cut the bullshit. I know you're here in Key West." He paused for a few beats. "And so is your boat. You know what I want. And, it better all be there. We're going to count it. Show up alone, and I mean alone, at the palm reader's at 8:30 sharp. Don't call the cops or bring anyone else. I get the money, you get your bride."

"How do I—"

The call ended. In a few seconds, his phone chimed, indicating a message.

The message had a short video attached. It was Molly, sitting in the little room off of Mysterie's shop. Her head was tilted and her eyes were glazed. She was moving, but like she was in a fog. He looked at the time. 8:00. He had thirty minutes.

39

Twenty-eight minutes later, Jack walked up to the door of Mysterie's shop carrying a faded red sail bag. The CLOSED sign was hanging in the window and the lights were out. He tried the doorknob and it was unlocked. Slowly, he opened the door.

"Hello?" he said, as he stuck his head in. No reply. He stepped inside and closed the door behind him, hearing it click. He waited, trying to hear something, anything, but there was nothing.

He walked across the shop and through the beaded curtains into the little room where Molly had been photographed. No one was there. It was darker, with only the ambient light from the shop leaking in between the columns of beads.

He walked over to the door marked PRIVATE and tried the doorknob. It, too, was unlocked. He walked through and before he could close it, he felt the cold steel of a gun barrel poking into his neck. He froze.

"Don't move." It was Randy's voice, coming from behind the door and on Jack's left.

Jack felt a hand expertly frisking him. Once Randy was satisfied that he was clean, the gun barrel slid around to the back of his neck and Randy closed the door.

"I'll take this." Randy took the sail bag from Jack and prodded him with the gun to move forward.

When they walked out on the patio, Jack's heart skipped a beat. Molly was tied to a chair, her head tilted to one side, and her mouth open. Her eyes were glassy and unfocused. He could see her chest moving with shallow breaths.

Next to her was Mysterie, also tied to a chair. She was alert, her eyes piercing, and focused on every move Randy made. Her eyes radiated pure hatred.

Jack breathed a sigh of relief when he saw the diving equipment still on the patio, next to the wall. The bang stick was propped up against the wall, powerhead down, and the safety pin inserted. He only hoped it was loaded.

Randy led Jack over to an empty chair next to Molly. "Sit."

"Don't you want me to open the bag so you can see?" Jack said, still standing, stalling.

Randy looked down at the bag, then back up at Jack. He grinned and shook his head. "You must really think I'm stupid. I'm going to hand the bag to you and let you open it so you can reach inside and grab the gun or whatever it is you've stashed inside?"

Jack held his breath, trying to will Randy to open the bag while he was still free to move. He had gone by Doug's on the way over, and the two of them had cobbled together a plan in the span of a few minutes.

Randy set the bag on the table in front of everyone and waved the gun at Jack. "Sit down."

"I thought you were going to open the bag?" Jack asked, still not moving.

"I am," Randy said, "but first, I'm tying your ass to the chair." He pointed his pistol at Jack. "I'm not telling you again."

Jack turned and looked at the chair he was supposed to sit in. It was an all-plastic chair, green, the kind you see at any of the big-box stores in the patio section. Not particularly sturdy, but adequate. If his arms were tied to the chair arms, there would be little chance of getting loose in time.

Randy pulled out a black plastic electrical tie and handed it to Jack. "Tie your wrist to the chair arm."

Moving as slow as he dared, Jack reached out with his left hand and took it from Randy.

"The money's not in there," Jack said.

Randy cocked his head and looked at him.

"What did you say?"

Jack glanced down at the watch on his left wrist. Three more minutes to go. "The money is not in the bag."

Randy grabbed the bag and ripped the zipper open. He reached in and pulled out bundles of newsprint. In a rage, he pointed the gun at Jack.

"Where. Is. The. Money?"

Deliberately keeping his hands on the arms of the chair so as not to draw Randy's attention, Jack said as calmly as he could, "Don't shoot. Hear me out."

He kept talking, hoping to buy time.

"My phone's in the bag. A guy with the money—not the cops—is standing on the porch with the money. Call him and he can show it to you."

Randy jabbed the pistol barrel against Jack's temple hard enough to hurt. "If you're lying to me—"

Jack winced and tried to stay calm. "I swear, I'm not. I was afraid that if I walked in here with the money, you'd kill us both, so I left it outside with a friend."

"What's to keep me from killing you both now?"

"I know you what you want. You want the money and me. Here's the deal. You let Molly go. You've got me, just let her go."

Randy reached into the bag and pulled the phone out.

Encouraged, Jack said, "Just press the button marked Doug." He couldn't see the phone, but heard Doug answer. "Show him the money, Doug," Jack yelled. "Show him the money."

Doug had photoshopped the picture of the money over the live video of Doug standing on Mysterie's front porch. Jack didn't understand how he did it and didn't care, as long as Randy would buy it.

He watched Randy's expression. Randy's face lit up when he saw the money. He heard Doug yelling, "See, here it is, right here in the bag. I'm on your front porch."

Jack glanced at his watch. *Time up*. Doug would call 911 as soon as Randy hung up.

Randy disconnected the call and turned to face Jack. He handed Jack the phone.

"See?" Jack said. "The money's all there, just let Molly go."

Randy grinned. "New rules." He walked over to Molly and stuck the gun up to her temple.

"What are you doing?" Jack screamed. "The money's there, right outside—"

"Like I said, new rules. Call your friend and tell him to bring the money inside. I'm going to count to ten and if I don't hear that door open, your little red-headed bitch is dead."

No, no, no, no, no, Jack thought. *Please God, don't.*

"Ten."

Jack picked up the phone, hand shaking. There was a beeping sound as Doug's phone rang. *Shit,* he was on the phone, probably to 911.

"Nine."

He hung up and called again. Still busy.

"Eight."

Damn, why didn't he just call himself? He dialed 911.

"Seven."

Just as 911 operator answered, Jack heard a primal scream come from the opposite side of the patio.

"Six."

In a blur, Evens crashed through the door running full speed toward Randy, his arms outstretched to tackle the smaller man.

"Evens," Mysterie screamed at the top of her voice.

Momentarily confused, Randy hesitated before swiveling the gun toward Evens. The hesitation cost Randy the advantage as Evens hit him chest high before he could get the gun pointed at the big man.

Evens drove him several feet past the table, lifting him off the deck, and trying to drive him into the ground. Somehow, Randy managed to hold on to the gun and was attempting to point it at the larger, heavier man on top of him.

With one wrist tied to the chair, Jack struggled to stand. Dragging the chair behind him, he grabbed the bang stick with his free hand. He pulled out the safety pin, arming the powerhead. He turned to see Evens still wrestling with Randy.

Evens grabbed Randy's gun, which was pointed away from him. With his other hand now free, Randy began clawing the side of Evens's face with his fingers, trying to poke out the man's eyes.

Still dragging the chair tied to his left arm, Jack awkwardly made his way over to the two men tussling on the ground. Wielding the bang stick, he looked for an opening when Randy's pistol fired. Mysterie screamed. Jack instinctively ducked and raised his left arm to cover himself, whipping the chair against his head. He stumbled, dizzied and surprised.

Jack looked at Mysterie, thinking at first that she'd been shot. Realizing she wasn't hit, he turned back to the two men. Blood was pouring out of Evens's side. Randy was trying to get the gun out from under Evens, who lay on top of him.

As Randy rolled Evens off of him, Jack thrust the bang stick at Randy's chest. As soon as it made contact, it exploded with a deafening roar. The last expression on Randy's face was surprise as the muzzle blast from the .357 round tore through his chest.

Detective Stevens raced onto the patio, holding her gun out.

"Jack? You okay?" she said, coming up next to Jack. He looked at her strangely. It sounded like she was talking in a barrel, his ears still ringing from the discharge of the weapon.

Jack dropped the bang stick and surveyed the scene. Randy was still and not of this world, a gaping hole where his chest had been. Jack bent over Evens, but it didn't look good. Evens was on his back next to Randy. His breath was shallow, and blood gurgled out of the wound in his side.

The detective was on her radio, calling for medical help, but Jack shook his head.

It was too late for Evens.

40

Three days later, Jack walked into the little shop on Petronia Street.

"Can I help you?" the young girl asked as she looked up. "Oh," she said, "it's you."

She had visible piercings and tattoos in places that made Jack wince. He didn't want to think about the others.

"I'm looking for Mysterie."

The girl stood. "You're . . ."

"Jack Davis."

The girl nodded and disappeared through the beads and into the back. In a few minutes, she emerged, trailed by Mysterie.

"I'm sorry, Mysterie," he said. "Your brother was a good man. He saved our lives." He heard a sniffle and saw a teardrop roll down her cheek.

"I'm sorry I got you and Molly involved," she said in an unsteady voice.

He looked around, then back at her. "Is there somewhere we can talk?" he asked.

She motioned him back through the curtain in silence, through the door back to the patio where he'd seen two people die, one at his own hand. She motioned to a seat, and after he sat, she pulled up a chair at an angle to him.

"I don't know you, and you don't know me," Jack said, his voice catching. "But, it doesn't matter. I wanted to tell you how sorry I am about your brother. He was a good man and saved a lot of lives. In the end, he did the right thing, and that's what really counts."

Mysterie lowered her head and spoke softly. "I'm sorry about Molly. I was just trying to save him. He was the only brother I had."

He nodded. "I understand. I don't blame you." His voice caught, and he swallowed. "I had one brother, too. If I had tried to do more to save him, maybe he'd still be alive."

As he rose to leave, he nodded toward the flowering shrub in front of them. "That is a beautiful plant. What is that?"

"Angel's trumpet."

He turned to walk out, and she said, "Mr. Davis?"

He stopped and looked back over his shoulder.

"Is there anything I can do?"

He thought for a moment, then nodded. "I'm not sure I completely believe in what you do, but if you have any magic to help me get Molly back, I sure would appreciate it."

She studied him, then held out her hand. "Give me your hand."

He hesitated, then stepped over and placed his hand in hers. She closed her eyes for a few seconds, then opened them and smiled. "Everything's going to work out for you two. Don't worry."

Jack walked out to Duval, still shaking his head. He didn't feel any different than when he'd walked into

Mysterie's shop, but the strength of her conviction had impressed him. He hoped she was right.

When he got to Seth's store, he stepped inside and the doorbell chimed. Seth looked up from his desk in the back.

"Jack, how are you?" he said. He met Jack halfway across the small shop. "What a horrible thing."

"I'm okay . . . no, I'm not. You have a few minutes?"

"Certainly. Come on back. Coffee?"

"Yes, thank you." He followed Seth back to his desk and sat.

Seth turned and popped a K-cup into the Keurig on his credenza. He placed a coffee mug underneath and pressed the button.

"Lee refuses to use one of these, but they are so convenient." The machine hissed and Seth turned back around, giving Jack his full attention. "You look like you have the weight of the world on your shoulders."

Jack forced a laugh. "I miss Molly. Tell me what to do, Seth."

Seth swiveled around, took the steaming cup of coffee, and set it front of Jack. "Black, right?"

Jack nodded. "Thanks."

Seth took a sip from his coffee mug before speaking. "I have never seen two people so miserable." He shook his head. "Don't you dare tell her I said this, but she misses you, too."

"Really?" Jack said, unable to hide his enthusiasm.

"Oh, yes. You two are made for each other. I told Lee that the first time we had you over. Refreshing, actually, to see two people so moon-eyed over each other."

Jack grinned. "Okay, so how do I get her back?"

"Grovel." Seth put his index finger on his chin. "And, beg." He thought for a minute, then added. "I think I know just the right setting. What are you doing tonight?"

Later that evening, just before dark, Jack walked over to Seth and Lee's house, carrying a bouquet of fresh daisies. He was as nervous as he'd ever been.

Seth had taken him out shopping that afternoon and picked out a new shirt, slacks, and shoes. Then, he'd sent Jack over to his salon for a haircut and manicure. Jack had tried to protest, but Seth would have none of that. He insisted that Jack follow his instructions precisely, guaranteeing the results.

Jack had to admit, the silk shirt and linen trousers felt good. He rang the doorbell, and Seth answered, his finger to his lips. "Follow me," he whispered.

Silently, Jack followed Seth into the house and up the stairs. The smells emanating from the kitchen were delicious, and Jack wondered what Lee was preparing. On the second floor, Seth led him into what looked like a library, with bookshelves lining three sides of the room. Soft music was playing in the background.

The patio doors were open and led to a small balcony overlooking the courtyard behind their house. There was a table set for three on the balcony, with a candle in the center of the table. He paused when he saw Molly sitting at the table, staring out over the courtyard, a glass of wine on the table in front of her. He looked over at Seth, who held his hand up and moved it slowly down. He bowed, rolling his hand over toward Molly, then turned and walked out of the room.

Jack stood there, mesmerized by the scene. The candlelight was illuminating the side of Molly's face with a soft glow. He could see her bare shoulders, and noticed the dress she wore. It was black, and from what little he could see, clingy and brief.

He took a deep breath and walked through the open French doors.

"The wine is lovely—" Molly stopped in mid-sentence as she turned and saw Jack.

"Hello, Molly." He held the daisies out to her. She looked around. For a minute, he thought she was going to reject them, just like she had at the hospital. Then, she gingerly extended her hand and took them. A brief smile crossed her face.

He wanted to touch her, to kiss her, to hold her, but he didn't want to screw things up. He tried to remember Seth's instructions. He pulled out the chair opposite her. She gave him a quick once-over before he sat.

"I need to speak with Seth," she said. She set the flowers down at the empty place at the table and started to rise.

"Molly, please. Don't leave."

She paused, studying him. Slowly, she pulled her chair back up to the table and eased down into her seat.

"You look incredible. I love that dress." He thought he saw a smile crack the façade for a second, then disappear.

"You look nice," she said, appraising his hair. "I see Seth's been spending some time with you."

He shrugged. "I couldn't talk him into a new t-shirt and flip-flops." Again, he saw a glimpse of a smile cross her face.

"Molly . . . I miss you." She tilted her head and opened her mouth to speak, but he held up his hand. "I know I screwed up, and I am sorry. I've told you everything and I promise I'll never keep secrets from you again." He took a deep breath, then continued. "Please come back home."

Before she could respond, Seth walked through the door with an open bottle of wine and a plate of appetizers. "Well, I see you're both still sitting here. That's a good start," he said, setting the appetizers on the table between them.

"You and I need to talk," Molly said to him in a stern voice.

"A little nibble from the chef," he said, ignoring her comment. He poured them each a healthy glassful of wine and set the bottle on the table. "I know—more than is proper, but I figure it will help lubricate the discussion."

"My compliments to you on his outfit, Seth," Molly said, "considering what you had to work with. I'm glad you didn't let him talk you into a new t-shirt."

"Oh, no. In fact, I had to burn the outfit he had on. Absolutely atrocious."

A snicker escaped her lips, and the smile stayed there for a bit longer than before.

Jack looked at her and licked his lips. "The dress is stunning. I'd wear a tutu and tights to see her in that outfit."

Molly's grin got broader, and she gave a slight shake of her head and rolled her eyes.

Seth put his hand on Jack's shoulder. "You're such a tease. Well, enjoy your appetizers. The entrees will be up shortly."

As he walked away, Molly looked at Jack and he saw a glimpse of that familiar twinkle in her eyes. "A tutu and tights? Where did you come up with that line?"

He shrugged. "Sorry, that was the best I could do on the spur-of-the-moment."

She reached over, picked up a spring roll from the plate, and took a bite. "Whose idea was this?" Her face was tight and the smile disappeared.

Jack grabbed one and followed suit, stalling for time. "Umm. These are delicious." He finished it with one more bite, licked his fingers, and then wiped them on his napkin.

"I went by Seth's shop and asked him for advice," he said. "We were co-conspirators." He studied her face. "Don't be mad at him."

They finished the appetizers, then Seth appeared with entrees, red snapper en papillote. He refilled their wine glasses and cautioned them to save room for dessert before disappearing again.

"Thank you for what you did at Mysterie's," she said, her features softening as darkness crept in, combined with the fabulous wine. "That was very brave."

She smiled, and he thought he would melt. "Of course, I don't remember much. Mysterie's special tea has a punch to it."

"Probably a good thing. I went by to see her this morning."

"You did?" Molly was surprised.

He nodded. "I wanted to tell her how sorry I was, and to thank her for her brother's sacrifice. He saved us all. If it hadn't been for him . . ."

They talked over dinner, and Jack felt better than he had in weeks. As Seth had predicted, the food and wine in a romantic setting were working. Seeing glimpses of the old Molly made him smile, and he recalled Mysterie's words. Maybe she was right, maybe they were going to be okay.

As they finished dinner, Jack took a deep breath and pushed his plate aside. He folded his hands underneath his chin, resting his elbows on the table and looking at Molly.

"There's something I need to tell you before dessert."

She set her fork down and folded her arms across her chest, shaking her head as if expecting the worst.

He laid the newspaper clipping on the table and pushed it across for her to read. The headline said, "Anonymous Benefactor Leaves Money."

He watched as she read the article he'd clipped out of the *Miami Herald*. Someone had left almost half a million dollars at the shelter for abused women in Clearwater. They had notified the authorities, who were unaware of any robberies in the area.

"We don't know where it came from," said Detective Stanopolis of the Clearwater Police Department. "But no one has reported it missing and it was delivered to the Executive Director at the Shelter. If no one has claimed it within a reasonable period of time, we are going to petition the court to release it to the shelter."

When she finished reading, she looked at him, her eyes glistening in the candlelight.

"That's the shelter where Wren stayed," she said.

He nodded. "They deserve it, and that was the only way I could figure out how to get it to them. You're the only one who knows—nobody else. The money was nothing but trouble. I always intended to do something good with it, and this was the right thing to do."

She put her hand on top of his.

"I love you, Molly. I'm sorry, and I hope you'll forgive me."

Before she could answer, Seth and Lee both appeared in the doorway.

"Well, you're both still here and even sitting closer. That's encouraging," Seth said.

Molly smiled and left her hand over Jack's. "That was a fabulous dinner. Thank you so much—in spite of the deception," she said, cutting her eyes at Seth.

"Yes, it was. Thank you guys," Jack said. "I explained that it was my doing."

He started to rise, and Seth put his hand on Jack's shoulder, pushing him back down into his chair.

"Not so fast. After all the wine you've consumed, you're in no condition to walk. You're staying here tonight." He looked over at Lee, who nodded.

Seth continued. "This side of the top floor is yours. Molly has her room, and you'll be in the adjoining room. I see you each have a little port left, so if you require nothing else, Lee and I will be retiring to our quarters. Sweet dreams."

As they walked away, Jack reached over, took Molly's other hand, and looked her in the eyes.

"You want to show me your room?"

Epilogue

It was a beautiful day in Fort Myers, that in-between time on the calendar where it's not too hot but not cool enough even for long sleeves. Jack and Molly were walking up the steps to the fellowship hall at the Catholic Church near Tony and Connie's condo. Nick, still using a cane, was behind them with Wren holding his arm.

Tony's funeral had been both solemn and joyful, the way Tony would have wanted it. In his heart, Jack was glad that his friend had not lingered. He never regained consciousness after the stroke, which was a blessing. Tony would not have wanted Connie or his friends to see him that way.

"Are doing you okay?" Molly asked as they entered the hall.

He nodded and pulled her close. "We knew this was going to be the outcome. I'm just glad he didn't suffer long."

They stood off to one side, waiting for Wren and Nick to catch up. Nick had suffered nerve damage from the curare and was still undergoing physical therapy. It was too early to tell if the damage was permanent, but he was slowly improving and had graduated to using a cane to get around.

In a few minutes, Nick hobbled up to them, with Wren on his arm.

"How are you feeling, Nick?" Molly asked.

He smiled and patted Wren's arm. "As long as I have my nurse, here, I'm fine."

"Shall we get something to eat and sit down?" Jack asked as he moved toward the buffet line.

As they made their way over, Connie approached, along with a man in a wheelchair accompanied by a hulk.

"Jack. I want you and Molly to meet someone special," she said. "This is Frankie Crispino, Tony's friend and business partner from Miami."

Jack maintained his poker face and stuck out his hand. "Frankie. I'm Jack Davis. This is my wife, Molly, and our friends, Wren, and Nick."

Frankie shook Jack's hand, giving no indication of familiarity. "Jack, a pleasure. Connie speaks highly of you."

I wish I could say the same, Jack thought. He noticed the hulk staring at him and Jack flashed him a big smile.

"Jack has been so helpful," Connie said. "I don't know what I would've done without him."

"Anytime, Connie. You know you can always call," Jack said. He stole a glance toward Frankie and could sense the animosity emanating from him.

"Well, I think we'll grab a bite if you don't mind," Frankie said, turning toward the buffet line. "Nice to meet all of you."

"Likewise." It was the best Jack could muster.

After they left, Nick leaned over and whispered in Jack's ear, "The big guy was eyeing you like a hungry dog eyes a steak."

"Maybe I reminded him of someone he knew."

"So, that was the infamous Frankie Crispino you told me about?" Molly asked.

"The one and only."

"I don't think he cares much for you."

Jack laughed. "You think?"

Walter Dobbs walked in and when he saw Jack and Molly, he came over. He hugged Molly, then Jack, and introduced himself to Nick and Wren.

"Excuse me, but I'm taking my patient over to sit down and then feed him," Wren said, ushering Nick toward a nearby table.

"You're spoiling him," Jack said as they walked away.

Walter looked at Molly and Jack. "Good to see you both, although I would've preferred a more cheerful occasion for this reunion."

"I agree. But, it was a beautiful service. Walter, you're looking well, as always," Jack said.

"Thank you. You two look great. Key West must be agreeing with you."

Molly smiled and said, "Thank you. It's been an adjustment." She looked at Jack. "But we've managed and are doing fine."

Walter looked at Molly, then Jack. "Interesting news item from the Tampa area a few weeks ago," he said, lowering his voice. "Apparently someone dropped off a bag of money at the women's shelter in Clearwater." A barely noticeable smile creased his face as he looked at them.

"I heard," Jack said. "They ever figure out where it came from?" He felt Molly squeeze his hand, but he kept his eyes on Walter.

"No, so it's going to the shelter. I guess the donor didn't want the publicity."

"It doesn't matter," said Molly, again squeezing Jack's hand. "The important thing is that the money is going to a good cause."

"Do right and God will know," Jack said. "Tony's words."

Acknowledgments

While writing is a solitary endeavor, once again I am indebted to countless others for their help and generosity in indulging my questions.

Many thanks to the following people for taking the time to read my manuscript and offer much-needed feedback and support: Mary Jo Burkhalter Persons, Otis Scarbary, Cindy Deane, Shirley Scarbary, Clara Blanquet, Fred Blanquet, Barry McIntosh, Jay Holmes, and Donna Jennings. You guys are the best.

Thanks to Karl Steele and Scott Cherry for putting up with my questions on police procedures.

Carl Graves once again delivered a stunning cover. Thanks to Anitra Mayhann Photography for the picture on the back.

Thanks to Kieran Sultan, M.D. for setting me straight on pathology issues.

Another huge thanks to my editor, Heather Whitaker. She pushes me to make my writing better, and I appreciate her advice and counsel. As always, any mistakes that remain are mine.

My granddaughter Breanna is now a sophomore in college, even closer to that point where she can start buying me books.

Thanks to my wife, June, for supporting me and having faith in my writing. I couldn't do it without you.